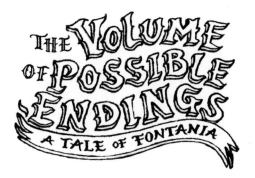

THE VOLUME OF POSSIBLE ENDINGS
A TALE OF FONTANIA

Books in the Tales of Fontania series
The Traveling Restaurant
The Queen and the Nobody Boy
The Volume of Possible Endings

www.TalesOfFontania.com

First published in 2014 by Gecko Press
PO Box 9335, Marion Square, Wellington 6141, New Zealand
info@geckopress.com

Text © 2014 Barbara Else
Cover and illustrations © 2014 Sam Broad

© Gecko Press Ltd

First American edition published in 2015 by Gecko Press USA,
an imprint of Gecko Press Ltd.

Distributed in the United States and Canada by Lerner Publishing Group,
www.lernerbooks.com

Distributed in the United Kingdom by Bounce Sales and Marketing,
www.bouncemarketing.co.uk

Distributed in Australia by Scholastic Australia,
www.scholastic.com.au

Distributed in New Zealand by Random House NZ,
www.randomhouse.co.nz

A catalogue record for this book is available from the
National Library of New Zealand

≋creative*nz*
ARTS COUNCIL OF NEW ZEALAND TOI AOTEAROA

The author and Gecko Press acknowledge the generous support of
Creative New Zealand

Design by Luke Kelly, Wellington, New Zealand
Printed in China by Everbest Printing Co Ltd,
an accredited ISO 14001 & FSC certified printer

ISBN hardback (USA): 978-1-927271-61-2
ISBN paperback: 978-1-927271-37-7
E-book available

For more curiously good books, visit www.geckopress.com

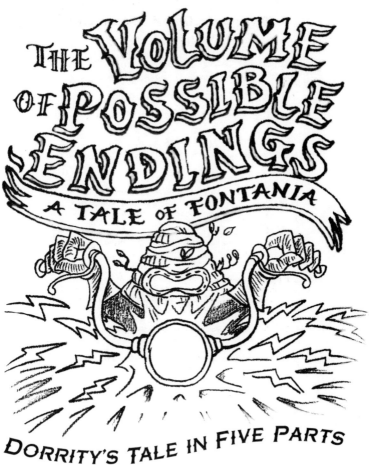

THE VOLUME OF POSSIBLE ENDINGS

A TALE OF FONTANIA

DORRITY'S TALE IN FIVE PARTS

BY BARBARA ELSE

~ WITH ILLUSTRATIONS BY SAM BROAD ~

GECKO PRESS

DEDICATION

for brothers and librarians

Once upon a time, the world was rich in magic. It was used wisely, not wasted on anything selfish or mean-spirited. It was saved for important things like making sure babies slept safe in their cots, that people had enough to eat, and that the world was peaceful. There were dangers, as there always is with magic. But there was also common sense. Some people began to experiment with science and machines, and that was all right. You see, everyone thought somebody was in charge.

— Polly, *The Traveling Restaurant*

CONTENTS

PART ONE
THE TOWN WITHOUT MAGIC

Part Two
NEVER GO TO THE BEASTLY DARK

Part Three
STRANGERS AND VILLAINS

Part Four
Home Life, ha ha ha

Part Five
Mistakes and Experiments

Appendices

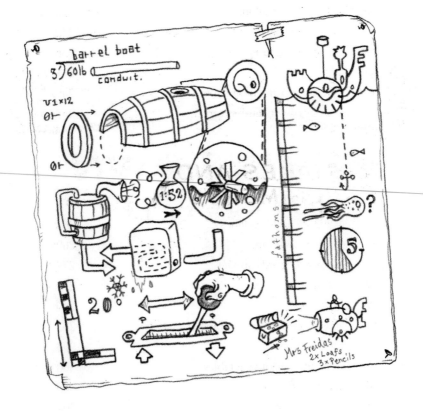

barrel boat

3)60lb

conduit.

V1×12

20°

fathoms

1:52

?

5

Mrs Freidas
2× Loafs
3× Pencils

PART ONE OF DORRITY'S TALE

THE TOWN WITHOUT MAGIC

THE KING'S WORKSHOP

Red dust from the grindstone shimmered in the air over King Jasper's workbench. Rulers and screwdrivers lay there along with hammers and pliers of all sizes, a soldering iron, and a blowtorch. On a shelf was an open box lined with velvet. It held a feather made of silver and lighter than thistledown. The King's own mechanical message-birds perched on a rack by the door and a large waste bin spilled over with mistakes.

The King rummaged in his toolbox for three gold screws to fit the blood-red jasper heart he had made for the clockwork boy. He had chosen it not because its name was the same as his own, but because the stone was meant to give the bearer courage.

Three seconds after the King set the heart in the boy's chest and began turning the first screw, the clockwork boy thought—*Courage. That must mean there will be danger.*

When the King turned the second screw, a chill traced down the boy's metal spine. A heart could be trouble. It might be better without a brain, too. Already he felt that it had been far better when he was just an experiment that the

King's family and friends came to admire, and said:

"So it's not in the waste bin yet."

"Are you sure it will ever be useful?"

"What deep gray eyes it has."

"Good grief, what a bald metal head."

"Isn't it time you gave it trousers?"

The King began turning the third screw to fix the jasper heart in place. Midday sun shone through the skylight.

"The dragon-eagles said this was a good idea, but even they know magic's a mystery," the King muttered as if he was talking to the clockwork boy. "It will be slow to get going. But time is an important part of magic. Please gather information for me from dangerous places. It's too risky for anyone else to try..."

The dust made the King want to sneeze. He turned aside and held his arm over a huge *ker-choo!* that made an eddy in the air. The feather, purest silver, lifted from the box on the shelf. By the time the King turned back, the feather had tucked itself behind the heart of the metal boy.

The King closed up the boy's chest-plate with four more gold screws and patted his head. "There. That's as good as I can manage. I hope it will do."

It was only later, when the sun had moved from the skylight, that the King glanced at the box and saw that the dragon-eagle feather had gone.

He scanned the floor, hunted over the workbench. How could it be lost? In his mind he said, *Dragon-eagles, what have I done? If your magic gift falls into the wrong hands it could be used for terrible things.*

The King heard a whisper like a silver chime, the voice of the first dragon-eagle ~ *Do not worry* ~

~ *Do not worry* ~ the second dragon-eagle echoed, then added ~ *not too much, not yet* ~

The King didn't think to ask the clockwork boy where the silver feather might be, so the boy was unable to answer. That was a problem with questions, the boy realized. Before they could be answered, they had to be asked.

The moon rose that night in perfect fullness and shone through the skylight on the boy's metal head.

At last dawn washed across the sky. The boy blinked for the first time since he'd been put together. Soon the King might come in carrying a bowl of porridge and stewed plums. Would he say the heart was ready? What danger did the King expect him to face? When would the danger come? Next month? Next week? Today? Another chill traced down the boy's back. The new heart jolted once inside his chest.

~

The King's clocks said half-past eight when he came into the workshop in his overalls and denim cap. He carried only a mug of coffee and a sheaf of royal papers. A no-breakfast morning? The boy didn't know exactly why, but he took that as a bad sign.

The papers were letters and memos that trailed ribbons stuck on with sealing wax by the royal secretary. King Jasper never brought paper clips into the workshop in case they fell off and wedged into an experiment. He didn't count on any accident being a lucky one. Green ribbons meant good news. Orange ribbons meant news that required keen thinking. Red ribbons meant bad news, and that often needed something done at once. A black ribbon meant someone important was dead.

Today the ribbons were all orange and red.

The King shut the workshop door behind him. "I must find that feather," he muttered. But first he sat beside the clockwork boy and read the letter with the widest red ribbon. "What?" He set his mug down with a slam—then wiped up spilled coffee with his shirt sleeve and read on. The clockwork boy saw the King's jaw tighten.

In the Grand Palace grounds, seven guards marched past humming their marching song, four not in tune and three out of step.

Until—or unless—his heart began to work properly, the boy could only speak when spoken to and obey orders. But as he listened to the guards and watched the King reading the letter, he felt something very new. His metal lips pressed together, turned down a little at each end, and he let out a sound like *hmmph*.

King Jasper glanced at the boy, but just then someone rapped on the workshop door.

"Go away, annoying little sister!" called the King.

Queen Sibilla ignored that and strode in. She wasn't little at all. She was nearly grown up, taller than a lot of other women, taller than the metal boy. Today her hair was elasticked into bunches. She wore boots up to her knees, and down to her knees she had a green skirt so stiff it looked like a lamp shade.

The clockwork boy knew a lot of things already. For instance, it took real people a long time to grow up—

seventeen years in the Queen's case. The boy himself had been made in just one year—plus the three days it took for the King to carve and set in the jasper heart. He wondered if he would ever be able to tell the King about the silver feather-scale tucked in behind it.

"It's time you dusted in here, but I say that every morning." Queen Sibilla sat down and shuffled through the pile of letters.

"Try this." The King handed her the one with the widest red ribbon.

The Queen studied the page and turned more pale with every paragraph. "Count Bale's people have been seen all over the kingdom! They're hunting for the girl. This is terrible news. If they find her, they'll use her against us."

"We should have looked harder for her ourselves," said the King. "We'll look harder right away." He sprang up and counted the message-birds. "The secretary's office will have at least thirty more. We'll send alerts to every outpost."

"Send warnings everywhere," said Queen Sibilla. "Poor girl. If Bale's people find her, she's a danger to every single person in Fontania."

The King's worry lines grew deeper as he looked at the clockwork boy. "I hope I haven't taken too long."

Queen Sibilla frowned at the boy too. "How soon could you send him?"

"He's nearly ready, which doesn't mean ready," growled the King. "And I don't dare rush things."

He marched from the workshop, those ominous ribbons flapping on the papers bunched in his hand.

Queen Sibilla stepped up to the clockwork boy. Being stared at so closely had never worried him before. Today it made him uncomfortable. The Queen rested her fingers on his shoulders and bent down to kiss his forehead.

"Poor metal boy. Good luck," she said. "Very good luck, for everyone's sake." She ran after her brother.

The workshop door swung almost shut, which meant it stayed slightly open. A palace cat strolled past and the boy heard it lap at a puddle.

It stayed warm where the Queen had kissed him. And by midday the sun again shone through the skylight onto the clockwork boy. The jasper heart gave a judder, a great throb, and this time continued to beat.

The boy felt all sorts of new things. The beating in his chest was just one of them. So was being slightly cold. Annoyance and impatience were two others, but they were only itches compared to his fear. The fear wasn't exactly new—he'd felt it slinking through him the day before. But by now it was so huge he thought all his bolts would unscrew with squeaks of terror. If they did, he would end up in the bin of mistakes.

He took his first movement by himself. Near the door he bumped the rack of message-birds. One of them fell and a wing broke off. He picked it up, fixed the wing, and listened. Nobody had heard.

He was already ashamed of running away. But nothing would stop him. Not even the fact he had no clothes. With luck he'd find a jacket as well as a cap to hide his metal head. He hoped it wouldn't be too difficult to climb into a pair of stolen trousers.

～

THE MISFITS OF OWL TOWN

Good day! Giddy-giddy! sang the red and white gidibirds as they sped along the banks of the Forgotten River. Blue-bellied starlings answered with *Watch-out-watch-out, be caa-aareful!* Owl Town lay between the Forgotten River and the Beastly Dark. The people who lived there claimed that around here there was not even a bean or a skerrick, not a flea-pinch of magic.

Dorrity lived at at the very end of Lower High Street. She had freckles and straight brown hair and had just turned twelve. She had lived here since she was four, with her three grown brothers. Their market garden was squashed into the last patch of land before the Beastly Dark came down to meet the river. Lettuces from their garden were as beautiful as roses and some of them were even red.

Dorrity always liked to wear something with hand-sewn cross-stitch. She also liked to hear stories about the rest of the world—for instance, about magic and the Royals. But she was very happy here in quiet Owl Town—quiet except for dances in the town hall, Miss Honey Dearborn's piano, and at weekends the noise from the Owl and Pie tavern.

Each year Dorrity's brothers journeyed across the bridge over the Forgotten River to Fribbleton, and every year she asked, "Why do you all go and why do I stay?"

Each year her biggest brother, Birkett, said in a growl, "We have to go. That's that."

Her second brother, Mike, always tossed his head. "Such a ruddy chore but that's the way of it."

The other brothers usually frowned because *ruddy* was sort of a swear word.

Her third brother, Yorky, always said, "You've just had your birthday but we'll squeeze the wallet for another present."

Each year Dorrity shivered with relief because she didn't want to go as well. When her brothers were ready she said, "See you in a week. Kiss-kiss." Then, her pajamas in a basket, she ran along to stay in the spare room at Mrs. Freida's house.

"Let's spoil that girl rotten," Miss Honey said each year to Mrs. Freida.

Mrs. Freida always replied, "It would be astonishing if the only child in a town was not already spoiled far past rotten."

Over the years, Mrs. Freida, who had lived in Owl Town the longest of anyone, taught Dorrity many things about life and brothers. She said that folk who didn't know better reckoned Owl Town was a clutch of misfits, but the fact was that everyone fit like a charm.

She also told stories about Fontania and magic. Every

story arose from one of the stamps in her twenty-one-volume stamp collection. She said that most of them were true, which of course meant several must be invented. Dorrity preferred the ones that were made up. More of them had happy endings. She was in her own happy ending already, or so she felt, and never made herself examine why.

~

Every year, two days before Dorrity's brothers went to Fribbleton, they had to have First Shave. They gave their faces one day to recover, then they'd have Second Shave the morning they actually left. When they returned, they'd start growing beards again.

Today, as always, they lined shaving bowls up at the bathroom mirror and paid close attention because their razors were old-fashioned cut-throats. A year of beards had to come off, so this was much more interesting than Second Shave.

Dorrity sat on the bathroom stool to watch the foam rasped off in patches and stripes from their cheeks and chins.

She began her annual question. "Why do you all go and why…"

A bird landed on the sill outside the window. It might have been a starling but its shape shivered and blurred through the wavy glass. Its chirp sounded odd, more like a whirr. Dorrity's brothers startled up, then looked down at her, Birkett's brown eyes, Mike's blue eyes, Yorky with a worried gaze of yellowy hazel.

She finished her question: "…why do I stay?"

Birkett glanced at the bird again. "We must go and that's that." He whipped up more shaving soap.

"It's a ruddy big chore." Mike swished his razor in the middle bowl. Birkett frowned and Dorrity chuckled.

"We'll bring back a special present." Yorky leaned close to the mirror to scrape the tricky bit under his nose.

At last, Dorrity saw that year after year they'd never answered properly. They never said exactly why they went to Fribbleton at all. And that was because she asked two questions in one sentence.

The bird on the sill chirped again. There was a whirr, a clank. *Re-wuh-wuh-wuh*, it chirped. *Find the gu-gu-girl. Re-wuh-wuh-ward.* It spread its wings and lurched from sight.

Dorrity laughed. "Maybe that was one of the King's spy-birds."

Her brothers frowned at each other over the shaving foam.

"I was being sarcastic," she said. "It will be an ordinary message-bird. It could belong to anyone who can afford one."

They stared at her, still not moving. They might just be trying to keep the soap out of their eyes, but she didn't want them to have an accident with those cut-throat razors. Maybe she should change the subject.

"You know how I've just turned twelve? In some of Mrs. Freida's stories, turning twelve is a huge event. Would it be possible to bring back an extra-special present?"

"I gave you red boots for your birthday," Birkett growled.

"I gave you a new overdress with cross-stitch," mumbled Mike.

"I gave you the blue hat with green feathers," Yorky said.

"I love my boots and the overdress." She stood up and did a twirl in them. "It's been too windy for the hat but I've sewn strings and a toggle on and I'll wear it today. I don't know what there is to buy in Fribbleton anyway. An extra-special present was just a thought."

Her brothers scowled close to the mirror, razors scritching their bristles.

She sat on the stool again and pleated the hem of the overdress. The line of cross-stitch under her fingers felt like an encouraging message. "Even if it sounds like nagging, I've got another question. Exactly why do all three of you go to Fribbleton at the same time every year?"

The bathroom went so quiet she heard foam frothing on her brothers' cheeks and chins.

Birkett moved first. He pulled his lower lip up over his teeth to scrape the crease in his chin, and growled, "Ee haff to ss-ign the ss-ame bi' of ph-apher."

"Why?" asked Dorrity.

"*Mmph…*" Mike slathered more foam on his cheeks. "To show we agree."

"Agree about what?" she asked. "I know it's business, but what sort precisely?"

There was more scraping of razors.

"Yorky?" she asked.

"Oh…let's say…about bringing you up," he said.

She jolted upright on the stool. "Who do you have to show that you agree?"

"The authorities," growled Birkett after a moment.

"Ha," said Mike, "authorities. Too right."

"What authorities!" It was a question but she shouted it.

"You know the townsfolk don't like visitors. So we… have to go to the authorities." Yorky usually explained things better than the other two. Mike tended to go off on his own and kick things, and Birkett tended to sulk. But Dorrity could tell that right now he was dodging and fudging. She could also tell it would be useless to shout again.

The sun dazzled on the rim of the mirror. Birkett tipped out his shaving water and wiped at his scattering of shaved-off beard. Mike wiped at his scattering of sandy-blond whiskers. Yorky squinted in the mirror, first at one side of his face, then at the other. Then he dabbed up his red beard scrapings along with any mess left over by the others. They each patted on lots of lotion, very intent. They looked so different without beards. Dorrity had never wondered before, but now she did—why did they have to be clean-shaven to see the authorities?

Mike gave his face a final pat. "It's the last time, anyway," he muttered.

Yorky nudged his elbow, Birkett growled, and Mike turned red.

It was a warm morning but Dorrity shivered. "Last time for seeing authorities? Or…for what?"

Birkett shot Mike another dark look before he answered. "As soon as we're back we're going to think about new arrangements. Like moving off. You need friends your own age!" he added as if he'd just thought of it.

"I've got plenty of friends," she managed to say. "I've got

Miss Honey and she's quite young. There's Mrs. Freida and Mr. Coop."

"No point in talking about it till we're back from Fribbleton. In the meantime, not a word. Not one. Not to anyone." Birkett narrowed his eyes at Mike and Yorky, then the three of them narrowed their eyes at her.

A steamboat whistled down at the wharves. The rumble of steam trucks echoed over the bridge.

"Hurry it up," said Birkett to the other two. "Any rain while we're away, the weeds will strangle the garden. If the place doesn't look good, we'll be out of pocket."

They really were thinking of moving away! Dorrity followed as they shoved to the back porch to find their work boots. "But I like living in…" she began.

"Not a word!" Birkett sounded so fierce it was frightening.

~

THE BOOK WITH NO TITLE

By now Mike and Yorky had barged into the yard. She heard Mike grumbling, "Where's that can of paint? It was at the shed door."

"Where the blazes is my axe?" said Birkett as he joined them. "I must have left it down by the fence posts."

Dorrity stood at the back door as he strode off to find it.

"Get ready for Mrs. Freida's," Yorky said. "I'll come round and watch you go."

She didn't need to be watched, not just along High Street. But she fetched her birthday hat and her basket of daily bits and pieces, like a cardigan and spare handkerchief.

Yorky was at the front gate. "Work hard," he said. "Keep yourself busy." He leaned down for a goodbye peck, but she nipped past with her chin in the air and marched off.

Her brothers were bossy enough. Why were "authorities" involved? Though she wouldn't say so to her brothers, she mostly agreed with the way they were bringing her up. She thought she'd grow into a very good and useful young woman. Then she intended to be a very good and sensible old one who still rollicked and hopped at the Owl Town dances.

At Miss Honey's gate she stopped and listened. The sewing machine was already whirring, busy and breathless like the piano. Across Lower High Street a horse waited outside Dr. Oxford's surgery. A farmhand held tight to the reins, but Dorrity edged past on this side of the road. Last time her brothers had gone to Fribbleton, Dr. Oxford had to take a huge splinter out of Dorrity's elbow. He'd spread the wound with an ointment of his own invention, *Oxford's Special Balm For Man and Horse*. By the time her brothers were back there was only a tiny red mark.

Those brothers—they'd never before said they had to see authorities, just that they had to do business. They'd even said so to the new policeman a few days ago. Officer Edgar had asked, *What business?* Birkett had replied as if he were an entry in a dictionary, *Business means, for instance, to do with organizing supplies and buying and selling.*

Dorrity supposed that talking to authorities could sort-of be business. She understood that all three brothers might have to put their signatures on the same piece of paper, which must be like a license for bringing up a younger sister. All the same, a lump came into her throat. She never liked to think about not having parents and had never asked anything about them.

She glanced back down the street. Yorky still watched from the gate, as if there might be trouble in Owl Town.

Rubbish. This was the safest place in all Fontania. There were no river pirates. The only visitor of any sort in the last two years had been an ogre, trudging downriver to the West

March Engineering College. He'd asked for third helpings of Miss Honey's pumpkin pie and then spent the night on her fold-out sofa. Everyone else said they didn't have a spare bed suitable. In most cases that had been true. Occasionally from the Dark came a far-off roaring that choked down into *koff-koff-koff*. But nothing had ever hurtled out of the Beastly Dark to gobble up anyone. And there was no danger of a cat or dog being snaffled by something like a panther because no one in Owl Town kept pets at all.

So her brothers were being baffling and upsetting.

Outside the Necessary Shop and Post Office, the newspaper hoarding for the *Two-Daily Blast* said KING'S EXPERIMENT STILL MISSING.

Inside, Mrs. Freida was serving five early customers and her gray curls hadn't been brushed. Button, the shop assistant, was reaching for things on the high shelves. He was a squat middle-aged troll so shy that he only did the jobs that needed extremely long arms or a point and a nod, like serving ice cream cones.

Of course the customers were gossiping. For the last two weeks they'd chewed over the story that King Jasper and Queen Sibilla would reopen Eagle Hall, an old royal family holiday home somewhere up in the Beastly Dark. "It's in ruins," Mrs. Freida had said. "They've always said someday they'll clear it out. But there's been nothing in the papers. I wonder where the story started?"

This morning the gossip had fresh bits. There'd been burglaries around town—a couple of cushions, a pair of pliers, a mat left outside for an airing, that sort of thing.

Mrs. Freida didn't even glance at Dorrity. But the craft lady, who had lost her broom for sweeping down cobwebs, nodded to her.

"Nice hat." She had probably made it.

"Hang on to it, lest it vanish like my best knickerbockers," said gruff Farmer Ember. "Best pair ever seen around Owl Town. Biggest pair, too."

"We never had a thimble pinched before," said the craft lady. "This week it's as bad as the city."

"Even the King lost that experiment from his own workshop," said a river fisherman. "The papers say he was working on something to save Fontania from danger."

Another fisherman laughed. "I heard it was a mechanical scarecrow!"

"If the Grand Palace isn't safe, how could the Royals manage Eagle Hall?" cried Dr. Oxford's assistant.

"We don't want any Royals back near here," said the craft lady. "Magic would wreck our contentment."

Dorrity ducked past the counter and through the connecting door into the house. She hung her hat on the peg by the kitchen door. Usually things were so tidy they made Dorrity's teeth hurt, but Mrs. Freida's breakfast dishes were still in the sink. A cup of tea had gone cold on the bench. She carried her basket of books into the dining room to work on parentheses (sometimes called brackets). Mrs. Freida hadn't even cleared the table for school. A brown paper package lay there, old and torn so that it showed part of what was inside—a large green book half-wrapped in a silky blue cloth.

For a moment Dorrity thought it was one of Mrs. Freida's twenty-one stamp albums. But there wasn't a gap on the shelf—the albums were as crammed as usual. She looked again at the book on the table. It was fatter than the albums, too, and more rectangular. The brown paper had a note in shaky old writing—*personal delivery please.*

She pulled the paper and silky cloth down a bit to see the title. *Ouch!* Her fingernails stung like a burn where they had grazed the book.

The cover was blank. Her fingertips really hurt, and Dorrity knew it was wrong to snoop, but she flicked the cloth further aside. On the spine of the book there seemed to be five words, so faded and tiny she couldn't read them. At the bottom were two initials. She made out an *Ɛ.* and an *ℋ.*

By now, her whole hand stung. She'd gone very shivery. But she dug a magnifying glass with a brass handle out of a dresser drawer and squinted through it. She bent her head this way and that. The words on the spine were still no more than dips and hollows in the leather.

At last she reached out just with her fingernails to lift the cover— *ouch!* She wrapped her fingers in her overdress. But what was the book cover doing? Instead of dropping shut again, it continued to lift—brown paper ripped—the book laid itself open. The first couple of blank pages fluttered over as well. There was the title page.

At first Dorrity couldn't read that lettering either. But after a moment the whole book started to glow a soft reddish gold.

This had to be magic, in Mrs. Freida's dining room.

Actual magic, right in the middle of Owl Town. Dorrity started to shake.

The lettering grew larger until at the top of the page she could see *Property of Royal Family Library, Eagle Hall.* Then, in the middle of the page, in much larger letters, the title appeared: *The Volume of Possible Endings.*

"Endings for what?" Dorrity whispered.

Something seemed to whisper back— "Dorrity's Tale."

"Dorrity's Tale?" she said more loudly. "My tale?"

The pages of the book began turning by themselves again, slowly, then faster and faster. The glow turned into a shimmer that made Dorrity's eyes feel they saw the boundary between the ordinary world and the world of magic. Her heart raced, her throat tightened. As if something huge breathed on their edges, the pages continued to flutter. Dorrity caught glimpses of lettering, some silver, some a rich, inky blue, some purple, some green. She thought she saw pictures, too, or at least what might be the first scratches of a talented pencil.

The pages stopped fluttering. The two spread before her were creamy and blank. As she stared, words began to form on the left-hand page.

One ~ Dorrity stayed in Owl Town and did nothing. She never saw Birkett and Mike again. Yorky lived with one arm and one wing for the rest of his life but never, not once, did he blame her. ~ The End ~

Her shaking grew worse. More words started to form.

Two ~ Dorrity returned from the Beastly Dark and the dangerous ways she'd had to go. Birkett and Mike thanked Dorrity with all their

*hearts, and Yorky welcomed her back with two whole arms. ~
The End ~*

"This is a bad joke." Dorrity's voice quivered.

Another set of words took shape, and then another.

*Three ~ At last Dorrity had discovered who she was and all came
clear. ~ The End ~*

*Four ~ Dorrity, with a sad lonely heart, was crowned Queen of
Fontania. ~ The End ~*

"Stop, please stop," she said in a high, thin voice.

*Five ~ Dorrity thought about her doll and wished she had
remembered it sooner. ~ The End ~*

"But I've never had a doll," Dorrity cried.

~

JOTTING

The door between the shop and house banged open. Mrs. Freida's slippers slapped on the floor. Dorrity slammed the book shut, whipped the cloth back and did her best to smooth the brown paper over it all. She darted to the window, scorched fingers nursed in the skirt of her overdress.

Mrs. Freida flung into the room and stopped with a gasp. "Dorrity—you snuck in without me noticing. Good morning. How are you?"

Dorrity hoped Mrs. Freida wouldn't see how she was shaking. "I was…staring at your scarecrow. It's terribly ragged."

"Don't be rude," said Mrs. Freida.

"Sorry," said Dorrity. "We could make a new one."

"Good. I mean yes. One day soon." Mrs. Freida checked the wrapping around the book—Dorrity noted that she didn't actually touch the book itself—and set it all carefully in a drawer in the middle of a cabinet. She turned a lock on it and tucked the tiny key into the checked pocket of her shop apron.

Dorrity cleared her throat but her voice still wobbled. "Is that a book?"

Mrs. Freida didn't meet her eyes. "It's just something the postmistress has charge of, and I'd forgotten. If the Royals do end up coming, I can hand it over. Now, today's lessons."

The gossip about the return of the Royals must have reminded Mrs. Freida that the book should go back to the Eagle Hall library. She couldn't have delivered it personally when the Hall had been closed for countless years. She obviously knew the book was dangerous, and must just have been checking it was all right.

The shop bell dinged again. Mrs. Freida hurried out, hand over the pocket with the key in it.

Dorrity opened her exercise book to the back page and jotted down as much as she could remember of the five endings of her own tale.

1 — *did nothing, and Yorky had a wing*. Ridiculous.

2 — *returned from the Beastly Dark*. But she'd been inside the Dark lots of times—well, just on the edges.

3 — *discovered who she was and all came clear*. Even more ridiculous.

4 — *was crowned Queen, sad and lonely*. Even more than even more ridiculous.

5 — *remembered a doll*. Rubbish. Dorrity much preferred playing dress-up.

A LITTLE FRIEND

By lunchtime, Dorrity had managed to do parentheses (easy), commas, and dashes—easy as well—though she still felt upset and her hand hurt.

Mrs. Freida bustled in and looked over her shoulder.

It just popped out: "This afternoon I'll write my own story. That's *Dorrity's Tale*. How should it end?"

Mrs. Freida's eyes, a faded blue, looked shocked, then worried.

Dorrity felt ashamed that she'd been a bit mean. "No, I'll try a poem with no punctuation. Not even a dot at the end."

Mrs. Freida sounded old as well as uneasy. "The shop's still very busy. Come in while you have lunch."

"If it's crowded, I'd rather have lunch by the fountain," Dorrity said.

Mrs. Freida nodded, put her hand over the pocket in her apron again and sort-of tottered back into the shop.

Dorrity felt more ashamed. But in the kitchen she chose a plate with a feather-shaped scroll around the rim. She filled a matching mug with milk. On the plate she set seven round crackers with small squares of cheese, segments of a red and a green apple from last summer's harvest, and seven almonds because seven was a lucky number. So was three, but three almonds were hardly any. She put the food on a tray with a tea cloth over it in case of flies. She jammed her birthday hat well down over her face so she wouldn't catch anyone's eye and left the house by the back door.

From the side path she saw the midday riverboat tied up at the main wharf. She waited till High Street was clear of steam trucks bringing the weekly meat, dry goods, and what-nots over the bridge, then crossed to the fountain in the plaza.

The rim of the fountain was chipped here and there, but the town couldn't afford to mend it. The chips added to its charm, so Dorrity thought. The statue in the middle was a dragon-eagle, just a small one because of the cost—of the marble, of course. Nobody could ever buy a real dragon-eagle. Such things were far too powerful to own, and Owl Town had struggled even to save the dolleros for new carpet in the town hall meeting room.

Around the fountain were seats separated by four big urns that spilled with all-year ivy and springtime flowers. Dorrity sat beside the shadiest urn where she wouldn't be noticed. She crunched the crackers and thought about her brothers, who would be back at the house eating lettuce sandwiches.

She hardly ever cried, but the inside of her nose started to smart. She shrank further under her hat. Keeping secrets was close to lying. That meant her brothers had lied to her—about no magic in Owl Town, and about deciding without telling her that they'd leave here. Dorrity wiped her nose on the hem of her overdress. Her fingers still stung.

When she lifted her head again, she saw Birkett march out of the shop. He wasn't having lunch at all. He had a new axe with the price tag dangling. What had happened to the old one? He was always so careful with dangerous things.

Not noticing her among the ivy, he strode on, arguing to himself. Dr. Oxford whizzed past on his red bicycle. The law clerk sped home for lunch on her blue one. The craft lady trundled by with her hand cart. A starling sang, *Be caa-aareful.*

Dorrity saw a tall stranger in a cap with a feather-shaped badge and a dark blue brass-buttoned jacket standing nearby. He squinted after Birkett as he disappeared down Lower High Street.

After another moment, footsteps knocked on the cobblestones. Dorrity glanced under the brim of her feathery hat. It was Officer Edgar in his hard-heeled boots. People hadn't decided yet whether he was a plus for the town or a pest.

A cold voice spoke. It must be the stranger. "Officer? Who is that with the axe?"

"A market gardener," said Officer Edgar. "And who are you, sir?"

"Don't you recognize my badge?" The stranger sounded stern as well as cold. Dorrity peered through the ivy.

"No," said Edgar. "It's similar to the badge of the Grand Palace. Is it a new issue?"

"Underground Branch," said the stranger. "What do you know about that gardener? How long has he lived here?"

Edgar paused for a moment. "I'm fairly new myself. All I can say is he has two brothers and a sister. Why are you asking?"

"Official business," the man snapped.

Dorrity knew she was eavesdropping but she dared another look. The official had a chilly half-smile.

"Hmm," said Edgar. "I had part of a garbled message from the Palace early this morning, but the bird flew off again. Faulty equipment doesn't help communications."

"Do you want me to complain about the equipment to His and Her Majesties?" the man asked in his hard voice.

"Not especially, unless it will help," Edgar said.

"I want to see the sister for myself. I'm in a hurry. Where will I find her?" The Underground Branch man sounded colder with every sentence.

Dorrity dared another look.

Edgar had folded his arms. "As far as I know there's only one child in Owl Town. It doesn't seem right, but that appears to be the case. You can possibly find her in the shop."

She kept very still, huddled back under the urn.

"Say nothing," said the man. "Not to anyone. Not even another message to the King and Queen. Is that understood?"

Dorrity could tell Edgar was annoyed by the man being bossy, but he pointed to the Necessary Shop. The stranger had another hard look down High Street after Birkett. Then he headed for the shop, Edgar more slowly behind him.

Dorrity set the lunch tray on the cobblestones and dashed for the bridge. She scrambled under the ramparts to the lower path. When she was under the willows she started running home to tell her brothers…

She skidded to a stop in a patch of mud. The Underground man must be one of the authorities. Her brothers might actually use him as another reason to argue how important it was to leave Owl Town.

But if the man was in a hurry, it probably meant he had to return on the riverboat when it left at one o'clock. That at least was easy to deal with.

~

Dorrity raced along the lower path and from the shelter of a flowering cherry peered across the road to her own cottage. All she saw of her brothers was their backs in their overalls. Mike and Yorky were clomping down to the market garden and Birkett marching over to the beehives. They didn't spot her.

In half a minute she was through the front door where wavery green light came through a panel beside it. Last year's hat hung on the hallway pegs. Edgar would recognize its blue and red checks and purple ribbon. She grabbed it and put it on. With the new hat under her arm, she rushed out the back gate, down to the Dark Road, along to Arrow Street and finally to Mrs. Freida's little back gate.

There, under the apple tree, was the swing. It was half-hidden from Mrs. Freida's kitchen door by the blueberry hedge. Every summer that hedge needed the scarecrow to keep the gidibirds from stripping the fruit.

Dorrity's idea had come from a stamp in one of Mrs. Freida's albums. It had a picture about a historical moment when some monkeys in hats had fooled sailors into thinking they were children. The monkeys hadn't done it deliberately.

They were just monkeys that were nuts about hats (as well as nuts). Dorrity needed to fool the man on purpose.

She heaved the scarecrow off its pole and tied her new birthday hat with its green feathers onto its head. Then she sat on the swing, the scarecrow beside her, and gently worked her legs so both hats would sway back and forth above the blueberries. Under the brim of the old hat, she kept an eye on the side path.

There was the Underground man now, still with Edgar behind him.

Dorrity was used to doing various voices. It helped when she played by herself. She especially liked copying the squabbling families she'd heard on the riverboats.

"*Too hii-iigh*," she squeaked. "*You're scaa-arin' me!*"

"Don't be silly," she said in her own voice. "I'm not going to drop you."

Edgar started to stride down the garden. The stranger put a hand out and kept him there.

Dorrity kept the swing dipping and squeaked again. "*You're bein' mean! I don't want to plaa-ay!*"

"You're no fun today," she said in her natural voice. "Go home then. See if I care."

She stopped the swing, dropped the scarecrow and birthday hat under the apple tree, and rattled the back gate as if someone was leaving. Still wearing last year's checked hat, she marched up the garden.

The Underground Branch man pulled his cap low on his brow.

Dorrity put on a bright smile and spoke around him to

Edgar. "Hello, Officer. Are you here for law and order?"

Edgar frowned. "Who was that with you just now?"

She wanted to be careful not to lie. "Nobody. Young children get into moods easily, don't they?"

The Underground man dipped his cap even lower as if he didn't want to have a face at all. "The police officer said there was only one child in Owl Town. Is that not correct?"

Hadn't he asked in the shop? Dorrity smiled politely. "Officer Edgar can't know everything yet. He's only been here a few weeks."

Edgar's face turned red like a beet stain.

It was lucky that a whistle came from the river—the steamboat, ready to leave.

"That's your call, isn't it?" said Edgar. "Doesn't pay to be late."

The Underground man went *tcha!* like a very cross kiss. Before he stamped off, he also eyed Dorrity in a way that made her skin shrink.

She whisked herself to the back doorstep. "Lesson time! Mustn't annoy Mrs. Freida!" She pulled the door shut behind her and crossed her burnt fingers.

Through the window she saw Edgar stand for a moment, then stride away. He'd be annoyed at being made to look a fool. She'd better keep out of his sight till he calmed down. And she'd better not wear her new hat for a couple more days.

She'd also annoyed an important man from the Grand Palace.

—

6

A FEW QUESTIONS

By next afternoon, Dorrity had managed to stay out of Edgar's way. Once her brothers left the following day, it wouldn't matter so much.

"Give me something new?" she asked Mrs. Freida after lunch in the kitchen. "Some history? Something quite difficult that will keep me inside?"

"That's a sign of an inquiring mind," said Mrs. Freida. "A spot of history wouldn't hurt. The battles of Battle Island. Or foreign relations with Um'Binnia."

Despite herself, Dorrity glanced through the dining-room door. She could just see the locked drawer of the dresser. "Is there anything about the history of Eagle Hall?"

Mrs. Freida wiped her hands on her apron. "You are twelve now. I daresay you're ready." She went through to the dining room.

Dorrity followed.

Mrs. Freida touched a couple of books on an upper shelf, then took one down. "Bring it into the shop. I can keep an eye on you, and you can ask questions."

Dorrity didn't want to be out in the shop but she sat under the counter so no one would see her. It smelled of licorice, coffee, and soap, and Mrs. Freida's shop slippers. Button bent down and gave her a smile.

There was only one chapter on Eagle Hall, mostly about how it was a beloved holiday home of King Vincent, the three times great-grandfather of King Jasper and Queen Sibilla. His older brother, Count Bale, had been his adviser. Why hadn't the older brother been King instead of Vincent? Oh—Count Bale had been so late coming into his magical power that Vincent had to be made King first.

Dorrity skimmed a few paragraphs till she saw the words "shape-changing" and "animals." She wanted to skim them as well because they made her too shivery. The King's brother, Count Bale, had done some experiments. It sounded like bad magic. Then Vincent had died and Count Bale had been banished from Fontania for all time. *For all time*? Why not just "till he died?"

She slapped the book shut. For a few minutes she stayed there under the counter. Mrs. Freida's ankles, the hem of her skirt, and the comforting checked apron passed up and down. Then Dorrity slipped into the house, put the book back on the shelf, and looked out the dining-room window at sunshine bright as butter on the terracotta pots and geraniums.

From here she could see over the scarecrow, down Arrow Street to the Dark Road, the ditch, and even a bit of the wasteland.

Something glinted near the ditch and disappeared. It had looked like someone lugging something large and thin like…a placard? For a moment she thought it was the Underground Branch man—she was sure she glimpsed a dark blue jacket—but this person seemed much too short. Not as chunky as a dwarf, and definitely too small to be an ogre or troll unless it was a toddler and under-fed.

The more she thought about it, the more she felt it might have been a boy. But how could that be? Anyway, there was no more movement. No other glint.

"Dorrity?" called Mrs. Freida from the shop. "Please come and help."

She hurried back. The shop was even busier than yesterday. There was either a rash of petty burglaries or an epidemic of bad memory. Townsfolk wanted replacements of all sorts: a pot of glue, a punnet of violet seedlings. What's more, the meeting-room door from the town hall was missing. That couldn't be bad memory. Mr. Coop had taken it off its hinges at lunchtime and set it outside while the new carpet was laid. Half an hour later, the door had vanished.

"Astonishing nerve," Mr. Coop was saying to Mrs. Freida and Button. "You can almost admire it. Whoever took it must have strong friends. It took me and two hefty others, along with Button and his long arms—" he nodded at the troll, who blushed at once—"to move the door outside in the first place, especially without breaking the glass."

Dorrity loved that meeting-room door. It had green and red glass strips and two panels, each with an image of a dragon-eagle. Its huge brass handle had been perfect to swing on when she was little. Could that person in the ditch have been stealing the door? Impossible. He was only one person and whatever he'd been carrying was too light to be any door.

A customer spilled a box of needles. Dorrity had to scramble through everyone's legs to gather them up—very tricky with the fingertips that had been scorched on *The Volume of Possible Endings*. Another customer started an argument with Mrs. Freida over not getting discounts. Dorrity saw everyone listen. Of course they pretended they weren't interested. They just examined the price tags on nail clippers or the list of ingredients on bags of sugar (very short lists) while their ears flapped, which was just an expression.

~

Dorrity ran home at the end of the day. Her brothers clomped round the kitchen in their work socks, doing the usual things for the night before they left for "business" in Fribbleton, *ha ha*.

Birkett stirred masses of chopped-up parsley into butter and breadcrumbs to make a crust for baking fish. Today it was a medium-sized spotty plumpoe, tastiest fish in the river. Mike jumbled a salad out of grated carrot, shredded lettuce, chunks of apple, and a scattering of seeds from last year's sunflowers.

Once again words just popped out. "I don't need friends my own age."

Yorky's freckled nose was smudged with flour. Into a cake pan he pressed a mixture of dough with grated lemon. "But you might like a few chocolate sprinkles."

"I'm wise to being ignored and also pampered," Dorrity said.

Yorky just chuckled. So she scattered chocolate over the lemon dough. Yorky poured lemon custardy stuff over the top and clanged the pan into the oven.

The plumpoe was plump and delicious. The salad had all the right crunchy bits. The lemon slice was...

"Hold your fork properly," growled Birkett.

"Have you hurt those fingers?" Yorky asked.

"In fact, I have something to tell—" she began.

There was a knock on the front door.

Birkett raised his eyebrows, clattered down his dessert fork and went to answer. Mike and Yorky held their forkfuls untasted, ears turned in the direction of the hallway. Dorrity listened too.

"Edgar? Come in," Birkett said with a deeper growl.

His socks padded back down the hall. Edgar's hard heels clacked. They came into the kitchen. Edgar carried a stove-pipe hat, not his helmet, and wore a leather jacket, so he must be off duty.

"Sit down if you like," growled Birkett again. "Have a piece of lemon slice."

"Thank you, but no." Edgar turned his hat in his hands. "I would have come yesterday but with all these burglaries—well, I'd just like an unofficial word."

"Let it rip," said Mike.

"Oh, to Birkett will do," said Edgar. "Good evening, Dorrity. How is your imaginary friend?"

"Imaginary friend?" asked Yorky.

Her three brothers looked at her.

Dorrity widened her eyes back. "Miss Honey used to

have ten when she was a child. She told me. She believed they lived in the piano and when she touched the keys they ran about inside to push the tune out. That would be one friend for each finger, so it makes a peculiar sense."

"I was asking about yours," said the off-duty officer in a dark tone.

All right—she could tell the truth. "Twelve's too old to have an imaginary friend. I might have had one when I was four." She frowned at her brothers. "If I did, it's too long ago. I don't want to know."

Her brothers shrugged and stared at Edgar. He beetled his eyebrows. "If I could have that word," he said to Birkett. "Back on the doorstep."

Birkett showed the police officer out of the kitchen. After a moment or two the front door closed and the bolt clanked. Yorky reached to the kitchen door bolt and clanked that too.

~

Birkett strode back into the kitchen. He looked as grim as when they'd been shaving the previous morning and the bird had landed on the sill. Dorrity bet Edgar's word had been to do with the Underground Branch man.

"Early bed," growled Birkett. "Never too old for reading aloud, but a very short story tonight. We've talking to do. Brotherly talking."

Dorrity bet they did. She chose the story of the lollipop house and the witch in the forest for Mike to read. He always used it as an excuse to say, *So never go into the Beastly Dark*. But it was only three pages and she was keen to hear if Edgar had mentioned the Underground man. After her brothers had said good night, she'd slip out of the room and hide where the coats hung near the door halfway down the hall.

Two eavesdroppings in two days. Why not?

~

It actually stayed at one eavesdropping. Mike rattled through the story and the brothers said their good nights. Birkett shut Dorrity's bedroom door behind them. She heard the door by the coats close as well. *Cuss.* When that door was opened, the hinges gave a groan of agony. No amount of oil ever helped.

All she could hear was raised voices. They'd never sounded so angry before, angry and worried. She lay there in her blue pajamas with their cross-stitch bodice and put two fingers in her mouth to soothe them where they still stung from *The Volume of Possible Endings*.

~

GOODBYE, GOODBYE

Dorrity was not ready to wake when she heard her brothers clattering into the bathroom and Yorky calling, "Second Shave!"

They'd be off to Fribbleton straight after breakfast. Dorrity had to pack a week-full basket for Mrs. Freida's.

Over their toast and boiled eggs, her brothers were silent again till Birkett pushed his chair back. "We'll walk you to the shop," he said in his deep voice.

"I can wave goodbye from our own gate," Dorrity said. "I can watch you go over the bridge. I'd like to see you go while I'm still at home."

Mike slapped the table and stood up. "We're walking you."

"We'd like a word with Mrs. Freida," Yorky explained. "And a word with Mr. Coop."

"What sort of word?" Dorrity asked.

Yorky gave his crow of laughter. "Do you want your last half of toast? Too late. It's mine." He snaffled it off her plate, spread it with far too much honey and stuffed it in his mouth.

Birkett bustled them to rinse their dishes and gather their

packs and spare boots. The more her brothers pretended things were normal, the more Dorrity worried. Maybe she should say something about seeing the Underground man, and about that *Volume*.

She tugged Yorky's sleeve.

"What's the matter?" he asked.

Mike pushed between them to pick up his hiking stick and all the sticks fell over. Birkett got a swipe on the ear by accident, and Mike said hang on a tick, he'd forgotten his toothbrush.

This was not a good time to say anything. She put a cross-stitched hanky in her overdress pocket, fastened the toggle of her feathery hat, then Birkett had them all out the door and the key turned.

Her brothers hurried her up Lower High Street. Their boots made such a noise that she couldn't hear the cries of the starlings or gidibirds. An arrow of crows flew out of the Beastly Dark, followed by so many more that they looked like a veil with a few holes torn to show the sky.

She could say something when they all got to Mrs. Freida's—oh, not about *The Volume*. Mrs. Freida would know that Dorrity had snooped at it.

"Stop lagging."

"Get a move on."

"Rattle your sit-upon."

"Shut up, I'm not four any more," Dorrity said between her teeth.

Outside the shop, Birkett gave her a hug and a kiss, then thundered off up High Street to Mr. Coop's. Mike and

Yorky sprinted her down Mrs. Freida's side path and rapped on the back door.

Mrs. Freida was still in her flannel nightgown, decorated down the front with toast crumbs.

"Morning, Mrs. Freida, lovely day for it." Mike hustled Dorrity through to the spare room, picked her up under the armpits and dumped her down on the bed. "I'll unpack your stuff."

"I can do it later." Dorrity wanted to hear what Yorky was saying to Mrs. Freida.

"Pajamas!" Mike hauled them out of the basket. "Under the pillow?"

"Just like at home," Dorrity said.

"Hairbrush!" He flourished it and gazed around.

"On the dressing table," Dorrity said, "just like at home."

"Did you bring anything to read? Ah, Mrs. Freida has piled library books up on the bedside table." He gave her a breath-squeezing hug and hurried out.

Dorrity followed. He was already stomping on the back path.

Yorky's hug scooped her right off her feet. She was furious with all of them. But when he bumped her down, she saw a smudge of honey at the corner of his mouth. She took the hanky from her overdress, dabbed his face with it and tucked it into the top pocket of his jacket. She didn't think he'd realized, but he'd find it later on when he needed a nose-blow.

He pecked her cheek. "No worrying, right?"

So of course questions lined up in her head. What if the

authorities didn't like what her brothers said this year? How many more years were they meant to talk to them about bringing her up? Four more, till she was sixteen? Six more, till she was eighteen? What would the authorities say about them all leaving Owl Town?

She hissed in his ear. "Would leaving Owl Town mean we'd get away from the authorities? Is that why it has to be secret?"

The expression on his face reminded her of when he had opened the flour bin to get a cupful to make a cake and found it wriggling with weevils. "Good questions," he said. "Answers when we get back home. Bye!" He hurried out too.

Mrs. Freida closed the door and put an arm around Dorrity's shoulders. "We can watch them from the front of the shop." She unlatched the connecting door at the end of her hallway and hurried through.

Dorrity followed to the shop door and looked over the *Closed* sign from the side that said *Open*. The Forgotten River sparkled silver in the morning sun. The gidibirds called *Good day*.

Watch-out-watch-out-watch-out! the starlings shrieked.

There was Birkett thundering back across the plaza from Mr. Coop's. He joined the others near the fountain. They did some brotherly buffeting as if they needed special encouragement. Then they strode down to the bridge: brown-haired Birkett, sandy-haired Mike, red-haired Yorky. By the time they were halfway over the bridge, it looked as if the buffeting had turned to arguing. As they set off up the road, there was even a punch. Two punches. Three.

She clambered onto some boxes of canned beans and saw them disappear round the corner of the hill faster than they'd ever hiked before. It made her shivery again. Then Mr. Coop appeared down High Street in his smart black going-out beanie, and Mrs. Freida opened the shop door.

"Your brothers want you to spend a day with mathematics," Mr. Coop said to Dorrity. "Can you stand it?"

Mathematics nearly always ended up with Mr. Coop talking about the barrel-boat he was constructing in the same way as his leak-proof barrels. The answer was yes.

~

Dorrity and Mr. Coop walked up High Street. There was a difficult moment passing the Watch House. Edgar, in his official jacket and helmet, was on the step. He narrowed his eyes at Dorrity's feathery hat.

"How's your little friend today?" he called.

She was tempted to whine *Got a headache* in the voice of the imaginary friend who was really the scarecrow. But she smiled, gave a wave and didn't glance back.

"I'm asking no questions," said Mr. Coop in his sawdusty voice. That was good because it was too complicated for any answers.

~

Dorrity hadn't been in the workshop for three days. Had he done anything new?

Yes. A scroll of paper was spread on a shelf, weighted down with a jar of copper screws, a tack hammer, and a wooden ruler. It would be improvements for the barrel-boat. In the end it might make Mr. Coop a ship-load of money. He'd built most of it years ago but had run out of dolleros. All the bankers who could have loaned more had fallen about laughing at the idea of a boat that could travel underwater.

Dorrity had no great opinion of bankers. Mr. Coop's barrels were famous for being airtight and therefore bugtight. After Yorky had found those weevils in the flour, he'd decided to store dry goods in little barrels from Mr. Coop. Those barrels could also store vinegar and other liquids. If they could keep liquid in, it should be obvious to bankers that they'd keep water out as well.

She had a good look at this latest plan. He'd installed a chemical burner inside to heat water for steam. Brilliant— the chemicals would also make oxygen for the people in the boat, and that would be especially important when they had to pump air into the buoyancy tanks. There'd be no point in being underwater and suffocating rather than drowning.

His calculations down the side of the plan reckoned on the boat being able to stay underwater, below ordinary steam ships, for up to five hours. Sailing in secret could be a huge advantage if you wanted to sneak up…

"Mr. Coop," she called, "can you say 'sailing' when a boat doesn't have sails?"

He had his green work beanie on now. Through his beard, a line-up of rivets clamped in his lips looked like metal teeth. Steel hoops of all sizes hung over his arm. He nodded.

"You could have a mast and sail folded down on top of your boat, and flip it up when necessary," Dorrity said.

He spat the rivets into his palm. "Another good idea from Dorrity. Now, nine times table."

She'd been doing this for years. But Mr. Coop liked to start simple and work upward. She started writing. It would be weird to do lessons with other children. Would they whisper, give each other secret nudges, or even copy someone else's answer? She wrote 9 x 12 = 108, then chewed a pencil till bits of wood—*ptha!*—came off on her tongue

"Mr. Coop," she asked, "why am I the only child in Owl Town?"

He looked startled and scratched his head. The hoops fell down his arm in a musical clash.

"It just so happened," he said. "The townsfolk weren't keen to have any child, in fact. But your brothers begged. And it's hard to turn a little child away."

"Thank you. But that's not quite what I meant," Dorrity said. "I heard Edgar say that it didn't seem right for a child to be the only one."

"There's right and there's wrong." Mr Coop began hammering. "If a child is well and happy, there's no call for anyone to pry."

"But why didn't the townsfolk want any children at all?" she asked. "Is no children really unusual?"

"There is usual and unusual," said Mr. Coop.

She was finding him very frustrating. "I think Birkett must have asked you to take care of me particularly this time. Did he say why?"

Mr. Coop shook his head and began hammering a middle hoop into place around the staves.

Dorrity may as well ask one of the other questions twisting inside. "You know how Owl Town is proud of not having even a spit of magic? What if someone here turned out to have something magical hidden away?"

He frowned at her. "Six times nine."

"Fifty-four." She felt her jaw go stubborn. At least that was better than being afraid. "Mr. Coop, what if someone in the town is looking after a tiny spit of magic or even a big spit, and the magic mentions somebody else who lives in the town?"

He'd gone frowny. "Eight times table, starting at eight times one."

By the time Dorrity had written $8 \times 12 = 96$, Mr. Coop had switched on his bench saw. Its whine was tremendous. He sawed new staves so hard that she worried he might burst a boiler (she didn't want to think *his heart* instead of *boiler*). Why hadn't he answered? What was he hiding?

There were too many secrets. She might have to do some deliberate spying to find out why everyone seemed determined to keep something from her—oh! She remembered that message-bird. What if it had been a spy-bird sent by the authorities? How could she tell?

She eased off the stool. "I'm running back to Mrs. Freida's."

With the wail of staves being cut, Mr. Coop didn't hear. She grabbed her hat off the hook and flourished it. He still didn't notice, mainly because she flourished it only a bit as well as behind his back. But Dorrity had said what she was doing. At least, she'd said the first part of it.

⁓

HELLO!

Dorrity hurried down High Street past steam trucks and hand carts, and stopped outside the shop. There—she had done what she said and so far she hadn't been noticed. She took the next side street, then Scabbard Lane, and headed along Beak Avenue back up to Lower High Street. From Miss Honey's front room she heard bouncing runs from the piano. Miss Honey's brown curls would be bouncing too.

She ducked to her own cottage and around to the bathroom window. If the mechanical bird hadn't soared off but had toppled, it might be under the gooseberry. Birkett had planted the bush there so nobody could climb in. Yorky had argued that they might need to climb in themselves if they lost the key. Mike argued that if they needed a spiky bush under one window, they should have one under every ruddy window. Dorrity had asked who would ever want to climb into their cottage in the first place? The brothers had gone quiet and dark on it. She hadn't mentioned the ancient dog-door down beside the washtub in the laundry. She was pretty certain she was the only one who knew about it anyway.

She mustn't let out a single squeak. For one thing, no brothers were here to haul her out of the prickles. For the main thing, she didn't want Officer Edgar to hear her.

She took off her hat so it wouldn't be ripped to pieces, knelt and tried to see if anything lay on the ground. There was an orange-spotted ball they'd lost months ago. There was an old brick. There was a striped cotton sock that must have blown off the clothesline. Just behind that was the glint of metal.

The branches snagged while she wriggled in. She tossed the ball out behind her, reached past the sock and scrabbled several scraps of metal into her hand. She wriggled further and found several more, sort-of triangular. They might be bits of a wing. She squirmed backwards past the same snags and prickles (*ouch!*—one in her scalp!), and sat up with the pieces.

"I can put you together," she muttered. "I'm the most resourceful child in town."

Still, if it was a spy-bird, it might fly off and tell whomever had sent it about her and her brothers. After all, the three of them had gone silent at the idea of spy-birds. She had that feeling again of darkness and things creeping closer. But for goodness' sake, there was nothing to tell. If this was one of the King's birds, he wouldn't be interested in an ordinary girl and her ordinary brothers.

Cross-legged in her grubby overdress, she used her hat as a basin to hold the pieces so she could examine them. The bird was made of coils of brass, silver screws, tiny wheels and tinier levers. How cunningly the parts had been packed to fit inside the little round body. She would put it together except for one wing so that it couldn't fly off.

First she fitted the wing bits together. Nothing was missing. Then she started on the body. She'd had plenty of fun at Mr. Coop's over the years, helping him with handyman jobs. Now her fingers seemed to sense by themselves which broken bit to fit with which other piece.

There was a little feather-scale mark on the bird's underside—the King's mark. It wasn't quite the same as the one the Underground Branch man had on his cap.

She shivered. A cloud had passed under the sun. Most people said over the sun, but Dorrity liked to get things right. Was it midday already? She couldn't see how to fix the bird's legs tight, but began to get up. *Ow.* Pins and needles.

Footsteps crunched on the front path. It sounded like Officer Edgar. He knew her brothers were away. Was he snooping? In those noisy boots?

As fast as she could—not very fast at all with pins and needles—she hobbled beside the garden shed, holding the hat with the clockwork pieces against her chest. From there she peered at the house. Yes, Edgar. He snooped here, snooped there, even tried looking through the windows, and turned to the shed.

She eased further down the garden, unlatched the back gate and slunk through without making a sound. If she took the clockwork bits to Mr. Coop, he might decide to send a message to the Grand Palace to say he had come upon some royal property, and that might bring back the Underground man. Dorrity would sneak across the Dark Road, over the ditch and the wasteland, and find a hollow at the base of a tree to store the bird.

Never go into the Beastly Dark, her brothers had said.

"I'll never go," she had answered and always added to herself, *not far enough to get into trouble.*

~

The ditch was five man-strides wide but ten of Dorrity's. One of her red birthday boots slipped into mud. Her overdress caught on burrs. When she hauled herself up the other side, she snagged some cross-stitch.

Now she had to be careful of the briars on the wasteland. It took longer than usual to reach the forest because of carrying the hat with the bits of bird. From the river came the call of blue-bellied starlings. *Watch-out-watch-out.*

That second ending from *The Volume* came into her mind. *She returned from the Beastly Dark and the dangerous ways…*

She shivered again. She could hardly *return from the Beastly Dark* if she only ever tinkered round its edge. How far in should she go? It had to be further than usual, or else Edgar might spot her.

The ground sloped up. Thick leaves muffled the rush of the river and sounds of the town. She climbed higher and looked back. Through a gap in the branches she saw the bridge below, white huffs coming out each side from where a boat steamed underneath.

She climbed several more paces. The ground led to a hollow. Though she was more scared with every step, it would be better to go further—out of this dip, into the next, perhaps up again.

After a few minutes, there, higher up, was a tiny house. Her heart gave a horrible jolt.

Could she really be seeing this? She wanted to run—nobody had mentioned a house in this part of the Dark. At least, not to Dorrity. It could be an out-building of Eagle Hall, though she'd always thought the Hall was much further along, behind Mr. Coop's end of the town.

From a tree above her head came a soft *oo*, like an owl surprised in a dream. By now her feet had carried her on even nearer the building. It felt deserted, so she dared to go even closer.

On this side it had no windows. She came to a pile of logs and a small workbench with an axe like Birkett's. She skirted the logs. On the second side, the tiny house had one high window. In a few more careful steps, Dorrity had turned a corner and was around at the front. Here a larger window reflected a sheen of forest gloom. A row of violets sat in fresh-turned earth beside the porch. The porch itself was half-finished, one wall the same brown as the fence paint that Mike had lost.

And the door…was a very fine door for anywhere. It was especially fine for such a small house in a forest. A door with glass strips of red and green, panels each with an image of a dragon-eagle. The varnished wood was carved like feather-scales. The handle was a big brass one, just right to swing on if you were small.

From inside the house came a struggle of music. Somebody was trying to play scales. It sounded nothing like Birkett's ukulele, nothing like Mike's mouth organ or Miss Honey's piano. It could almost be singing. But it wasn't like Dorrity's voice (ordinary), Mrs. Freida's (rich and wobbly) or

Mr. Coop's (like an echo from an empty barrel).

Whatever it was, the music stopped. Somebody crossed behind the window. The person inside must have seen her. The only thing to do was go and knock.

Dorrity held the hat like a bowl in one arm and tapped on the glass. After a couple of heartbeats, the door opened.

At first Dorrity thought it was a man, but he was too short and skinny. It was a boy!

She let out a scream. It was just a small one, but it still made her very embarrassed.

~

POCKET OF CHANGE

Dorrity started to step off the porch to run away. But the boy hadn't said a word yet. And he didn't look like the children she'd seen on riverboats. What was it about him? He was just a little taller than her. His face and hands were pale, with a silvery look. His jacket, too big for him, was the same dark blue as the Underground Branch man's. His trousers, bunched at the waist, were over-sized knickerbockers in a green and brown check like Farmer Ember's missing pair. He wore a cap almost the same shade as the Underground man's. It looked as if it had lost a badge—there was a darker patch where the cap hadn't faded. It came down half over his ears. None of his hair poked out at all.

The boy didn't step out onto the porch. He still hadn't said anything. There was no expression on his face. But all the same he seemed horrified to see her on the doorstep.

Dorrity had better let him know that she was harmless. A compliment might do the job. "I liked the…music." It was only sort-of a lie.

"I…am…try-ing…my…voice." It was all on one slow level as if he'd never used his voice even for speaking. There was a faint sound like tiny gears grinding. "I am not ready. To meet. Anyone yet."

"When you are ready, you might like to sing with Miss Honey and my brothers." What was she saying? She didn't want to see or hear the boy again. More words burst out anyway. "Yorky squawks rather than sings but nobody minds."

The faintest flush appeared on the boy's neck. "I am a quick learner," he said in his slow way. "But I have learned that quick does not mean instant."

A puff of wind ruffled the green feathers of the birthday hat so they tickled Dorrity's hands. The boy looked down.

"Feathers." He seemed a little surprised, though his eyebrows didn't go up. Now she thought of it, how could they? He didn't have any.

The boy glanced into the bowl of the hat and seemed startled again. She folded down the brim to hide the clockwork. She'd better distract him.

"My name is Dorrity. What's yours?"

"A name…" There was a sort of clank like a metal burp, *clur-urp*. "I have been called Metal Boy."

Metalboy? Dorrity laughed. Her hand reached out by itself and rapped his arm. There was another clank, as if he wore a suit of metal under his jacket. Why? And how had the town hall door appeared here?

She thought it best to carry on as if things were normal and she was used to children her own age. "I live sort-of nearby. Let me know if there's anything I can do. For instance, do you need something from the Necessary Shop?" With luck, he'd shake his head and go inside. Then she could escape.

The boy was stock-still. "Nec-ess-ary," he said.

"You know, soap, scissors. Toilet paper. Ice cream," Dorrity said. "All the essentials."

The boy bowed a little. "It would be kind of you to bring me an oil-can. It is the one thing I have not man-aged to—"

To steal? Like the door? Dorrity decided to hold her tongue—just an expression—but was horrified to see her hand go out again, this time palm up. "An oil-can only costs about five dolleros."

His shoulders went straight, as shoulders do when someone is taken aback. "Mon-ey." He bent an arm and slid a hand into one of the pockets of his dark blue jacket. He brought it out, opened his palm and stared at the coins there as if he had been wondering what on earth they were for. Then he tipped them into her hand: six dolleros, a three-cent piece and a rattle of single cents. She jingled them into her pocket.

Without warning, the boy grabbed her hat and picked up the body of the broken mechanical bird.

"Hey…" But Dorrity couldn't say the bird was hers when it wasn't.

In a blink of time he'd fitted those tricky legs tighter. Then he fitted the second wing. The bird started to whirr. Words grated from it, impossible to understand at first, then clearer only in patches.

"*The…whirr…every official…whirr…girl must be found. Whirr…at wuh-wuh-once…reward…rewuh-wuh-wuh…*"

"Is it the King's?" Dorrity asked.

The bird's wings flapped, and the boy lost his grip on it. With another flap it landed at his feet. He was wearing one boot and one shoe. Was that usual for boys? A wing fluttered once.

"It could be a spy-bird," she continued. "But really I suppose it's just a message-bird."

He bent to scoop the bird up, but it flapped again. With a clatter of metal, a squawk, another whirr, it rose into an ogre-wood tree and perched for a moment. It squawked once more, then flew straight up and disappeared beyond the forest canopy.

The boy ducked back inside and slammed the door.

~

Wind rustled the tree tops. Dorrity ran, fast as she could, jumping over tree roots and ducking low branches. She didn't know why she'd agreed to come back here with an oil-can. All she wanted was to be safe with Mr. Coop and Mrs. Freida. She should tell them at once about the town hall door—but then they would know she'd been here in the Beastly Dark.

Hang on—she stopped under an ogre-wood. That person she'd seen carrying something yesterday. Had it been the boy? With the door? Boys couldn't be stronger than men, could they?

Above her came the slapping sound of a falling ogre blossom. She looked up and jumped aside. It fell where she'd been standing and bounced three times. This was a good one, plenty big enough, so fresh it smelled like soap.

She checked it for insects. Only a small community of earwigs. She scooped them out with *Excuse me, ew-ew-ew*. Then she heaved the ogre-wood flower so the bit where the petals joined pointed downhill, straight towards Mr. Coop's end of town. She tightened her hat toggle. Now she was ready.

She climbed in the open part, stuck a foot out between the petals to give a shove, pulled her foot in and sped off.

The blossom-sled was so leathery it shielded her from a bump against a rock, three bumps against trees. A fallen branch lay in her path—she heaved up on the petals and kicked so the sled bounced over. She coaxed it down another short slope, then steered it around so it faced uphill and stopped.

She wriggled out. The blossom wouldn't last another ride. From here she could easily get down to the town and no one would ever know she'd been up in the Dark on her own.

But her pocket clinked. Metalboy's money. He wanted that oil-can. *Cuss.*

—

10

SHADOW OF CROWS

After a few steps Dorrity came to an old brick bench half-covered with ivy. She could be on the old road to Eagle Hall. Here and there were fragments of pavers. There was a stonework edge, crumbling with age. She hurried down till the briars of the wasteland showed through the trees. From here she could see that the road had led to the ditch and the old ramp that was no longer used. She teetered across the broken planks, passed the side road to Ember Farm, and at last reached Mr. Coop's end of High Street.

At Mr. Coop's workshop door she kicked off her muddy boots and tried to sneak in. On the floor was a heap of fresh sawdust, but Mr. Coop wasn't working—he was wearing his going-out beanie.

"Dorrity!" he said. "Where have you been? You look like a mud child."

"I'm…wet from the fountain," she said.

He peered under his curly white eyebrows. "I hadn't realized you'd gone. I rushed along to the shop and couldn't find you. I was going to start a proper search."

She squeaked, "Sorry!" and ducked into the bathroom.

In the mirror she saw splatters of mud like a hundred more freckles. Her clothes had give-away smears of yellow pollen from the ogre blossom. She cracked open the door. "Mr. Coop? Can I borrow a shirt?"

The answer was a coughing rumble, part growl and part chuckle. Maybe he'd muddied himself now and then as a boy. How long ago must that have been? Thirty years? His eyebrows and beard were so white, it could be more like sixty years or even seventy.

After she dirtied his towel, she buttoned on a shirt from his ironing basket, rolled up its cuffs and smoothed the hat feathers. When she went back into the workshop, Mr. Coop tapped the side of a newly finished barrel and it boomed a rich note.

"I'll take you back to Mrs. Freida's," he said. He scraped the worst of the mud off one of her boots, she did the other.

While they walked, he gave a gentle scolding. Maybe grown-ups worried just as much or even more about children as the children grew older. But what was the harm? She was here, safe. He didn't know she'd been in the Dark, and he couldn't know anything about that second ending in the magical book at Mrs. Freida's—*the Beastly Dark and the dangerous ways*.

None of those endings made sense. Like the one about remembering a doll. Had she ever owned one? Another ending said she'd be Queen but sad and lonely. Fontania had a good King and Queen already, and they were young so they'd live for ages. Even if they died, Dorrity wouldn't be Queen. Not all stories were true, anyway. She'd like her real ending to be: *Dorrity lived all her life in Owl Town, dared to help Mr. Coop launch the first barrel-boat, and was famous because of it.*

"What's going on?" asked Mr. Coop.

Dorrity jumped—but he didn't mean what was going on inside her head. He meant what were people doing outside the Necessary Shop and Post Office?

~

They were staring and pointing at the sky on the far side of the Forgotten River. Mr Coop hobbled to a stop beside them and shaded his eyes. High above the hills were gray streaks of cloud. There was a low black cloud as well, breaking up and then re-forming. It took several moments for Dorrity to realize it must be a flock of birds, circling, far away—so they had to be huge ones.

"They're attacking," said Mr. Coop. "It could be something on—"

He cut himself short. But Dorrity knew what words he had kept in his mouth: *the Fribbleton Road.* Where her brothers were. Dorrity felt a squeeze around her heart. How far would they have hiked in the last four hours?

The wind blew a sharp gust and the sun appeared. Even at this distance the cloud of birds gleamed with an oily sheen. Something about it reminded Dorrity of the glow around *The Volume of Possible Endings.* But that had been a golden shimmer. The birds had the shine she sometimes saw in very bad dreams. Her fingertips tingled and she felt a pain round her heart again, like remembering being miserable and scared and having to run when she was little. How silly. She couldn't actually remember being miserable except with colds and general snuffles. But she found she was stepping slowly backwards, eyes on the faraway birds.

"Dorrity!" Mrs. Freida ran up and gave her a shake. "Mr. Coop said you ran off. Where did you go?"

"You're not the boss of me," Dorrity said.

Mrs. Freida looked ready to dance a jig of pure annoyance. "While your brothers are away, I certainly am. Don't you dare run off again. And don't pout. I'm old, very old, and I know what's best."

Mrs. Freida glanced at the crowd of birds, then back at Dorrity. "You're shivering. Have you had any lunch? Let's warm you up with double hot chocolate."

Dorrity let her hustle her through the shop door, but she stayed close to the window.

Out in the plaza the townsfolk were joined by the captain of a small steamboat. One of his crew, a sailor with a spade-shaped beard, must have been to the Owl and Pie because he held a twelve-pack of small-roar. There was more pointing, shaking and scratching of heads. Gradually the crowd focused around Officer Edgar. Dorrity opened the window a crack so she could hear.

Mr. Coop, hands on his hips, was speaking. "Something's badly wrong along that road. You'd better check."

Edgar put both hands on his helmet as if it would soar off any moment. "Whatever it is, it's beyond the town boundary. I have no authority."

"We'll go with you," came the butcher's voice. "Or

somebody will. I'm halfway through making sausages. Can't close my shop."

"Nor me." That was the hairdresser. "I'm doing a perm."

"I've left something in the kiln," the craft lady said.

"I'm unloading a load of roar-juice," said Chippy O'Now from the Owl and Pie.

The steamboat captain gave a shout. "I don't have to be off till tomorrow. I'm up for a look. I've got a rifle and a bulletproof hat—it ought to be peck-proof. Any of you oddballs changed your minds?"

The townsfolk shuffled and mumbled and looked sideways.

"Let's wait till the next truck arrives and ask if they saw anything," suggested the lawyer.

The steamboat captain and the bearded sailor snorted and clomped down to the wharf. Dorrity felt brave enough to leave the shop. She saw them disappear into their steamboat. Their dog, tied up to its kennel on deck, lay with its ears flat against its skull. The captain and the sailor came out again with a cabin boy. He looked very wary of Owl Town. But all three of them wore protective hats and carried rifles. The captain held up a well-stuffed backpack. "Bandages! Just in case!" He laughed. The dog whined and wriggled backwards into its kennel.

Mr. Coop began to hobble to join them, but Mrs. Freida came running out and tugged him to stop. "Not with your leg! You'll spend a week in bed and a month in a terrible temper."

The captain and crew already had their feet on the approach to the bridge.

"To the town boundary but no further!" Edgar clutched his helmet and ran after them.

Mrs. Freida marched Dorrity back to the shop. "Now sit down with your punctuation. I'm still annoyed that you ran off from Mr. Coop's."

Dorrity flounced through the connecting door. Why on earth didn't Mrs. Freida ask about why she'd run off? Then Dorrity would have to confess and everything would sort itself out. Honestly, trying to hold her own temper, trying to keep questions in, was like knowing a cork would explode from a ginger-beer bottle. How did other children ever cope with grown-ups?

She wouldn't get a chance to ask that cabin boy. But she had to take that oil-can to Metalboy. She could ask him.

—

11

A GOAT AND A PUZZLE

While Dorrity waited for another chance to sneak away, she sat at the dining-room table, scowled at quote marks, and played with the buttons of the shirt she'd borrowed from Mr. Coop. It was hard to concentrate. That cabin boy had looked too scared to stay in Owl Town on his own, even on his boat. But he was brave to head towards the gathering of crows—though of course he was with two strong men. Was Metalboy alone, up in the Dark? That would be scary, so surely not. He wasn't old enough, hardly bigger than her. Why had she imagined for a second that he could have carried that heavy door all by himself?

"I'm sorry I snapped," said Mrs. Freida from the doorway, though she still sounded cranky. "But come in the shop and stay under my eye. You can sit by the window." Her tone added, *Don't argue*. It was definitely not a tone that made Dorrity want to say she'd been to the Dark and met an odd boy who had the town hall door.

~

From a chair near the shop window, Dorrity could just see

Officer Edgar standing at the far end of the bridge. The cloud of birds had disappeared. Two steam trucks had trundled into town with no news of any kind. The road was empty. No sign of the steamboat captain and crew.

The aisles were full of people not choosing and buying, just using the shop as an excuse to stay out of the wind while they watched the bridge. Button, long arms folded up like insects' legs, peered at the crossword in the *Owl Town Crier*. The librarian muttered with the craft lady next to the newspapers and magazines. There was whispering up by the soap powders. Dorrity had the feeling that everyone in the shop knew more than she did. If it was like this for children everywhere, maybe Metalboy had run away because he was fed up with grown-ups. Maybe he did live on his own. But right now Dorrity's stomach hurt with missing her brothers.

She leaned her forehead on the window. On the cliffs downriver from the bridge, blue and white daisies quivered in the breeze. The glass misted from her breath. There was still no movement on the Fribbleton Road...

A four-legged creature appeared around the bend in a stumbling rush. It shot out of sight behind a hillock, then reappeared. People crowded at the window beside Dorrity and squashed the breath out of her. At the sight of a loose animal she felt breathless anyway.

"A dog!" said somebody. "Bii-iig dog."

"Wild dog?"

"Lost dog?"

"No dogs allowed here."

"Rope round its neck."

"Funny shape for a dog."

"It's a goat!"

"That explains it. Good shape for a goat."

"Bii-iig goat. Is Edgar all right?"

"Got a sore leg. Not Edgar. The goat."

"Shut up," muttered the librarian.

Through a gap between someone's hefty arm and someone else's hefty belly, Dorrity saw Edgar standing firm. By now the goat had reached the bridge in limping dashes. Its coat was cream with patchy brown. It had a short whiskery beard and curly horns. The rope round its neck was bright shiny red. It stumbled and stared at Edgar. Then it shook itself and trotted past him, over the bridge and up into High Street.

Each step seemed an effort for the goat now. Edgar followed it to the town end of the bridge but stayed well back as the goat, in a fit of energy, headed for the fountain. There it struggled its front hooves up on the seat and had a slurp. Its back legs folded in a collapse. *Maa-aa.* It lowered its head.

"Can't trust goats at the best of times."

"Can't trust you."

"You're a goat."

"Watch it!"

"It was a joke."

"You'd better make the next one funny."

"Will the pair of you shut up," said the librarian.

Edgar stayed near the bridge and glanced back up at the Fribbleton Road. Mr. Coop, in his work beanie, was hobbling across the plaza towards the fountain. Arms held low, he was ready to pick up the end of the rope.

"Coop'll do it."

"Nah, he'll spook it."

"We'll all spook it if we rush out."

"I'm spooked myself. I'm staying put."

Just before Mr. Coop reached it, the goat scrambled to its feet. It was easily as big as Mr. Coop.

"Be careful," whispered Dorrity.

The goat backed across the plaza, bobbing its head. Mr. Coop took another step. The goat stamped once, turned and limped down Lower High Street, trailing the red rope. It stumbled again. Mr. Coop hobbled faster. They looked equally lame and determined.

Edgar stayed at this end of the bridge. But the townsfolk crowded out of the shop and along to the bend, craning to see but also jostling to stay behind somebody else. Dorrity nerved herself to go outside too, just as far as the bend. She watched as the goat limped past Dr. Oxford's, past Miss Honey's, past Beak Street, to the last house—hers— and stumbled on beyond that. Then its head swayed from side to side. It turned back.

Mr. Coop edged over to pick up the rope, but the goat nosed open the gate to Dorrity's house and staggered in. Mr. Coop hesitated.

"Say ta-ta to your lettuces," said the butcher.

"They've already bolted," said Dorrity. "Mike was going to pull them out and dig them in."

The townsfolk mumbled and muttered.

"Let's go and see."

"Not a chance. We might get butted."

"It looks tame."

"But a butt still hurts."

"It's just a goat. I've seen goats before."

"You see one in the mirror every morning."

"Go sit on your butt."

The librarian hissed, "The pair of you, *cussing* shut up!"

Dorrity left them to their bickering and ran light on her feet down High Street. By the time Mr. Coop saw her and flapped for her to stop, too late, she'd reached him.

"Stay here at the gate," he said. Then he glanced over her shoulder and touched a finger to his beanie. It was Miss Honey, brown curls in a bounce, petticoats in a flutter. She had something folded in her hands. "You stay behind me," he said to her. Miss Honey nodded. They went with gentle steps around the house, out of Dorrity's sight.

She crept after them.

The goat lay by the shed. Its sides were trembling. Its head and back were blotched with blood as if something had stabbed it. When it saw Mr. Coop and Miss Honey, it tried to scramble up but fell again.

It was terrifying and exciting to see an animal up so close.

"It needs fresh water." Dorrity knew that much about animals from stories.

"Wait," said Miss Honey.

But Dorrity was already filling a bucket at the outside tap. She set it as close to the goat as she dared and darted back behind Mr. Coop.

The goat bobbed its head as if it meant thank you. It shook its horns—it was plain that the red rope bothered it. After a moment it managed to stumble to the bucket and lowered its head. It raised its chin, little beard dripping, and watched Dorrity for another moment—not the others, just her. Its eyes were gray with strange narrow pupils. It let out another bleat.

Dorrity called from behind Mr. Coop. "Mister Goat, do have the lettuces."

Miss Honey unfolded the cloth in her hands and held it so the goat could see. It was a collar, gray with blue stitching. The goat edged back. "I'll try to take that rope," she said to the goat. "A collar will show you mustn't be harmed."

"It won't understand you." Dorrity had told it to eat the lettuces but that had felt different.

Carefully Miss Honey slipped the rope off the goat's neck and let it drop. The goat bleated and shook its horns as if a load had lifted. With her other hand, Miss Honey dropped the collar down around the fleecy neck. She blew on the fingers that had touched the rope and pulled her sleeve down over them before she picked it up again.

"Is the rope sticky?" Dorrity asked.

Mr. Coop glanced at Miss Honey. She glanced back at him. "Sticky," he said. "Of course."

How would he know when he hadn't touched it? He and Miss Honey avoided Dorrity's eye.

The goat backed far down beside the shed and folded all four legs to have a rest.

"It needs the vet," said Dorrity.

"Poor thing's tuckered out," said Mr. Coop. "It can snooze here, since you're not worried about Mike's lettuces. Dr. Oxford can check it later. Dorrity, we'll get you back to Mrs. Freida's."

The sun was starting to sink behind the foresty hills to the west. It was much colder. An early owl called—*hoo-oo?* Dorrity had a secret huff on her own fingertips because they stung again from *The Volume of Possible Endings*.

On the way up High Street, Dorrity heard Mr. Coop whisper to Miss Honey, something about the furnace in his workshop. Miss Honey looked grateful. He pulled a handkerchief from his pocket and wrapped it around his hand before he took the rope from her. He whispered something else to Miss Honey about Edgar and a message to the King.

Grown-ups and secrets again. Cussed if Dorrity would mention anything now to a grown-up about *The Volume*, the town hall door, or Metalboy. She'd hang onto her secrets like they kept theirs.

Miss Honey gave her a suspicious look. "What's going on in that head?"

Dorrity had better be careful. After all, it was obvious that a grown-up had once been young and might still have a slight insight into a child's mind.

She was saved by more movement on the Fribbleton Road. "Look!"

The steamboat captain and the bearded sailor were running full pelt for the bridge. They had the cabin boy hoisted by the arms to help his shorter legs keep up.

"What's the matter?" called the police officer and hurried after them.

They didn't answer, just ran over the bridge and plunged down the path to the wharf. Their dog set up a howl.

"What did you see?" Mr. Coop shouted.

Edgar reached the wharf but the boat's engine started with a *gruff-gruff-koff*. The sailor whipped the ropes off the bollards. Within moments the steamboat was heading back under the bridge.

"You said you didn't have to leave until tomorrow!" bellowed Edgar.

The answer was a wave of an arm, more howling from the dog and a frothy wake as the boat arced out of sight around the cliffs.

"What's your guess?" Mr. Coop murmured to Miss Honey.

Miss Honey glanced at Dorrity, lips pinched back as if she had buttoned them.

Mr. Coop buttoned his lips too. Then he unbuttoned them. "Just scared of their own shadows," he said to Dorrity.

—

GOSSIP AND BEARS

Mrs. Freida's spare bed was warm and comfortable, but Dorrity didn't sleep well. That magical book had scorched her fingers, the goat's rope had scorched Miss Honey's hand. The book was locked away, and by now Mr. Coop would have burned the rope—there was no way of knowing what it all meant. And she hadn't taken the oil-can to Metalboy...was he stuck in a metal suit under that jacket? His skin was so pale...he talked in that strange way...who could be living with him...

At last she woke up, which meant at some stage she had fallen asleep. Morning boats whistled. Gidibirds and starlings screamed back at them. The only thing to wear was her second-best overdress and old red leggings.

At breakfast Mrs. Freida didn't look as if she had slept well either. There wasn't fluffy egg-scramble or Um'Binnian toast. There was burnt scramble and charred ordinary toast, which Mrs. Freida said could go to the goat later if nobody wanted it.

Mr. Coop came trudging down the side path and Mrs.

Freida let him in. He carried the *Fontanian Daily Watch*, just off the steamboat. Mrs. Freida offered him toast, he said thank you, sat down and cut off the black corners.

"What are the headlines?" asked Mrs. Freida.

Mr. Coop shook the newspaper to straighten the fold marks. "They're two days old of course but...*hrmph*...the King's Experiment still isn't found...some say it could be in the hands of the King's enemies...*hrmph*...it won't do them much good because it's an experiment dedicated to one special purpose that nobody knows except King Jasper and Queen Sibilla. And they're not telling."

He shook the paper again. "They're a good king and queen. But they're still young. With a scientist for a father, they can't be blamed for thinking that inventions will improve the world. They could be right, they could be wrong. Their father didn't invent a great deal that was useful."

"We won't mention your barrel-boat," said Mrs. Freida with her first tiny smile for a day or two.

Mr. Coop gave a tiny grin too. "Without disrespect, only chumps and children criticize things half done."

Mrs. Freida made a playful swipe at him with a wooden spoon. Dorrity felt they were rather putting it on to make everything seem usual.

He ate a bite of toast that put crumbs in his whiskers. "*Hmm*...a side column says that vats of the first beauteen are whispered to be stored beneath a royal residence."

Mrs. Freida snorted. "Beauteen! What good does it do anyone to be unwrinkled at seventy-three?"

Mr. Coop turned slightly red in a mischievous, more truly

normal way. "In my opinion a woman doesn't come into her true beauty till the wisdom of age shines in her eyes."

Mrs. Freida's cheeks went rosy too. Dorrity caught her squinting at the side of the kettle. Its particular curves made anyone's face look very wide from side to side, scarily narrow from forehead to chin, and did nothing for anyone's eyes.

"*Er-hem*, it was Count Bale who invented that first version of beauteen, by dark magic," Mrs. Freida said to Dorrity. "The King and Queen's father managed to reproduce it scientifically."

"I know," Dorrity said. "It was a scientific accident in the Workroom of Knowledge."

Mr. Coop ate another bite of toast and turned the page. "Some say there may be truth to the gossip that old royal holiday homes will be reopened."

"Gossip has been saying that for weeks," said Mrs. Freida. "I've seen no sign. Of course they'd be reluctant about Eagle Hall." She lowered her voice. "Because of Count Bale. You read about that, Dorrity. We don't really talk about it. The one who was banished. He spent a lot of time at Eagle Hall. His brother, the old King, died there."

Dark magic in Eagle Hall. Dorrity's fingertips hurt. She paid great attention to spreading cranberry jelly over a patch of nicely toasted toast.

Mrs. Freida clattered dishes into the sink. "Someone should take the scraps and check on the goat. Then have a word with Officer Edgar."

Mr. Coop was on his feet at once.

Sometimes Dorrity was scared of something but still

wanted to do it—the goat, not the word with Edgar. She slipped down from her chair and into her cleaned birthday boots. She put on her feathery hat and picked up the scrap bucket.

"By the way," said Mr. Coop to Mrs. Freida. "There is— ah—another story not in the paper. The riverboat captain heard it in Fribbleton from the steamboat that left in such a rush yesterday. Bears."

"Bears?" cried Dorrity.

"That's why they ran back so fast. The sailor said three bears. The captain says one. The boy only heard ferocious growling, but he swears never to come near Owl Town again."

"There cannot be a bear around here." Mrs. Freida spoke like someone trying to carry a wobbly jelly.

"The only wild bears in Fontania live in the High Murisons where they are very wild indeed," Dorrity said. "Their growling has been measured as the deepest from any living throat. I forget how deep that actually is or how they measure it. Anyway, the main thing is there are none near here."

Mrs. Freida patted her hand. "If you ask me, that captain had too long in the sun and his eyesight was addled. And that sailor had been guzzling small-roar. Now off you go, the pair of you, very carefully."

———

CIRCUS OR ZOO?

Townsfolk trotted along to the shop or cycled to work. Another steamboat was tying up beside the boat that brought the newspapers. Blue-bellied starlings winged over the river.

Dorrity and Mr. Coop were past the edge of the plaza. Her fingers prickled. She switched the scrap bucket to her other hand and squinted at the shaded far end of the bridge. It looked as if a huge furry bedspread was draped over the wall. It must have fallen off a steam truck. How glossy it was.

She nudged Mr. Coop. "Whoever lost that will be furious."

He looked where she pointed.

"It is a bedspread, isn't it?" said Dorrity. "Or a rug or…"

The furry lump heaved around and grew taller. It wasn't a bedspread. It was a bear trying to stand. It staggered back against the parapet. For a moment it looked like a rug again, tossed for an airing.

"A bear," whispered Dorrity. "Really a bear?"

"Keep facing it," breathed Mr. Coop. "Now…slowly… step…backwards…"

THE VOLUME OF POSSIBLE ENDINGS

Shouts sounded along High Street.

"Bear!"

"Get behind a stout door!"

"Who's got a rifle?"

"Cuss me eyes! It can't be a bear!"

Dorrity clung to Mr. Coop's hand. The bear tried to stand again but fell on its forepaws and slowly began to pad over the bridge towards them. Dorrity bent and set the bucket of breakfast scraps on the road. She hoped bears liked burnt toast and burnt scrambled egg. She and Mr. Coop eased back another few steps. By now the bear was midway on the bridge.

The braver townsfolk (three younger ones—the butcher, the baker's assistant, and Miss Honey Dearborn) appeared near the plaza. The butcher had a rifle. The baker's assistant carried a long oven paddle. Miss Honey was empty-handed.

The bear reached the town side of the bridge. It swung its head to peer up at the plaza. The butcher aimed his rifle. The bear, looking straight at him, reared on its hind legs. It swayed its front paws from side to side. Its hind legs shuffled.

"A dancing bear," said the baker's assistant.

The butcher lowered his rifle. "A circus bear. Or…or one that's learned how to beg for buns in a zoo."

Dorrity thought they both sounded doubtful.

Miss Honey crept up beside Dorrity and Mr. Coop. The bear squinted at the three of them. It swayed its front paws again and shuffled its feet.

"My brothers dance like that at the town hall parties," Dorrity whispered.

"Birkett especially." Miss Honey's face was drawn and intent.

"But the bear does it better," said Dorrity.

Joking in the face of danger made her feel braver by only a very tiny fraction.

—

WITHOUT THAT
DOOR

The bear had started padding up towards the plaza and High Street.

Miss Honey edged a hand to the long purple scarf she wore around her neck, drew it off, and tied it in a loop. She walked as slowly as possible to meet the bear. It lowered its head.

"It's tame," she called in a soft voice. "Tame enough, anyway." She slipped the scarf over its head and eased backwards again. "That should show nobody must harm it unless there's no choice," she said.

Whumph, went the bear. It looked very much as if it would like to follow Miss Honey and sniff her. With a *whuffle* it stayed put.

Dorrity's heart banged against her ribs. "If it belongs to somebody then it's been lost," she whispered. "If it hasn't got a home it will be scared."

"It's wounded the same way as the goat," Miss Honey murmured to Mr. Coop. "Dried blood on its shoulders and head."

The bear shook its head as if something buzzed in its ears.

"Dorrity, go inside to Mrs. Freida," said Mr. Coop.

Dorrity wanted to go, but she still set her jaw. Mr. Coop—kind Mr. Coop who never showed temper—looked as if he'd like to shake her. He and Miss Honey began a discussion with the butcher and the baker's assistant. The other townsfolk were in doorways, still ready to hide.

The bear patted the purple scarf then licked its paw. It turned and paced down Lower High Street, head swaying, smelling the breeze. Dorrity had read that bears didn't have good eyesight. She sidled behind it, though very far back, and checked all the places along the road for safety if the bear turned bad (a very large waste bin, a tree to climb). Behind her she heard Mr. Coop give a curse and start hobbling after her.

Still sniffing, the bear passed the banker's villa, the law clerk's cottage. It lumbered past Miss Honey Dearborn's, further and further. It might be heading for where the Beastly Dark came down to the river. At Dorrity's own gate the bear stopped and sniffed harder.

The bees! Birkett would be furious if the bear destroyed the hives.

The bear pushed against the gate till it opened—less than a split second—then lumbered down the side path.

Heart thudding, Dorrity followed, trying to be light on her feet so it wouldn't hear. What if the bear was wild after all? What if it tore the goat to pieces? What if it turned on her? Somehow she knew it wouldn't. But she was very nearly fainting in case she was wrong.

She heard the goat bleat, a *whuff* from the bear. She

pressed against the side of the cottage and risked peering round to the back.

The goat stamped once and tossed its horns. The bear turned aside with another *whuff*. It padded down to the beehives, where it subsided onto its backside. Its head turned towards the hives a couple of times but it seemed ready for sleep.

Dorrity crept backwards around the house. Mr. Coop grabbed her and hurried her to the front gate. Miss Honey, the butcher, and the baker's assistant were there, hissing her name. Dorrity's knees buckled. Miss Honey hugged her so tight that it hurt. Then the baker's assistant gripped one of her arms and the butcher the other. Just like the cabin boy yesterday, Dorrity was hoisted up and carried at a run back up High Street to the town hall.

~

There was a huddle in the meeting room with the missing door. Dorrity crept in too. Always before the grown-ups had left her outside, which was why the door handle had been such fun when she was small.

"Order!" said Officer Edgar.

"Explain the bear!" somebody called.

"Catch it first and then explain," called somebody else.

"Catch it and kill it!" cried another voice.

"It's tame," Miss Honey said. "I put a scarf around its neck."

"As long as there's no magical explanation for the bear," said the butcher. "It's an unwritten by-law that there is no magic in Owl Town."

"Rubbish," said a voice in the crowd. "It's just the way the town has to be kept."

"And I'm keeping an eye out for it," called yet another voice. "So are we all."

The room rumbled with *too right, you bet, on the money*. Mrs. Freida blushed again. Mr. Coop and the librarian eyed her as if they'd always known about the magic library book from Eagle Hall. Then Mr. Coop and Miss Honey exchanged the same look they'd had over the red rope from the goat.

"Order!" called Officer Edgar again. He stood there holding his helmet. "We need to talk about the bear and bear alone."

"We're wary of animals of every kind," said the craft lady. "Noted and numbered, that's what they must be around Owl Town."

"Like my sheep," said Farmer Ember. "Ten and ten only. Round number. Easy to count."

Button, wearing a hood because he'd had to cross the street in sunshine which was always a danger for trolls, raised a very long arm. "Magical explanation?" he whispered. "For the bear? And the goat?"

"The explanation is most likely it escaped from a circus!" shouted the craft lady, as if she seriously hoped so and didn't believe it. "It might want to ride someone's bicycle."

"First step, message to the King," cried the hairdresser.

"Already taken care of," said Mr. Coop. "Two message-birds and two back-ups."

"And I've sent telegrams," said Mrs. Freida. "One of my own, and one for Edgar."

The lawyer nodded. "Second step, advertise in the papers about a lost bear and goat. We can't risk being sued for someone's lost property."

"What's 'sued?'" asked the stream-truck garage-hand.

"Being taken to court in front of a judge," the lawyer said. "And made to pay money."

"Who'll pay for a newspaper ad?" asked Farmer Ember.

"You're not asking the right questions," Dorrity cried.

Everyone stared as if they'd forgotten her.

"Like what happened on the Fribbleton Road?" Her voice sounded weak. "That cloud of birds. Now the goat and the bear. I want my brothers to be home safe."

Mrs. Freida gave her a warm little jog. Apart from that, all the grown-ups behaved as if Dorrity had said the right thing but they wished it hadn't been aloud, and anyway they would ignore it.

She felt helpless. She could throw a tantrum but that would be exhausting. She could sulk but that would be boring when nobody was noticing her anyway. If she burst into tears, they'd just say *there-there* and give her a couple of double hot chocolates.

But something strange and possibly terrible had happened on the Fribbleton Road. For a moment she would have dared run up the road as far as the bend, even further if it would give her a sign that her brothers were safe.

Her fingertips tingled. Something in her said, *Don't think of that direction. Think of the endings. Think about the Beastly Dark.*

—

NO QUESTION—MAGIC

The meeting broke up and Mrs. Freida arm-in-armed Dorrity across the plaza to the shop. "You and Button sort out the broken crackers for the bear and the goat. And open those packets of soup mix for lazy cooks. The goat should enjoy those."

There were plenty of packets past their *best by* date for ordinary people and almost at their *use by* date for trolls. Button handed down old goods from the top shelves and made comforting troll sounds to Dorrity. He offered silently to make her a double-scoop ice cream. She shook her head and glanced through the open door at the Fribbleton Road.

Something else had just come around the bend—a man, shambling and staggering. His head was low, jacket half on, with the left side wrapped over his arm. He nearly fell but struggled on to the far end of the bridge. There he fell against the parapet, just like the bear.

It was Yorky. Dorrity flung out of the shop and screamed his name.

He looked up. Still holding his left arm tight under the jacket, he lurched to his feet.

"Go back!" he shouted. "Keep away!"

Hood on again, Button ran past her. The butcher joined him. They took hold of Yorky. Button gathered him into his long arms and carried him back all the way to set him down beside the fountain.

Dorrity stumbled over to them. Blood had dried on Yorky's temple. The butcher tried to ease her brother's jacket off, but Yorky kept holding his left arm against his side under the jacket.

Mrs. Freida had rushed from the shop. Other townsfolk crowded around. Mr. Coop was here too, as well as Miss Honey.

"What happened?" Dorrity was hot with fright. "Yorky, what is it?"

"He's bleeding," said Mr. Coop. "Let's have a look…"

Yorky reeled but raised a foot and pushed the old man back a step. "No…listen…Birkett and Mike—" He reeled again.

"Where are they?" Miss Honey said. "Yorky, what happened?"

Mr. Coop put a hand on Yorky's shoulder and tried again to ease the jacket from the injured arm.

"No!" Yorky gripped his jacket tight. His eyes closed and he let out a groan. It was the groan people gave when something had happened that they'd deeply hoped would never come to pass, though even deeper down they'd known it would. The very worst thing was how he whispered again. "Dorrity—keep her away."

~

"Carry him to the cottage," Miss Honey said. "Somebody, find Dr. Oxford."

Yorky held his arm even closer under his jacket.

Officer Edgar shoved through the crowd. "What's going on? Everyone, back three steps. Do you want to push the man into the fountain?"

"Button, pick him up again," snapped Mrs. Freida. "Please hurry, and keep your hood on. Dorrity, run!"

Dorrity sped to the cottage and found the spare back-door key under the third brick of the third stack where it belonged. She was inside with the front door open just as Button carried Yorky down the path.

Miss Honey whipped in ahead of them, and rushed to the linen cupboard for an armful of towels. Mrs. Freida was nearly as swift. They both whisked to the brothers' bedroom. There were two beds and a set of bunks because Yorky liked to use a top one. Mrs. Freida spread towels on the coverlet of the lower bunk. Button rested Yorky on them.

Officer Edgar pushed in past Mr. Coop and tried to edge Yorky's hand from the injured arm. Yorky managed to nudge him off and still keep the arm hidden.

"Not Edgar," Yorky whispered. "Get him out."

Button and the police officer left the room. Edgar's voice grew fainter, and Dorrity heard the front door slam. Mrs. Freida leaned to look at a crumple between Yorky's fingers in the hand that held the jacket tight. It was the handkerchief Dorrity had given him the previous morning. Yorky tried to speak but only gasps came out.

Dorrity fell on her knees beside the bunk. "Yorky, what happened? Where's Birkett? Where's Mike?"

Her brother was drained and gray. Even his curly auburn hair was gray with dust and dirt. He looked at her as if he was searching for words, then released his injured arm. Very gently Miss Honey pulled the jacket aside.

Dorrity thought her eyes could not be seeing right. Yorky's shirt was in tatters. Instead of a left arm, he had a wing, like a rooster's wing, but far larger, orange and black, feathers dusty, battered and broken.

He let out a groan. The wing flexed and shivered. Yorky's hazel gaze fixed on Dorrity. "Stay out of sight," he whispered. "Don't say anything to anyone." His eyes fluttered shut.

She remembered the first ending. *Dorrity stayed in Owl Town and did nothing. She never saw Birkett and Mike again. Yorky lived with one arm and one wing for the rest of his life and never, not once, did he blame her.*

———

PART TWO OF DORRITY'S TALE

NEVER GO TO THE BEASTLY DARK

MAGIC AND LIES

Dorrity ran from the room. She reached the coat nook in the hall and hid her face. She squeezed her eyes shut but still saw those terrible feathers.

Mrs. Freida hurried after her. "Dear!"

"I'm not crying!" Dorrity wept.

"No, dear," gasped Mrs. Freida. "Sometimes it is being angry that makes people's eyes leak. We have to wait for Dr. Oxford. It's lucky the doctor is also the vet. That is a benefit of a town with so few animals." Mrs. Freida sounded trembly and old but also determined. "Dorrity, wash your face and run to the shop. Behave as if nothing is wrong. We don't need gossip. I'll go off to the Watch House now to have a chat with that police officer."

Dorrity didn't want to wash her face—she couldn't bear to see that wing again—she didn't want to leave Yorky—but the notes she'd made about the five endings were in her room back at Mrs. Freida's. So she did wash her face, then sort-of stumbled up High Street.

Button must have heard her come in the back door

because he popped his head through into the corridor. He looked worried and held up another ice cream cone. She shook her head, crept to the spare bedroom and found what she'd scribbled.

She wished she'd written down the endings word for word. If she *did nothing*, the first ending must at least mean that Owl Town would be safe again fairly soon, though Yorky would always have a wing and she'd never see the other two again. Had her brothers known something dangerous and magical would happen? That could be why they'd wanted to sell up and leave. Why couldn't they have trusted her and told her what the matter was? She turned shivery again.

She looked at what she'd written from the second ending. The whole thing had been something like *Dorrity returned from the Dark and the dangerous ways she'd had to go. Birkett and Mike thanked Dorrity with all their hearts and Yorky welcomed her back with two whole arms.*

To keep her brothers safe, she would have to go again into the Dark.

~

All afternoon customers clutching long lists of essentials like toilet paper, batteries, ear plugs, and cans of beans waited in orderly lines. The only time Dorrity had seen such grim preparations was the previous year when there had been fears of a great flood which came to nothing.

But this time there was no gossip, just solemn expressions. Those looks had always accompanied people saying there'd be no magic in Owl Town. Now Dorrity realized it could always have meant *We'll make sure of that* and *Expecting it sometime, and then we'll deal with it.*

Dr. Oxford dropped in. He glanced at the number of customers, beckoned to Button, and pointed to the single-scoop cones and the bubble-gum ice cream. For a moment Dorrity hoped he'd visited Yorky and discovered they'd only imagined the wing. But behind the customers' backs Dr. Oxford signed to Dorrity and Mrs. Freida. He gave a shrug, a flap of his left arm, another shrug so big that all the customers startled and stared.

Then Dr. Oxford mimed writing a prescription and swallowing painkillers. He was silently saying that's all he could do. The wing was real. Real magic—and bad magic.

Dorrity pretended she must fetch something from the store room, which was true. The oil-can. For a moment she hid there, hands over her face.

How far into the Dark would she have to go now? It might have to be a great deal further than Metalboy's house, and by *dangerous ways*…She ought to go as soon as possible.

—

HELLO AGAIN
AND WHAT A SHOCK

Dorrity left a note for Mrs. Freida on the kitchen bench: *Thought I should check on Yorky*. Same old trick. It was the truth but not what she was in fact going to do.

She smoothed the green feathers on the birthday hat and crept down past the blueberry hedge. Nobody was about in Arrow Street. Nobody was sulking on the Dark Road. Everyone must be too busy preparing for the disaster.

It was tricky crossing the ditch because she carried a paper bag with the oil-can as well as a bottle of oil. Her second-best overdress gathered burrs, smudges of mud and a three-cornered rip. The bag ripped too. She tucked it under an arm and ducked up into the trees as fast as she could.

For a while she thought she might not be able to find Metalboy's house again. Far off was the *koff* of whatever lived far up the forest. The higher she climbed, the later the afternoon and the darker the Dark. She had to stop and take a breath when she thought about Yorky. That wing must hurt. He looked so ill. And where was Birkett? Where was

Mike? Worry nearly overwhelmed her till she made it work as an engine to help her trudge on.

At last the little house was there ahead. The only sound was a rustling of fresh leaves above, the crunch of twigs and fallen leaves underfoot, the thump of her heart. She reached the stolen town hall door and knocked.

"It's me. Dorrity."

The door opened. There stood the boy with his cap on. Those stolen knickerbockers were so long they bunched over the one shoe and one boot. He blinked at her hat.

"I brought your stuff." Her voice choked a bit, which was annoying in front of the boy. She held out the torn bag. "There was enough money for some oil too. I hope sewing-machine oil will do the job. There'd be twenty cents change but that's the delivery fee." A very fair one. Dorrity figured she'd earned it.

Metalboy didn't reach for the bag. She jiggled it at him.

"*He-ere*," she half-sang, hoping to coax him.

He still didn't take it.

"I don't care if you don't want to talk," Dorrity said. "In fact I'm going further on into the Dark, then dashing home."

The boy blinked slowly, once. "It must be…*whirr*…high machine-quality oil." His voice was still all on the same level.

"I already said, it's for sewing machines."

He was being very dense.

She jiggled the bag again. "It should be good for removing metal."

The boy blinked again, once. "Met-al."

Dorrity set the bag on the step. "If this is a game, I don't have time. Don't waste your voice on saying thank you." She hoped he would understand she was being sarcastic. But still he just stared at her.

What use were boys? She turned to go but felt a bit mean and turned back.

"I should warn you. There's a crisis in the town. They're stocking up in case of disaster. I've no idea why. Or maybe I sort-of do, but it's hard to explain. I just thought you'd better know."

He said just one word again with no expression. "Disaster."

"It's rude not to answer properly." Dorrity stepped off the porch. "But look, if you're rusted up and can't reach some tricky bits, I suppose I could help. You have to ask, though."

Again there was silence except for rustles in the trees, an *oo* from a bird.

"Disaster," Metalboy repeated in his flat voice. "Disaster means danger. I must face danger in the end. I am ashamed that I am not ready. Ashamed. Ashamed."

"For goodness' sake!" She jumped back on the porch. "Like it or not, I'll help with that oil-can."

Now that she was closer, he seemed bald under his dark blue cap. His face was smooth and stiff, with no wrinkles at all. Even Dorrity had a few normal twelve-year-old wrinkles from laughing and smiling, being puzzled or cross.

She tapped his arm. *Clunk.*

"Ashamed," said the boy. "Face danger. Ashamed. Make amends."

"Stop playing," Dorrity said. "Speak normally."

"Metalboy. Poor Metalboy. Face danger," Metalboy said. "*Whirr*—danger."

She looked at his jacket—the same blue as the Grand Palace guards'. And his cap—blue like the Grand Palace guards'. She looked at his face—pale and silvery like metal. That's why he was strange. He was was from the Palace—but he was clockwork.

"You're the King's stolen Experiment!" Dorrity said.

—

DO IT YOURSELF

Clockwork—and if the King had something to do with it, there could be magic involved too. Dorrity wanted to run.

"Danger...make amends...danger...dis–ast–er— must—face—dis–ast–er..." The boy's words came more and more slowly. He was either winding down or he needed that oil and probably both.

She made herself take him by the shoulders and waddle him into the house in a kind of dance.

She let him go, and the stolen door swung shut behind her. For a moment she just looked at him. A metal boy. It would be wonderful to take him to bits and see how he worked.

She'd better not. He belonged to the King. And whoever had stolen him was sure to return.

The banker's lost cushions were in a neat stack. There was a wooden chair and a rug that she recognized from the law clerk's dining room, and last week's *Owl Town Crier.* There was a pile of stolen clothing, and a stout pack bearing the sign of the Fontanian Army. Through a door she saw a kitchen. On the bench sat a bag marked ~~WALNITS~~ WALNUTS in Dorrity's own printing. One saucepan with a dent hung on a hook. Blue and white crockery sat on the shelves of a dresser. The kitchen could have been as inviting as Mrs. Freida's, Mr. Coop's, or Miss Honey Dearborn's, especially now that Dorrity recognized the china and the saucepan—chipped and a bit dinged—as ones they'd recently thrown out.

"How long before the thief comes back?" Dorrity asked.

Metalboy's deep gray eyes turned to look at her.

"I mean, it might be too long for you to wait, so I should oil you."

Now that she knew he was clockwork, it felt ridiculous trying to hold a conversation. She pushed her hat so it hung down her back and unwrapped the oil-can. Holding it over the sink, she poured in the oil. A drip fell. She turned the tap on to rinse it away—the tap spurted water. So far up into the Dark it was remarkable to have working plumbing. It was probably the pipes and taps—and the sink!—that the town plumber had lost last week. There must be a water barrel outside. And that stove looked like the old one from Dr. Oxford's villa. If it worked here, she had no idea how.

Being very curious now, she opened a drawer. There were two forks, a corkscrew, three spoons, a knife with a broken handle, and one of those kitchen implements that nobody can ever remember what to do with.

Metalboy's voice started again. "Dis–aaaast–errr…"

Dorrity ran to him with the oil-can. Where should she put a drop first? The back of his neck seemed a safe place to look. She yanked down his jacket collar. Yes—a tiny hole just like on a sewing machine. She let in two drops of oil and one for luck.

What about wrists? She pulled up the left sleeve of his jacket. There, where normal people had pulses, was another small hole. She let in another three drops, and the right wrist the same. He opened and closed his hands. So she must be doing something right. What about ankles? It was lucky he wasn't wearing stolen socks. On the foot that had a shoe the hole on the inside of his ankle was easy to see, more difficult on the boot one.

Dorrity stood back. Metalboy blinked several times. There was a quiet whirr inside him.

"That is much better. Thank you." His voice had a more natural rise and fall. "There are just one or two more places..."

She thrust the can into his hands. "Any more, you do it yourself."

His forehead, where he would have had eyebrows if he'd been human, raised a little.

"Do it yourself," she repeated.

His eyes shone as if he actually was human. "Do it myself," he whispered. "Of course. I have already done lots by myself!" Again his voice lifted in a more natural manner.

"Think ahead and make sure you're close to an oil-can before you run down again," Dorrity said. "Carry some oil around in a bag. It's common sense..." Again it felt silly, trying to give tips to a piece of equipment. To an experiment.

He began to unbutton his jacket. Dorrity felt just as

foolish for thinking a machine should have privacy, but turned her back. It meant she faced the boy's front door—the town hall door.

"I am done," said Metalboy.

She took back the can so he could fasten his buttons. "Look at all these things from the town. Just because something is put outside doesn't mean it can be stolen. Did the King leave you outside? Who would have the nerve to steal you out of the King's own workshop?"

"Steal…me," Metalboy said.

She peered at him more closely. There was still a silvery under-glow to his face, but he'd started to blush.

"Nobody stole me," said Metalboy.

Dorrity laughed. "Don't tell me you walked here all on your own."

"I walked many miles of the very long way." His flush looked like pride. "I hid on one steam ship. Three steam trucks. I had one hitch behind a steam bus. I hid on two riverboats."

"Oh, sure," said Dorrity. "Now you're going to say you built this house all by yourself in just a few weeks."

"The house was already here but very broken," Metalboy said. "I repaired it by myself in two weeks. It was not easy. I was careful only to take things that nobody wanted when nobody was looking."

"You can't have built it by yourself!" Dorrity shouted. "You're clockwork! You are an experiment!" She took the oil-can and shook it. "Look! You're a machine!"

"But the King used a little magic, even before the feather…" His hand went to his chest, he blinked very fast and started again. "I am learning to think for myself. I know about camouflage. I will be safe if I live like an ordinary boy with ordinary things in an ordinary house. Nobody noticed when I fetched the chair or the kitchen sink or even the door. I was surprised and pleased that such a beautiful door had been thrown away."

Dorrity felt she might burst with frustration. "I did notice you stealing the door. I just didn't understand what I was seeing."

She glanced at the door again and jumped. Through the glass there was a shape. The bear? Or another bear? Some sort of animal she'd never heard of? She hoped it was only the person who'd stolen Metalboy in shaggy headgear.

"If you live by yourself," she whispered, "who's on the doorstep?"

Metalboy's head jerked and he stared at the door. "Discovered," he mouthed. "I am a failure. I did not realize that running away was stealing myself. I will be punished. I will be taken back to the workshop, unbolted, unscrewed, and undone."

The figure on the doorstep raised a hand and gave a *rat-tat*.

Dorrity frowned. A thief wouldn't knock on the door of the house he had built himself from things he had stolen.

Another shaggy shape appeared in the glass and shoved the first one aside. With a bang and a bash, the door opened.

19

KOFF-KOFFS IN THE DARK

The two huge shaggy figures barged in, and a third one followed. They were nobody Dorrity had seen before. Metalboy seemed as confused as she was—it made him look far more human.

The three men nearly touched the ceiling. They wore thick knitted balaclavas that spread like capes over their shoulders. Twigs and leaves stuck all over the knitting made their heads look five times larger than normal, unless a creature was a warthog or rhinoceros, if the pictures Dorrity had seen were reliable. Below the headgear they had big leather jackets, black trousers on very thin legs, and workmen's boots.

"There are two of them!" said the smallest of the huge men.

"Nobody said there were two," the largest growled.

"Can't ever trust gossip," said the middle-sized large man who had tapped the door so politely.

"Then which one are we after?" the largest growled.

Dorrity took a step nearer Metalboy. "Who are they?" she whispered.

"Danger, danger…" he whispered back.

The smallest large man pointed at Dorrity. "I've a feeling the gossip said *she*." He pointed at Metalboy. "But that's an old Palace Guard cap the boy's wearing, so the King's likely to pay up for him. I say take them both."

"Right." The largest man grabbed Metalboy—"Aw, hard muscles for a kid!"—and hauled him outside.

The middle one pounced at Dorrity. She ducked and tripped over the stolen cushions. The hat cord was nearly strangling her. The man scooped her up. She tried to wriggle from his grip—wrench herself free—slide out of his grasp—nothing worked.

"Army pack!" he cried and scooped that up too. "And an oil-can—that'll be useful."

"Don't waste time," the leader growled. "Just bring the girlie."

Without losing hold of Dorrity, the man managed to stuff the oil-can into the pack, then he hauled her down the steps and deeper up into the Dark. She couldn't call out—his hand was over her mouth. She tried to slobber but it didn't seem to bother him. A glimpse of Metalboy's pale face—a jolt and plunge across a stream…Why didn't Metalboy wrench himself free? If he could carry that door, he was surely strong enough. Her hat cord still nearly strangled her. She wanted her brothers! The man had her over his shoulder now, her nose pressed against the stinky knitted headgear. Someone should slip these men a word about soap and regular rinsing.

At last they reached a track and stopped charging uphill.

The men set Metalboy and Dorrity down, and pushed those balaclavas off their faces. Sweat poured into their eyes.

"You smell terrible!" she gasped.

"Anarchists rule!" the largest man growled.

"No, Ruffgo," panted the one who'd been carrying Dorrity. "Try again."

"Brian's right," said the third. "Try again."

"Sorry, Dodger," Ruffgo growled. "Um—anarchists don't want a ruler."

"Got it," said Dodger.

"Anarchists!" said Metalboy. "You are anarchists!"

Dorrity didn't want to find out what anarchists were. She tried to scramble into the undergrowth, banged into something with wheels, flung herself aside, but her overdress snagged. Ruffgo caught her in one arm and yanked. Her overdress tore, though that didn't help her.

Puffing and grumbling, the anarchists hauled three machines out of the bushes. One had huge low handlebars—the next had high handlebars —the third, wide handlebars. They had narrow wheels, wooden panels, the glint of new metal, rivets, and patches. Twigs and leaves had been glued all over them—as a disguise? Three motorized bicycles! Dorrity was so surprised, she stopped struggling. In moments Metalboy was strapped on a bike behind Brian. She was strapped on behind Ruffgo. His balaclava smelled worse than Brian's.

Each anarchist kicked some sort of pedal. With *koff-koffs*, roars, and the stink of motor oil, the bikes sped uphill, swerving and juddering. The narrow track headed up and to the west, though it was hard to be sure. *Ouch!* They bounced over rocks on the path, rattled over a narrow bridge—the stream beneath was wide and fast.

By now they were miles from Owl Town. It grew darker under the trees. One by one, the men turned switches on their bikes—bright headlights fizzled and hissed, lit the path in front and made terrifying shadows in the forest.

Dorrity was scared and furious. All these years she'd believed the elderly coughing in the Dark was an ailing panther or maybe a wolf. All these years, it was motorized anarchists.

—

DINNER GUESTS

The bikes stopped at last in a gurgle of steam and the reek of oil. The men switched off the headlights. Through the branches of huge ogre-woods Dorrity saw orangey-pink clouds in a shade that said *sunset*. The rubbery-soapy smell of a thousand dropped blossoms made her nose sting all over again.

Metalboy was blinking fast. The jolts might have scrambled his insides. His cap had stayed on, which was surprising since it had no toggle. Her feathery hat still choked her throat.

Ruffgo unstrapped her. She had awful pins and needles. "Who are you exactly?" she cried. "What do you want?"

The smallest of the large men grinned and showed surprisingly white teeth. "We are the Dark Patrol. I'm Dodger—I'm captain this week. You won't have heard of us. We're not famous. Nor are we infamous. We are not looking for acclaim of any sort, good or bad."

"A bit of the good sort would be nice," growled Ruffgo.

Dorrity's brothers can't have known about the Dark

Patrol. Otherwise they would have wanted that kind of bike themselves. "Why is there a Dark Patrol?" she said.

Captain Dodger gave the same sort of look Mr. Coop had when Dorrity was bored with her times tables. "If we didn't patrol the Dark, unsteady types would make it their home. An unsteady Dark would spread rot to the rest of Fontania. A tidy Dark is what the country needs. A clean Dark is what we provide because we want to."

By beating on doors, wearing smelly balaclavas, and kidnapping children? Dorrity didn't say it, because she knew her face said it for her.

Captain Dodger eyed her for a moment, then adjusted his headgear. It made him look fearsome again, apart from those trousers which made his legs look like black bendy straws. He bowed, with obvious sarcasm.

"Girlie, how shall I put it? You are under our care. It's too dangerous for children to spend the night in the Dark on their own."

"We weren't out in the Dark till you brought us here," said Dorrity. But her heart lifted. Without even trying, she'd managed to get a long way into the Dark. This might be what the second ending meant. As soon as she was home, everything would be all right.

"Thank you," she said. "I really mean it. We'll stay under your roof tonight."

Ruffgo laughed behind a hand. "She said under our roof!"

Captain Dodger grinned too. "We call it our cave. Fair enough. That's what it is. And we don't go under it. We go into it, except for the one who stays on watch. He sits outside."

"And I go home tomorrow," Dorrity said loudly and clearly.

"Aw, a child who doesn't mumble." Brian smiled. "I understand most of what she says on the very first go."

"Brian, bring in the bikes. Ruffgo, bring the girlie and boy." Captain Dodger walked at a wall of rock and disappeared into a curtain of ivy.

Ruffgo grabbed the back of Metalboy's collar and Dorrity's arm. He tugged them towards the wall. Strands of ivy brushed Dorrity's face, then they were all standing in a clearing with rocks on three sides, a cliff on the fourth. In the cliff loomed a cave opening, and in front of it a round-shouldered man fed sticks to a campfire.

"It's a perfect hidey-hole!" said Dorrity.

Ruffgo growled in her ear. "Hidey-holes are for kids. This is a hide-out."

"Cooker, we have guests," said Captain Dodger.

"Guests!" The man at the campfire had a fit of coughing, perhaps from the smoke, though Dorrity had a sneaky feeling it was laughter.

"It will be their good luck to share tonight's fricassee," said Dodger. "Good luck, if there's enough. Cooker, what is it tonight?"

"Don't tell…!" Ruffgo sniffed the steam rising from a stout metal pot. "Mushroom and wild carrot."

"Right and right," said Cooker the cook. "But you didn't guess the shred of porcupine. Sorry, it's no more than a shred. It was hardly big enough to leave its mother."

"Take a seat," Captain Dodger said to Dorrity and Metalboy.

The only place to sit was stony ground. Brian wheeled

the bikes in, one by one. The men removed their balaclavas and used them as cushions. The cook set spoons down for everyone and began to ladle dinner into dented tin bowls.

Metalboy bent close to Dorrity. "I cannot eat. My kitchen was just camouflage. They will discover what I am. I do not like the chill of fear."

"If you can't eat, why did you steal those walnuts?" Dorrity hissed.

"I did not know they were food," whispered Metalboy. "I expected them to be nuts for screwing shelves to walls."

She picked up a spoon. "We mustn't offend them. Pretend to eat."

At first she couldn't eat anything herself. All she wanted was to be home with Yorky's lemon slice. The thought of his broken russet wing made her throat close up. At last she put a shred of porcupine fricassee onto her spoon. It almost melted on her tongue. That was a surprise.

Metalboy eased a small spoonful of fricassee into his mouth and sat with his eyes closed. After a few moments his eyelids flickered. He eased in another morsel.

"He's not a greedy-guts," said Brian.

Metalboy eased in a third shred of fricassee.

Now she'd started, Dorrity finished her meal quickly. "Thank you," she said. "Really delicious."

"I must remember table manners, even though we are not at a table," Metalboy said. "Thank you from the bottom of my—"

"Heart will be the word you're hunting for," said Cooker.

Metalboy pressed a hand to the left side of his chest.

"That's where most of us hope we might have 'em." Captain Dodger's smile was sly. It didn't make Dorrity feel comfortable.

"Why didn't you escape before?" she whispered to Metalboy.

He seemed surprised at the thought. "I seem to need to stay with you."

One twinkling star and an edge of moon showed through the pines on the cliff above. Dorrity longed to fall asleep because tomorrow would be...well, magically better. But it would be polite to have a scrap of conversation.

"It must make you proud to patrol the Dark for King Jasper and Queen Sibilla," she said to the anarchists.

"It's not for them," said Dodger. "I told you we're anarchists."

"We're not against the Royals," Brian said. "But we're not for anyone except us."

"I suppose you've got your orders, though," said Dorrity.

"Orders to keep the good food coming." Cooker saluted her with his spoon.

"Orders for a peaceful Dark," said Dodger. "And this week, I give them."

"Otherwise, it's *yah!* to rules," said Cooker "No one's in charge."

"Except me at the moment," said Dodger. "And of course that's a special arrangement."

The cook scraped the last morsel of fricassee from the pan into his bowl for a second helping. "And it depends what you mean by anarchists. I say it means law and freedom in little groups of our own, without any violence."

"What about that baby porcupine?" Dorrity asked.

Cooker gazed at the shred of moon just as Dorrity might if she was embarrassed. "I'm not talking about violence to an egg or vegetable or such. That's not violence, it's part of cooking."

"And I say," said Dodger, "that when we don't get what we want by peaceful means or trickery, it doesn't hurt to consider a bash in the name of freedom."

"It hurts the person who gets the bash," Dorrity muttered.

"My worry's the mushrooms and carrot," Brian said. "There are times when I'd swap anarchy and the Beastly Dark for an officer to keep order. I'd also like dinner with a tablecloth. Pork pie and cauliflower."

Sighs rose around the cooking fire. It crackled and sent sparks up.

Dorrity yawned. "Well, thank you again for letting us be your guests. And for taking us home tomorrow."

More sparks rose from the fire. So did more chuckling from the Patrol.

"We mentioned payment early on," Brian said. "But they still haven't guessed."

Dodger wagged a finger at Dorrity. "I used sarcasm. That means when I called you guests, I meant the opposite. There is a particular child who everyone's searching for. We plan to hold that child for ransom."

"Therefore, the word is hostages," Cooker explained.

In the shadows of the hide-out, in the flickering campfire, gleamed the smiles of the Dark Patrol and the handlebars of their motorized bikes.

~

21

ZERO TO TRIUMPH

Dorrity's spine went straight with the shock. Metalboy sat even straighter.

"The hostages are dead on their feet," the cook said.

"Nah," said Ruffgo, "they're sitting up and they're not dead."

Cooker grinned. "I mean their eyes look like poached eggs. They need to be tucked into their guest beds. Ha ha!"

"True. We'll get more dolleros if they look as if they're actually worth something." Dodger stared at Metalboy across the campfire. "Is it just me, or does the boy look abnormal?" He glanced at Dorrity. "I still think there was meant to be only a girl. Why did we pick up the wrong information?" He chewed his thumbnail for a moment, still staring at Dorrity, then shook his head. "Never mind. It's a riddle for tomorrow, after we've sent one message to the King and one to the Count."

"Count? What Count?" asked Dorrity.

"Count Bale," said Dodger.

"You can't frighten me with him," Dorrity said. "He's dead."

Dodger stretched. "That would be a problem, if it were true."

"Of course it's true, don't be ridiculous—oh, I didn't mean to be rude," said Dorrity. "But even if he was alive, he wouldn't want me."

Dodger cocked his head at Metalboy. "He must want the boy, then. My oath, he looks terrified. No wonder he was off his dinner."

"Yep, must be the boy."

"The boy after all."

Ruffgo and the others lounged beside the fire, sucking the last bits of fricassee out of their teeth until Captain Dodger stretched again. "Now, bedtime. Where are the extra blankets?"

"The wood lice are fond of those blankets," Cooker said. "I'll give them a shake—the blankets as well as the wood lice." With another laugh, he hunched off into the cave. He hunched out with an armful of bedding and flapped the blankets one by one too close to the fire. Wood lice like commas dropped into the flames and made tiny explosions. Smoke swirled gray and luminous into the night. The Dark Patrol coughed and cursed.

Dorrity shuffled closer to Metalboy. "They won't get a ransom for me. My brothers don't make much money." She realized she hadn't had a chance to tell Metalboy anything about her brothers. "I don't even know where Birkett and Mike are. I have to get home!"

"The King might pay to get me back," muttered Metalboy. "But he would be furious to find out I was the one who stole me. But—Count Bale. I heard Queen Sibilla say something about the Count's people…" A faint whirr sounded inside him. "Yes. The Queen read out a letter. It said the Count's people had been sighted all over Fontania."

"But that can't mean Count Bale himself," whispered Dorrity.

"It can," said Dodger, right behind her. Holding the pack with one hand, he shuffled her and Metalboy into the cave with the other.

"Count Bale died in history," said Dorrity.

"Dealing with children. The constant arguments." Dodger sighed. "Listen. Advice given us was that the Count wants a particular child for his campaign to re-enter Fontania. The advice was mostly gossip, but the stories of gossips sometimes hold a lick of truth. Here are your beds."

Two thin mattresses, tossed side by side on the hard cave floor, each had a thin blanket and yellowed pillow. Dodger dumped down the pack too. It clanked in a heavy manner. Dorrity didn't want to draw attention to it—Metalboy's oil was in there. She sat down, pulled her blanket over her legs, and tried to smooth the feathers on her hat.

Any stories the anarchists had heard must be to do with the King's lost Experiment. But the men seemed sure they were after a real child. If they realized that Metalboy was clockwork, they'd be certain Dorrity was the one to ransom. That would mean ages before she was back home to find Yorky with two arms and her other brothers safe. She had to keep back a sob that would explode into the air like a huge wood louse.

Metalboy's forehead had the faintest frown as if he was puzzled too. She whispered again. "Don't let them know you're the Experiment. Don't let them see that you're metal. For goodness' sake, keep your cap on."

She rested her hand on his wrist for a moment. It was warm, from the campfire probably, and steadied her. As if he was comforted too, he gave a small out-breath. That puzzled her all over again—he could breathe now?

Brian had settled himself out by the fire to stay on watch. The other anarchists straggled into the far side of the cave. There was a clatter and musical wheeze—Cooker had bumped a piano accordion. The men thumped very thick mattresses, tidied puffy fat pillows, and rolled their balaclava capes into neat bundles. They didn't change into pajamas to give their daytime clothes a chance to air. That, along with not having a bathroom, must be the reason for their sweaty and foresty smell.

"*Guests* instead of *hostages*." Dodger chuckled to Cooker. "Children have to learn to ask the right questions. Schools— *phoof*, not as good as they were in my day."

The cook wrestled with a boot lace. "I went to cooking school, as you'd have guessed. Learned to make do with the little we had. A meal out of nothing but pine needles and the foot of one mushroom. Turned zippo to triumph. They've forgotten to teach children to be resourceful."

Dodger grinned over at Metalboy and Dorrity. "That means creative and cunning."

The anarchists continued chuckling while they picked and swore at their boot laces. Dorrity wanted to cuss too.

But—*make do with what little we had? Creative and cunning?* The little that Dorrity and Metalboy had right now was in the pack. She pulled it towards her and undid a strap to see inside.

As well as the oil-can there were five heavy rectangular cans each with a picture of a cow in a wheat field. Above the wheat plants were letters that spelled *Army Rations*. A whiff of an idea came floating to her.

Ruffgo's chuckle turned into a startling roar. *Ha ha-aa-aahgh!* It was a yawn, though it sounded as if he was about to bite something and shake it to pieces. The other anarchists caught the yawn and made it a chorus. *Aa-aargh. A-ar-argh! Ah-hargh. Ya-harghh-ha-ha…*

Cooker grabbed up the accordion and made it wheeze music. The others more or less picked up the tune, then roared in a quick-march rhythm:

Ya-hah! Ya-hah! We do it all ourselves
Leave kings and queens on shelves
Shove prime ministers out the door
What the heck is a president for
'Cept to order us what to do?
Anarchists do it for themselves.
Quick march! No rules! Ya-hah to any rules.

Dorrity gulped down a laugh. They definitely didn't obey rules about singing, like ending a line at the same time, or being in tune, or even having much of a tune to start with. Metalboy looked startled again. His mouth opened and shut. Maybe he'd like to sing too but couldn't decide when to throw himself into it.

Cooker squeezed a last wheeze from the accordion, and the anarchists tucked themselves in.

"Tomorrow is another day," growled Ruffgo. "Another breakfast, lunch and dinner, a lot more mushrooms. *Aa-augh-yi-ih-ih-yüh.*"

"Another day, another ransom." Dodger lay flat and tugged his blanket up to his chin. "Goodnight, guests. Make yourselves comfy. Sweet—*aa-ou-aargh*—dreams."

By now Dorrity's idea was set in her head. But it was too dangerous to speak or even whisper. She hoped Metalboy would understand her when the time came. For the moment she had to stay awake till it was…well, as safe as it might ever be.

—

22

GIVE AWAY,
STEAL AWAY

At last the Dark Patrol seemed asleep, except for Brian out by the coals of the fire. The glow of embers was dotted with dancing moths. A small bat shape flitted above Brian's head, making its supper of night insects. The scene was so much like a picture from a storybook that Dorrity almost didn't want to ruin it. But tonight she had to be practical and resourceful.

Metalboy lay absolutely straight under his blanket. Dorrity felt about on the cave floor then flicked a pebble at him (*clink!*). His head popped up. She waved her hand in the glow from the mouth of the cave, then poured an imaginary oil-can. She raised her hands in a silent question: *Do you need oiling?*

For a moment Metalboy did nothing. Then he shook his head.

She mimed to him to follow her at the right moment. It meant a lot of flapping and pointing in silence. At last he nodded.

Dorrity pulled the pack to her stomach and folded the

skirt of her overdress around it. The cross-stitch on the bodice reminded her of home and gave her courage. She climbed to her feet.

Ruffgo opened an eye. "Lie down," he growled.

Dorrity hunched the pack closer and took a step towards the fire. "It's that fricassee."

Ruffgo leaned up an elbow. "No tricks."

She let out a quiet moan. "But I might throw up."

Ruffgo lay down again at once and pulled his blanket over his head. "Do it outside," came his muffled voice.

Dorrity glanced behind her and saw Metalboy rise on one knee, ready to sneak out too. She grabbed her hat and hung it down her back. She wasn't going to leave it to be kicked about by anarchists.

Crouching as if she was desperate for the bathroom, she neared Brian at the mouth of the cave. Firelight flickered on his forehead and made him look scary. But she knelt beside him.

"That was a tasty fricassee." She brought a can of rations out of the pack. "Do you think this would be a good thank you?"

"*Property of the National Army of Fontania,*" breathed Brian. "I haven't a treat like that in years. Those were the days. Forced marches over The Stones of Beyond. Spooning into a can of rations while you soaked your aching feet in the nearest puddle."

She handed the can over and hoped he wouldn't notice Metalboy easing behind him towards the split in the rocks. "There are five cans. One each and a spare. You could hide the spare and have a tiny nibble now and then."

"What's the catch?" whispered Brian. "There's always a catch."

"Oh, just…while you sit here, could you have a little doze?" From the corner of her eye Dorrity saw Metalboy had almost reached the gap.

"Got anything else?" Brian fiddled in the pack and brought out the oil-can. He set it down. "Let's think," he muttered. "On the one hand, a treat all to myself. On the other, being disloyal to my brothers-in-arms."

"Think of it as a free giveaway?" She crossed her fingers.

He squeezed his eyes shut as if he really longed to say yes. "I just can't do it."

"Anarchists say *yah* to rules. Just once, couldn't you just say *yah* to the brotherhood?"

"Yah!" Brian flung himself backwards. He grabbed Metalboy, who fell in a clatter, and scrambled to his feet. "Hostages trying to nick off!"

Shouts echoed in the cave. The anarchists were struggling out of their blankets. Dorrity dived at Brian's skinny legs. The surprise of it made him fall in a twist, but he managed to snatch her ankle and hold on.

Metalboy lunged for the oil-can and tossed it in the fire. An orange *whoosh!* threw flames high and wide.

Brian let Dorrity's ankle go. She tugged Metalboy's arm, nearly fell on him, then they were both up. They fled through the gap in the rocks.

"After them!" yelled Dodger.

A shimmer from the moon lit up patches of forest.

Dorrity raced down the track, tripped, but Metalboy hoisted her to her feet again.

A motorized bike began to roar. A *koff-ugh-koff* joined in. Bright lights from the bikes flickered on the track. Dorrity pulled Metalboy into the uphill undergrowth—bracken, a fallen branch, a screen of creeper. Ruffgo and Brian zoomed past, heading downhill. The roar dwindled in the distance, and the stench of steam and oil hung round like a cloud.

"You shouldn't have flung the can on the fire," Dorrity gasped. "It was dangerous!"

"And now there is no oil," Metalboy said. "I might seize up. Poor boy. Poor Metalboy. I will not be able to make amends to the King. I will not be able to face danger when I am ready. I might never be ready."

It took a bucket of self-control not to give him a kick. But any more noise might bring Dodger and Cooker out on the hunt too.

—

DOWNHILL IN
THE DARK

A *flop!* meant an ogre-wood blossom had hit the forest floor nearby. Dorrity felt her heart lighten. But any new plan wouldn't work till it was dawn and she could see. Otherwise there'd be bruises or broken limbs—tree limbs and hers, even Metalboy's. She didn't want to be responsible for a wrecked experiment.

"Are we under an ogre-wood? It's too dark to see. It should be safe if you lean close to the trunk. All right?"

She settled down against the rough bark. Metalboy stayed standing. She just had to hope that Dodger and Cooker had tucked back to sleep and relied on Ruffgo and Brian to recapture the hostages.

The moon disappeared completely. It started to drizzle. Soon rain pattered on the forest canopy. Dorrity's hat brim sent drips down her neck. The ground grew damp. It grew damper. She started to shiver.

"Will you die from the cold?" asked Metalboy.

He sounded so normal she couldn't help giggling.

"What is funny?" Metalboy asked.

In the murk of the night she saw his head give a sudden tip. "What is it?" she asked.

"I have asked my first two questions!" he said. "One after the other! The King would be pleased. What a triumph. It is more important than ever that I nerve myself to face the danger I was made for. I must make full amends for running away."

"You've already faced danger," Dorrity said. "So have I. The anarchists were scary, though we'll probably laugh about them in years to come. First thing tomorrow we'll face danger again—and finish escaping, I hope."

Metalboy's face turned side to side, a glimmer in the gloom. "I do not think escaping will be enough. The danger I have to face is very great."

"For goodness' sake." Dorrity smothered a yawn. "Do your best to stay as dry as possible. The worst thing will be if you go rusty."

He was still muttering to himself.

"What?" asked Dorrity.

"I am searching for words to explain the danger I must face," he explained, "but the King did not reveal it in any detail."

"Then be quiet," said Dorrity. "I'm wet, cold, and grumpy. That could be dangerous. Would you like to find out?"

"Good night," said Metalboy.

~

The first light of morning seeped through the canopy of ogre-woods and pines. Dorrity had dreamed she tripped

Count Bale, then made him slip on a heap of spilled fricassee. The anarchists in her dream yawned like thunder over the Dark. Count Bale tumbled off an unfinished bridge and all that remained was a raft of bubbles. It was tiring to wake up and realize the adventure wasn't over.

Dorrity's hat had somehow kept her head dry. The rest of her was wetter, colder, and much more grumpy. But she thought of Yorky. If she managed to get home, his wing should be gone. Birkett and Mike would be there. Everything would be safe.

"Metalboy!" she hissed.

Eyes closed, he had slumped sideways, arm hooked over a low branch.

"Metalboy!" she said more loudly.

He gave a jerk and unhooked his arm. His knees wobbled. A few whirrs came out of his mouth. He spluttered, then stood straight. "Good morning," he said. "What is for breakfast?"

"Nothing," said Dorrity. "You don't have breakfast."

"What is for breakfast? What is for breakfast? How wonderful," he said. "What do you think of my questions? What is for breakfast?"

"Please don't ask the same one over and over," said Dorrity, "especially when the answer stays the same."

He still wore his cap. It had stayed on all through the wild ride uphill on the bike, through the scramble among the bracken and now in this rain.

"Is that glued to your head?" she asked.

His eyes gleamed. "It kept slipping off. I have good ideas."

"In fact, you do," said Dorrity.

His eyes glowed with pleasure. He gave a small chuckle. He grinned.

She chuckled too. Then she climbed to her feet and peered around.

Several ogre-wood flowers had hit the floor of the Dark some distance away. Dorrity investigated. Most of them were too wet to be useful. One blossom was small, not properly opened. But a few looked possible. She chose two that smelled very ripe indeed but still seemed sturdy.

"Hurry, before one falls on top of us." She beckoned Metalboy. "You said you were a quick learner. Copy me."

She sat down, slid herself inside a blossom and showed him how to grasp two petals like handles for steering. "Use your feet as well. Don't push too hard and don't leave your foot out or you'll break an ankle."

He hesitated.

"The oniony smell can't bother you. Get in!"

With creaks from his knee joints, Metalboy struggled into the other blossom. It was a neat fit. Dorrity's was a little large for her, but she'd had practice so she was sure she'd be all right.

"Now sort of bounce and slide…" she began.

Faint voices sounded through the trees. "Wretched brats…"

Dodger and Cooker!

"Quick," Dorrity hissed. "Keep up."

She shoved the blossom. The rubbery petals gave a bounce, a larger bounce—and she was off. She whizzed past ferns and rocks, gave a small deer a fright, and scattered some rabbits. A fallen tree was just ahead. She swerved at the very last moment.

It was best to avoid the tracks in case they bumped into the anarchists and their bikes. But the tracks zig-zagged, so now and then she had to bounce across an open path. She flashed around large and small trees, past more fallen trunks. She risked a glance over her shoulder. Metalboy was close behind. His clockwork brain must be very good if he'd learned this fast to ride an ogre-blossom sled. Dorrity swerved again to avoid a thorn bush.

There was so much noise from whishing over moss and fallen leaves, so much swishing from branches and fern fronds, so many *ouches* that she was afraid the anarchists would hear. And she couldn't listen out for a *koff-koff* or a *ya-hah!*

She glanced behind again, saw Metalboy veer away from another thorn bush and fall out. Her own sled was right on the edge of a bank. With no time to swerve, she bumped over and down. The blossom bounced her over another bank and onto a track. She tried to force it across to the other side but its oomph had gone. With a *slap!* a petal fell off the blossom. A second one followed—*flop-plop!*

At this stage it was usually fun to count bruises. But she was still nowhere near home. Dorrity wriggled out of the mangled blossom and scrabbled under a bush at the edge of the track.

She chanced a call. "Metalboy?"

On the other side of the track was a rustle of ferns. His

head came out of the undergrowth. He looked a bit different. The cap was sitting higher, on a sort of fuzz. She squinted.

"What is the matter?" he whispered.

"You," she said. "Feel your head."

He looked puzzled but raised his hand to the cap.

"Your head!" said Dorrity.

He pressed the cap down. It lifted again and came off in his hand, with some tufts stuck to it. He juddered a bit. "Fur," he said. "Fur! Did I hurt a small animal?"

"You're growing hair," she hissed.

His hand quivered—he stroked his head as if an animal lay there ready to bite. "It is really hair? What…what does it look like?"

"Sort of soft spikes," she whispered. "Did the King expect you to grow hair?"

In the distance was a *koff-koff-roar*. The sound faded for a moment, then grew louder.

"They're coming up the track." Dorrity shrank under the fern. "Hide."

"But I must be brave." He was blinking. "It was not brave to run away as I did last night."

"Stay out of sight or I'll be furious. And if they catch you, don't dare let them know where I am!" She ducked further down but found herself between a rock and a fallen tree. It meant extra cover but also that she had to stay close to the track.

Oh no! The blossom still lay on the road. The roar grew louder. She crouched right down, hands over her hat, and crossed her fingers.

There was a screech, a bang, an almighty shout, a few clatters, and a blast of steam. A lesser roar roared on, returned, and became a low growling from only one motor.

Dorrity turned her head enough to see. In the middle of the road Ruffgo lay on his back. Smoke twisted from the wreckage of his bike.

—

DOWNHILL IN
THE WET

Brian switched off his own bike and kicked down a small extra pedal. It made a steadying foot so the bike stood by itself. That was clever.

Slowly—very slowly—he tiptoed to Ruffgo. "Can you move?"

Ruffgo lay like a fallen tree. "I'll try in a bit."

"Fair enough." Brian put his hands in his pockets and sniffed the air. "Ah, steam and oil, it's my life-blood...but *phoof*. Onion, rubber, and soap."

Ruffgo raised a shaky hand to cover his own nose. "*Phoo-oof.*"

"Ogre-wood season." Brian scuffed his boots at the mashed petal around the wrecked wheel.

"There's no ogre-woods in this part of the Dark," said Ruffgo. "They're higher up or lower down."

"There's a mangled flower here," said Brian. "Your bike slipped on it."

"Lucky we didn't slip last night," grumbled Ruffgo. "Didn't even smell it. *Phoo-oof. Ow. Phoo-oof.*"

Brian peered at him. "Can you move yet?"

"No. *Ow*," said Ruffgo. "I played policemen in ogre blossoms when I was a kid."

"I used to slide in them till they fell apart." Brian started whistling the marching song but stopped after a few notes. "You don't suppose…No, not those kids."

"It takes bravery to slide in a blossom," said Ruffgo. "That boy wouldn't have the nerve."

On the far side of the track Dorrity saw a sharp movement of the bracken.

"And that girl could never do it," Brian said.

She nearly let out, *How dare you!*

"Probably neither of them is the one the Count wants," Brian said. "But he might pay up anyway."

"Not him," growled Ruffgo. "He's bad news. Bad blood. Very bad magic. He'll only pay for what he wants, and even then he might refuse."

"What about the King, then?" Brian began. "Which one of those children might he want?"

Ruffgo groaned. "I'm getting feeling in my legs. Nearly ready for a heave-up."

Brian hunkered beside him. "Let's tell the Captain we chased them into the stream and it carried them over rapids and dams all the watery way to the Forgotten River."

Ruffgo growled. "Lying's not right."

"Aw, no," said Brian, "but when you think about it, is it right to give a child up to the Count or to the King?"

Ruffgo groaned again. "I'm ready. Be gentle."

The heave-up meant plenty of groans and several swear

words. Ruffgo's back was bent like a bracket as he hobbled to the broken bike. He undid a panel and took out a screwdriver.

"You need pliers too," said Brian.

"Shut up," said Ruffgo.

On her backside Dorrity edged in shadow and shelter till she was behind the fallen tree. For a moment she wanted to sneak off without Metalboy—no, she couldn't. Slowly she lifted a hand to beckon him. The bracken across the track shivered again, and there was his face, eyes round and scared. He glanced at the anarchists. Their backs were towards him. He slid down to the track and darted across.

Dorrity kept backing downhill. Metalboy followed in a crouch. Her hat caught on a twig and the string dug into the side of her neck. She tripped. A branch cracked under her.

"The girl!" shouted Brian.

"Run!" she cried.

Metalboy charged through the undergrowth, cap clutched in a hand. Her overdress caught on twigs, branches whipped past her face, the hat bounced at her back. They fell onto the track again and scrambled across just before a bike shot past. Dorrity glanced back and saw Brian gripping the handlebars, Ruffgo clinging on behind him. She plunged on, down and down, till it seemed never-ending—there was a stream ahead, the track again, the wooden bridge they'd crossed the day before.

But the motorized bike was there too, resting against the bridge and steaming a bit. Dorrity managed to grab Metalboy's sleeve and make him stop.

Ruffgo and Brian stood each end of the bridge, glowering up and down the track and into the trees.

An oniony smell made her eyes water. More ogre-wood flowers lay nearby. She checked the state of them—full of holes already, as well as earwigs. They'd fall apart on the second skid.

Perhaps she and Metalboy could swim down the river. But it looked very rocky. Besides, Metalboy might seem more human now, but he was made of metal. Rust would definitely be the danger he'd have to face if he got soaked through.

Oh, why should he matter to her, anyway? You couldn't like an Experiment the way you liked people. Well—she supposed she could have a kind of friend that she didn't like much. Then it wouldn't be upsetting when he left, or she left, or whatever happened. Oh—yes, she'd better find a way to save them both.

So she hunched against a mossy boulder and chewed the side of her thumb—that was what Birkett did when he was thinking. *Think in logical chunks,* she told herself, *not scattery bits.*

The stream looked deep and wide and flowed south-west. It was probably the one that joined the Forgotten River well up past Mr. Coop's end of the town. It would be perfect if they could canoe down it. But there was no canoe and the blossoms would sink in ten seconds.

She stared at the stream, the anarchists scowling on the bridge, the eddies and swirling of water. Clumps of weed and twigs floated down, bumped into the bank and spun round. Then they shot on down to the Forgotten River, where they'd probably bump into Mr. Coop's boat shed before heading off under the bridge.

She found herself sitting straight. "Metalboy," she whispered, "I have an idea."

A breeze fluffed his fuzz of hair. "Will I have to be brave?"

She wanted to hit him and make him blink.

"Because I must work at how to be brave every chance that comes along. I would have had very few chances if I had stayed in the King's workshop." His eyes seemed to crinkle up. He still looked scared, but Dorrity thought it was his second smile.

~

They crept upstream till they were well out of the anarchists' sight and hearing.

Next they found stout fallen branches, not too stout, not very long and with plenty of leaves.

Third step was finding a way to lash the branches together with vines to make little rafts. Fourth was hoping the knots would last the distance to the boat shed.

Metalboy was excellent at making things. He started to tear the buttoned cuffs off his over-long knickerbockers. "I need those strings on your overdress too," he said.

"What for?" asked Dorrity.

"Straps. To help steer the rafts." He'd added the knickerbocker cuffs already.

It seemed to make sense, though it left her with rips in the side seams. Dorrity was sure to be in trouble over that and would have to try to mend them. But if the plan worked, at least she'd be doing her sewing back home.

Fifth step was to tell herself not to be stupid and worry about sewing and keep hunting for bracken and small leafy branches for camouflage.

Sixth would be setting the rafts in the river, climbing on, pulling the leafy stuff over themselves, then hoping like crazy that the plan would work.

—

25

ENDING WITH...

Should Dorrity launch her raft at the same time as Metalboy's? It didn't matter. Downstream was the only direction. What they needed was plenty of luck.

"Thank you." She held out her hand.

His forehead creased. "Why?"

"For not arguing. For being strong enough to fetch the branches, tie the knots really tight and everything, and for being so quick. Now you say, 'You are welcome, don't mention it, Dorrity. Thank you for the brilliant idea in the first place. If I don't see you again, thank you for the pleasure of your company.' Then shake my hand and let's get on with it."

Metalboy settled his cap. "Do not mention it, thank you for the brilliant idea. But it was not a pleasure altogether. It was difficult to stay out of the mud. I worried that my joints—"

"Don't whine," said Dorrity. "I'm covered in mud too. Look at my best boots. They'll get soaked again soon and never be the same. If you rust up, I promise to find more oil. Now I'm going."

"We did not shake hands yet," said Metalboy.

"If I hang about, I'll lose my nerve." She tightened her hat toggle and waded into the stream, pushing her raft in front of her. When the current began to tug, she half-lay on her stomach. *Ergh!*—in an instant her belly was wet.

She tugged the leafy branches over herself as well as she could, gripped the steering straps and kicked. Her raft raced to the bend, towards the bridge—she shot under it and out the other side. Ruffgo—or was it Brian?—yelled, but she was well past.

Another shout faded behind her. She hoped it meant that Metalboy was under the bridge too and away from the anarchists.

The stream was far too swift for more hoping. All she had the wit for was to hold tight and try to steer clear of snags and rocks. Bits of raft jabbed into her. The straps were a hopeless idea, pathetic. She nearly tipped off. She and Metalboy could share the blame for that.

Onward she plunged, bumped over a short set of rapids, around another bend, too close to a rock, just missed a mess of fallen trees—

The stream hurtled her on, down, down. To her right she had a glimpse of thicker green—was it a hedge? If so, it could be Eagle Hall...

Gradually the stream grew more steady and comfortable, like Mrs. Freida reaching a gentle mood after a fit of scolding. And there ahead was the swash and ripple where it flowed into the Forgotten River.

~

Dorrity still couldn't do more than hope and hang on.

Ducks and other river birds quacked and honked. Her raft bobbed past the Ember farm—she saw some of the sheep—then the old stonework in the riverbank that looked like the end of an ancient bridge. In another few moments she'd be coming up to Owl Town. A monstrous ogre-wood hung right over the river, nearly sweeping her off the raft— no, she was safe—no, she wasn't—yes! She passed the tree with no more than a few extra scratches.

In the distance Dorrity saw the roof of Mr. Coop's boat house, the bird-head finials at each end. She kicked towards the bank, rolled off the raft onto some mud and scrambled higher up into some grass. She lay there, lungs heaving. The raft floated away on its own.

It felt as if she'd never find the energy to move again. But she heard a bump and raised her head. Metalboy's raft had scooted on under the boat-house ramp. He was struggling to free it.

"Leave it," she called softly. "We're here."

He grabbed a strut under the ramp and swung himself to the bank. His raft yawed off into the river and out of sight.

"We are here!" Arms in the air, he jumped on the spot. "Hoo-roo-oo! We made it past danger, hoo-roo-oo!"

"Quiet!" The last thing she wanted was for Mr. Coop to hear his weird singing.

Metalboy clambered up and folded down beside her.

"I have to see Yorky…" She still hadn't told him about her brother's wing, about Birkett and Mike who were missing on the Fribbleton Road. But she couldn't take time now. She was shaking with cold. "I have to get home.

I need to warm up. You probably don't…Oh. You are cold."

Though his eyes still danced with excitement, his teeth were chattering. He pulled off his cap to wipe his face and his hair lay flat with the damp. He'd grown eyebrows—sketchy tufts at any rate. Dorrity wished she knew the next steps for the King's Experiment. How human would he be in the end?

"I cannot enter the town," Metalboy whispered. "I have faced enough danger for now and I'm shy. I—I'm only a piece of clockwork."

"Don't be feeble," said Dorrity. But that wasn't kind. "All right. You've grown feelings that can be hurt…"

"I have not," said Metalboy.

Her mouth opened to argue but longing to be home pulled at her.

She could see now that the boat shed was bolted. "I can squeeze under the door, so I'm sure you'll be able to. You should be safe in here. Go on," she said. "Let me see."

She watched as Metalboy laid himself flat on the ground and slid through the gap—yes, he made it. She hissed under the door after him. "I'm going home. There's oil in there if you think you need some. Wrap yourself in the rug on the chair." Already she was crawling up the grass behind the shed to reach the lower path.

Metalboy called through the gap. "Will you come back? I might be lonely!"

She didn't have time to answer. The second ending would have come true. Yorky would have two arms. Birkett and Mike would be home, and she would hug them.

~

THE VOLUME OF POSSIBLE ENDINGS

SHOCK

Dorrity was so certain she'd find her brothers safe that she raced as fast as a gidibird. She reached the wharf and sped up to the plaza.

But there were gossipers near the fountain.

"Dorrity?"

"What have you been doing? You're drenched!"

"Your poor birthday hat!"

No one seemed to know she'd been away all night, thank goodness. She scrambled past.

When she reached her own fence she saw her brothers' bedroom window was open a little. But she saw no movement, heard no sound. She crept in the front door.

In the greeny corridor light she snuck past her brothers' closed door to her own room. The hat was bedraggled, like a bird squashed by a steam truck. She didn't want to hurt Yorky's feelings. She slid it under the bed.

Now to see him! A laugh of joy waited to burst out. She tip-toed to the kitchen door and pushed it wide.

The room looked empty. The sink brimmed with dishes

to be washed. A stockpot simmered on the stove—probably soup. Then she saw Miss Honey huddled on the kitchen settle, curls in a mess, her eyes closed. She looked exhausted.

Where were the brothers? Dorrity stole down the corridor to their room and gave a rap.

"Yorky? I'm back! Yorky!" She opened the door wide for him to welcome her with his two good arms...

But it felt like a blow to her chest. There he lay on the lower bunk, eyes closed in a pain-filled face. On the coverlet lay one arm, and one wing of broken red feathers.

—

TERRIBLE SHOCK

"You're meant to be better! Where's Birkett? Where's Mike?" Dorrity cried.

Yorky's eyes flew open, and the wing spread with a crackle of feather and bone. He let out a howl of pain. Footsteps ran down the corridor. In came Miss Honey.

"Dorrity! What have you done to him?"

"Get away!" Yorky struggled to sit up. "Keep her away!"

"She's been away all night at Mrs. Freida's—" Miss Honey began.

"I mean out of sight!" he shouted. "Keep Dorrity hidden!"

"We're doing our best," Miss Honey snapped. "You should be grateful."

Yorky fell back on the pillow, hand over his eyes.

Miss Honey's hands went to her hips and her eyes narrowed to slits of dangerous blue. "If you're well enough to shout at me, you're well enough to say what you and your brothers have been up to. Why should your sister stay out of sight?"

Yorky groaned under his hand.

"It must be to do with…" Dorrity couldn't make herself

say magic. She tried to stop shivering and started again from a different angle. "There's not meant to be any magic in Owl Town."

"Exactly. So what's going on?" Miss Honey frowned at Yorky. "Well, you can explain to the police officer. At least your sister's shouting brought you around. She can look after you for half an hour. I need a wash and a change of clothes. Then I'll bring Edgar back with Dr. Oxford." Though she was cross, she still bent down and tucked his wing under the coverlet. "Think hard what you'll say. Make sure it's the truth."

Miss Honey turned to Dorrity and gave a hug as abrupt as a scolding. "I'll hurry back. Don't let anybody, or anything, in. I'll lock the front door."

Through the window Dorrity saw Miss Honey march a few paces along High Street, stop, rub her eyes and run a hand through her curls. Then she heaved a sigh and hurried on.

Dorrity turned to Yorky. "Why aren't you better?"

He rolled his head on the pillow and tried a fake laugh. "Nothing wrong with me! I'll get a job in a circus, fly half a trapeze. Listen, keep out of—"

"Out of sight, I know! Why?" she cried. "I'm not the one with the bad magic wing!"

But he just fell back and closed his eyes.

She may as well change into some dry clothes. She started to turn but heard a soft rattle as if someone else was slinking in the gate.

Yorky's eyes opened. He tensed on his pillow. "Who is it? No—don't go near a window. Hide in your room. Don't say a word. Promise, for your very life."

She backed out, but left his door ajar and stayed in the corridor.

~

Miss Honey wasn't stupid. Nobody could get in the front door unless they broke it down. The back door would be locked as well. And nobody knew about the dog-flap in the laundry.

A man—the Underground man, Dorrity saw his shape through the green side panel—knocked on the door. The next time, the knocking thundered.

His footsteps went away at last. Oh really? Dorrity listened.

For goodness' sake, Miss Honey was stupid after all, and so was she. The window catch rattled in the brothers' bedroom. Dorrity's skin shrank. She hid in the coats' nook and listened.

The Underground man spoke with a cold hard laugh. "At last, Officer of the Castle, there you are."

Why had he called Yorky an officer? Officer of what castle?

"And so, Captain Westrap, here you are as well," Yorky replied. How faint his voice sounded.

"You won't stand and salute?" The man's laugh sounded colder. "Don't tell me—you've been in some trouble."

Dorrity dared creep from the nook and peer through the crack in the door. She saw the Underground man—Captain Westrap—had unlatched the window and leaned his elbows on the sill. What a mean grin he had.

"Where is Officer Birkett? Where's Officer Michael?" he asked.

Yorky was so pale his freckles stood out like a rash. "I didn't see what happened to them."

Captain Westrap put a hand on the sill as if he'd hurdle in and sink his bony fingers into Yorky's throat. "Just give me the truth."

Yorky nodded and took in a breath. "The truth as I know it." The broken wing twitched and shivered under the cover. "I was behind the other two, blowing my nose. The others gave a yell—there was a bright light, a smell of ash. I knew what it was. Tried to run. Fell into a hollow. I heard a terrible deep groan—Birkett, I think. Nothing from Mike. Then a...a beating of wings that went on and on. I lay there, hours—all night—don't know how long."

Captain Westrap let out another laugh that made Dorrity's teeth grit. "Why did the three of you think you could get away with it, Officer Yorkman? You're lucky you weren't turned into three pigs already sliced into bacon."

Yorky gave a weak laugh of his own. "I'm surprised too."

Dorrity saw his right hand try to lift, but it fell back. The wing quivered again under the coverlet.

"I'm curious," said Captain Westrap in that chilly voice. "Where did you find her? The girl. Dorrity, is it?"

"An orphanage near Monkeyhop," said Yorky, each breath more shallow than the last.

"Her mother put her there before she died?" Captain Westrap's hand on the sill became a fist. "All right. How much does the girl know?"

Dorrity couldn't blink—it was like she was frozen.

Yorky's head turned in a *nothing*.

"Nothing at all?" asked the Captain. "No memories? Not even a dream that makes her wake screaming?"

Yorky said a very bad word.

The Captain gave a mocking grin. "Each year for seven years you met me and swore you were still hunting her. But seven years you've been here growing parsnips and beans. Clever. Seven years, under the royal spies' noses, right here in Owl Town."

Yorky swore even worse. The russet wing thrashed out from under the covers.

Captain Westrap's eyes widened. His bony jaw grinned. "Ha! Officer Yorkman, I give you points for getting away with it till now. But one scruffy rooster wing won't be enough punishment. You can imagine what Bale did to the officer he sent to stop the three of you when the fool confessed he'd botched the job."

Dorrity's breath jolted. The Captain didn't work for King Jasper and Queen Sibilla—he worked for the Count.

"But now it's my sorry carcass on the line," said Captain Westrap. "I'm the one who has to finish what you were sent to do seven years back. The Count wants her."

Yorky moaned. Blood pounded in Dorrity's ears.

The Captain laughed again. "That girl has a brain, a cunning way of attacking little problems—like she tackled me. If Bale decides to be kind to her, she'll do her job well. *Count Bale* and *kind*—no, the words don't often sit together." He slapped the sill. "All right, where is she?"

Yorky struggled to sit up. "I wouldn't tell you if both my arms were wings and both my sets of toes were chicken claws," he gasped. "Nor if I had to lay ten eggs for breakfast every morning."

"Roosters don't lay eggs," snapped the Captain. "Though that wouldn't stop the Count. You pack of thick-wits. Pretending to be the girl's brothers? She never had a single brother, let alone idiots like the three of you."

Dorrity sank to the hallway floor, breath finally knocked out of her.

"The brat will be flattened with shock," the Captain continued. "I can't stand to see a girl cry."

Yorky scoffed. "Catch her first!"

"I'll catch her," said Captain Westrap. "If I don't, it's me who'll be laying eggs for the Count until years beyond doomsday. I hope you're not fond of the girl by now. No, you can't be. All this time you've been hoping to push the price up. You reckoned that when you finally gave her to the Count, he'd pay triple dolleros."

Dorrity's breath still hadn't returned.

The Captain's voice was a snarl of disgust. "I'll take silence to mean yes, Officer Yorkman. Tough luck. You've waited seven years and all you've earned are some broken wing bones."

Dorrity knew that if the Captain came in now, he'd find her at once. And he might hear her if she tried to run back to the coat nook. But then from the back garden there came a deep growl. The bear! She'd forgotten the bear!

There was another moment of silence, then Captain Westrap gave a shout of laughter. It was just enough to allow her to sneak away from the bedroom door into her own room where she could peer through the window.

At first all she saw was the goat prancing sideways and back. Then the bear reared up and beat its chest. She heard

Captain Westrap still laughing. Dorrity had to crane to see in the other direction—he was striding to the gate, his shoulders shaking. He threw his head right back. His fist punched the air in a *Yes!*

She heard a thump in Yorky's bedroom and ran to his door. There he was struggling to get out of bed, coverlet wrapped over the wing. He reeled for a moment as if he might faint.

"I hate you! How could you!" Her breath left her again for a moment. Yorky took a step towards her. "You're not my brother! Don't dare to come near me!" she screamed.

He reached out. But the goat bleated. Yorky turned. Over his shoulder Dorrity saw the goat stamping its feet and shaking its horns. The bear lumbered towards the window. Yorky's good hand gripped his hair as if he wanted to rip off his own head.

"Oh, flaming fools! The three of us! I said this was the most dangerous year yet! I said we shouldn't go at all. I said we should just run, not wait anymore! Look at you! Flaming Mike's a flaming goat! And you…" He lunged at the window, punched at the bear and missed.

The bear growled, reared higher, and swung a paw. Yorky dodged, clouted it on the nose, then collapsed to the floor with a cry.

Dorrity swayed on her feet in the doorway. The goat was Mike. The bear was Birkett. They'd all been changed on the Fribbleton Road by Count Bale and his bad magic.

And for seven years they'd all been cheating her. They weren't her brothers.

—

PART THREE OF DORRITY'S TALE

STRANGERS
AND
VILLAINS

UH-OH...

The bear peered in the window, small yellow-brown eyes in the huge furry head.

Whumph. It glanced at the heap of Yorky on the floor. *Whumph*, it said again, even deeper, when it spotted Dorrity at the door. It bashed the window shut, dropped to all fours and shambled off.

Dorrity's breath was still ragged. Her limbs felt weak as straw. She stumbled up the hall. Her head swam and she sank to her knees.

Birkett and Mike were animals—magicked by Count Bale.

Time seemed to pleat up. She remembered all sorts of things she'd done with her brothers, games and jokes, the time she'd climbed up into the attic and they thought they'd lost her. How gently Birkett had carried her down again, with no scolding. No wonder. How upset they must have been to think they'd lose a great bucket of dolleros for finding her.

The front lock unclicked. In rushed Miss Honey with Mrs. Freida. Dorrity looked up from where she sat on the hallway runner.

"You said you were going to be with Mrs. Freida last night!" Miss Honey cried.

"What's the matter with the girl?" asked Mrs. Freida.

They swooped on Dorrity, carted her to the kitchen and propped her on a chair.

"She's soaked. She looks as if she'd been dragged through a thorn hedge. Where…" Mrs. Freida gave Dorrity a shake. "You haven't been to Eagle Hall?"

"Of course not," Dorrity managed.

"Then where were you?" Mrs. Freida did her irritated jig. "What's going on?"

Dorrity took in a shuddering breath.

"The girl's hungry," said Miss Honey. "Food first." She started bustling with a ladle and the pot of soup.

"Then a bath," said Mrs. Freida. "Then explanations. Get those boots off. Look at them—ruined."

Dorrity didn't know what to say or do, except wrestle the boots off. Mrs. Freida helped her out of the damp overdress and leggings and wrapped a blanket around her shoulders. Miss Honey ladled soup into a bowl, set it on a tray, and gave it to Dorrity.

She had a sip. Chicken soup, the smell of herbs and home—if only…if only things were normal and safe. A huge sob built up in her chest.

Miss Honey splashed more soup into another bowl. "Yorky might want some by now."

Dorrity's sob burst out in a shout. "Chicken soup? When he's got that wing?"

Miss Honey's mouth dropped open. "I didn't think! I'll

go and check on him." She swung out of the kitchen.

A moment later her voice rang down the hallway.

"Mrs. Freida! Quick! He's collapsed."

Mrs. Freida flurried out. There were noises of hauling and soothing and bustling. Why should Dorrity care? Yorky was a liar and cheat. He'd never been her brother. Nor had Birkett or Mike.

She had three more sips of soup but had no appetite. She put down the bowl and laid her head on the table.

"…seeing the bear must have given him a shock," Miss Honey was saying when she and Mrs. Freida returned. "Same with the goat…Hush, she's asleep."

Dorrity wasn't. But it solved the problem of what to say and do. She stayed with her eyes closed.

"I don't think she's realized, do you?" Miss Honey muttered.

Dorrity heard the women sidle to the kitchen window. They'd be looking out.

"Mike is a wonderful goat," breathed Mrs. Freida.

"I'd started to grow sweet on Birkett," Miss Honey whispered. "He's a truly magnificent bear."

"The butcher certainly shouldn't have shot it," said Mrs. Freida.

"But what's going on?" Miss Honey sounded close to tears.

"Obviously, something to do with magic or monarchy. And Count Bale."

"Dorrity's always dashing away," Miss Honey whispered. "If the Count's around again, what should we do?"

Through her eyelashes Dorrity saw the women look at her with anxious frowns.

"I'll speak to Officer Edgar," Mrs. Freida said. "The Watch House would be best without a doubt."

~

Lock her in the Watch House? *Cuss* to that!

Dorrity pretended to stretch and knocked the soup bowl. "I think I'll go to bed. I can have a bath later."

Again Miss Honey and Mrs. Freida exchanged a look. "Good idea," Miss Honey said.

"Come along," said Mrs. Freida. "Let's go to your room and find clean pajamas."

She locked the window and pulled the curtain while Dorrity sat on her bed and caught a false yawn in her hands. Then Mrs. Freida tip-toed out and shut the door. Through a chink in the curtain Dorrity saw her hurry up High Street. She'd be off to tell Edgar to get a cell ready.

Her friends might truly believe they were doing the right thing by wanting her locked in the Watch House. But Dorrity reckoned the right thing would depend whose side you were on. She knew where she stood—firm on her own side.

All she heard now was soft kitchen clack and clatter from Miss Honey. She edged to the wardrobe and changed into a gray tunic. On the wardrobe floor were her shoes, boxes of old clothes for playing dress-up, and old school books with scribbled notes for experiments she'd do when she grew up and became an inventor like Mr. Coop. It would never happen now. A lump came to her throat.

Right at the back of the wardrobe was the back of the wardrobe. If she shoved a metal comb between the second and third boards from the left, a bottom panel popped out.

She could climb through into the laundry, fit the panel again, and nobody would know.

The outside door of the laundry, as Dorrity had expected, was locked and bolted. She unlatched the ancient dog-flap. It was covered in cobwebs. With luck—and there was—she was still small enough to slide through without sticking. She left one foot inside while she rolled over, then eased it out. That way she stopped the flap from slamming to and fro to warn she'd escaped.

~

From the side path behind her, something said, *Whumph*. Dorrity jumped. The bear sat there, still with Miss Honey's purple scarf around its neck.

Its yellow-brown eyes watched her as she stood up outside the dog-flap. She tried not to tremble. The fur of the bear's forehead wrinkled. *Whumph*, it said again and sucked its long black claws. Such a huge glossy creature. Its smell burned the inside of her nose.

"Being lied to and cheated is disgusting!" she hissed to the bear.

Its paw lifted and rubbed its chest as if it had indigestion. Or perhaps it was hungry.

Dorrity took a step to see if this was it: *The bear pounced,* crunch, *Dorrity gone. The End.*

It just stared with those squinty yellow eyes.

She walked to the front gate. The bear didn't follow.

Keeping her chin up, trying not to let her knees give out again, trying to look normal, she crossed High Street and dodged to the low path. There beside the river, she strode with more purpose. She was Dorrity. She had no brothers. Grown-ups thought she had to be locked up. Her only friend had started as a piece of clockwork but he was a boy now, mostly or not. He might have an idea that would help.

—

29

A RULE ABOUT
LADDERS

Dorrity picked her way through curtains of willow and under the bridge. From there she had to scramble under the wharves, through more willows, then down the path that was always too muddy for the grown-ups.

The boat house seemed deserted. Ripples licked under the ramp. The bird-head finials on the roof kept an eye on the water.

"Metalboy?" she hissed. "Metalboy!"

She heard movement in the boat house, then his voice. "Dorrity?"

Who did he think it could be? Were all boys that dense? Ones that hadn't begun as experiments were possibly cleverer.

She squeezed under the door into the shed. Metalboy's boot and shoe sat drying in a patch of sunlight from a rectangular hole at the top of the wall. At this end there was a workbench. At the other end was the ramp, with wooden doors where the river made its lapping sounds. In the middle of the shed sat the barrel-boat on its cradle.

Dorrity had always been happy when she came in here.

She loved the huge wooden barrel for the outside of the boat. The staves came from the hugest of all ogre-woods. She loved the slightly smaller but still enormous barrel that fitted inside the first with space for all the necessary equipment to sit between them.

She loved the shiny brass pipes for the buoyancy chambers. And she loved the chambers themselves that filled with water to make the vessel heavy and take it down or filled with air to make the water squirt out so the boat could rise.

She absolutely loved the gears that turned a huge screw with paddles on. It propelled the vessel through the water. Mr. Coop didn't call it a screw—he said "a propeller".

If she ever got over the shocks about false brothers and the Count hunting her, she'd also love the new chemical furnace when she got to see it. Renewable, breathable air. And it would propel the propeller so the boat actually moved.

"Dorrity!" whispered Metalboy. He crept out from under the workbench. His cap was in his hand and his hair was soft peaks like whipped cream. His eyes gleamed, he trembled, his voice rose and fell in a chant of excitement. "There is oil. There are wrenches and pliers and hammers and screws. There is jar after jar of carefully sorted nails and nuts, all with their names on the jars. And tiny bolts. I climbed into the barrel, and checked the controls, fixed three knobs, and adjusted…"

"Keep your voice down." She nearly added *dumbo*. That would have been mean. He was just being happy. It wasn't his fault that she'd been so deceived by her brothers—the shock of it fell on her again. She crooked an arm over her eyes and crouched on the floor.

"What's the matter?" Metalboy asked. "Are you crying? Dorrity, what is the matter?"

He sounded so worried that she looked up. His hand had gone to his chest, the way it had done a few times over the last day.

"They're not my brothers," she said. "They tricked me. They just want money."

He peered at her. "Your voice is shaking. It must mean you are unhappy. Let me jolly you along. Cheer up, cheer up…"

She clenched her teeth.

Metalboy's forehead creased. "There may be something I have not learned yet about girls when they are unhappy. But it must be very upsetting to find that brothers…that they are not your brothers at all." He stood straight. "Dorrity, I'm learning new things all the time. I have learned from the anarchists and from you that people give each other advice and comments."

His face seemed plump and pink as Dorrity had seen many a face when the person it belonged to was being smug.

"My advice is to ask questions," Metalboy continued. "Which ones to ask, I am not sure. Nor am I sure who you should ask. That's the trouble with questions. I learned early in my life—my life with a heart, that is to say—that questions have problems."

Metalboy had a heart? That must be why he kept putting his hand on his chest, not indigestion from the porcupine fricassee.

She climbed into the old cane chair. "I haven't told you everything, give me a chance. Captain Westrap…no, I haven't explained anything yet. I thought he'd been sent by the King. So did Officer Edgar. But I heard the Captain talking to Yorky. He kept saying 'Count Bale.'"

"The dead Count? So he really is alive. Yes, because a dead Count wouldn't count…A joke!" Metalboy jammed his cap on at a jaunty angle. "Ha! I just made a joke!"

Dorrity gritted her teeth so hard she thought they'd crack. But a boat whistle sounded downriver. If it was the regular afternoon riverboat, Captain Westrap might be ready to leave on it.

Three ladders rested against the barrel-boat. She'd climbed up and down those with Mr. Coop, even entered the hatch and pretended she was steering underwater. If she moved one of the ladders against the wall, she could see through the gap near the top and spy out. She tried to shift the shortest ladder. It was far too heavy.

Without even being asked, Metalboy padded over on his bare feet, lifted the ladder and rested it where she wanted, no trouble at all. "I will hold it steady."

"Promise," said Dorrity.

He nodded.

Was she still too shaky? She scooted six rungs, seven, eight, nine, and reached the gap.

A family of gidibirds flew past singing, *gidday*, *giddy giddy*. Blue and white daisies swayed on the far side of the river, but afternoon shadow made it tricky to see much on this bank. The wharf was only just in view.

"I'm holding the ladder very steady," Metalboy said.

"Good on you," she muttered. "Shut up."

The riverboat swinging into the wharf was the afternoon steamer. There was no sign of Captain Westrap waiting. Dorrity wanted to be absolutely sure he was leaving.

Mr. Coop and her fake brothers always warned her never to go further than three rungs from the top. She climbed another one now.

She made out Farmer Ember's steam truck heading to the wharf, Dr. Oxford on his bicycle near the plaza, Chippy O'Now sweeping the tavern steps. A dark cap bobbed out of sight behind a tree, then she saw it again. Was it Captain Westrap? If so, he was heading fast away from the river.

With a blur of wings a cloud of starlings hurtled out of the Beastly Dark from the direction of Eagle Hall. Of course, she knew that on the other side of the Beastly Dark was Lake Riversea. At the furthest end of Lake Riversea was the boundary of Fontania, and just over the boundary was the City of Canals and Castle Bale. That's where Count Bale had been banished—from Eagle Hall to the City of Canals.

Dorrity clung to the ladder, puzzling it out. The Count had been banished so long ago that he should be dead. Now she knew he was definitely alive, and probably because of magic. But why was he interested in her? Why on earth would he pay anyone to find her?

She stretched just a little higher to see if the Captain entered the Dark. The ladder shifted.

"Be careful!" cried Metalboy.

But the ladder started to slide. Dorrity screamed and tried

to fling herself in the other direction. The ladder crashed to the decking, and she found herself sprawled on top of the barrel-boat.

"You said you'd hold it!"

"I tried," called Metalboy. "But you climbed too high. Therefore it is also your fault and you too should be ashamed."

"You're the stupidest thing I've ever met!"

Metalboy jerked his head. "Someone is coming. Slide down. I'll catch you."

No matter how stupid he was, she knew he was strong. She gathered her nerve and pushed off, and he caught her easily.

She shoved him towards the workbench. "Hide behind that box of tools!"

He ducked into the shadow under the bench. She dived behind a jumble of equipment that one day, if Mr. Coop found time, he would make into a clever device to poke up from the barrel-boat so you could check what was there above water.

A key rasped in the shed-door lock.

~

WORSE TERRIBLE
SHOCK

The door swung open and late sunlight rippled gold all over the decking. The shape of Mr. Coop stood there. "Anyone here?" He creaked his knees to see under the workbench. "A cat?" he said. "We don't like strange and stray animals in Owl Town. We've already got a bear and a goat and a man with a wing... Puss? No?"

He straightened up, scratched his head through his beanie and let out a sigh. In a slow step or two he reached the side of the barrel-boat and patted it.

"Nearly ready, my girl. Ah, would anyone be brave enough to come with us?"

He moved out of sight. Dorrity saw the ladder being heaved up off the decking and set down lengthways against the wall. Mr. Coop stepped back into view. His hunched old shoulders gave a start.

"Dorrity?" But Mr. Coop was looking under the bench again. He gave a shout of surprise, reached in and pulled out Metalboy.

"This is private property! What boat are you from? Stand up, boy. What are you doing?"

Metalboy stammered and climbed to his feet.

"Take your cap off when you talk to me!" said Mr Coop as if he was used to being obeyed.

Dorrity flinched. This wasn't the Mr. Coop she'd always known. But then, the brothers she'd always known were now that bear, that goat, and the one-quarter rooster.

Metalboy grabbed the cap off with one hand. His other arm went up in a salute. A breeze through the door ruffled his hair. He looked almost entirely like an ordinary boy—though only almost.

"Hmm." Mr. Coop leaned closer. He walked around Metalboy, gave a tap on the saluting elbow, a rap on the right shoulder. "For goodness' sake…" Dorrity saw a smile creep over his face. "Excellent workmanship. There's a touch of old Rocket about it—old Rocket John, excellent craftsman…" He peered again at Metalboy, pulled down the saluting arm, and examined the hand. "But you can't have been made by my old friend Rocket. He's been retired for years…Ah."

Mr. Coop steadied himself on the back of the chair, grinned and rubbed a hand over his beard. "A boy-machine. My goodness. Rocket John, grandfather of the King and Queen. You were made by the King, I have no doubt."

"Sir!" Metalboy stood to attention.

"The question is," said Mr. Coop, "what did he make you for?"

Metalboy saluted again. "The King made me to face danger." His voice was natural, up-and-down.

"This is wonderful. You answer questions! Exactly what danger are you to face?" asked Mr. Coop.

"The King did not say exactly," Metalboy answered.

"Just repeat what you know," said Mr. Coop.

Dorrity wished she'd thought to ask that.

Metalboy nodded. "The King showed his sister an important letter. Count Bale's people have been seen all over the Kingdom. They are probably hunting for the girl. The King said he and the Queen should have looked harder. They would have to send message-birds and warn every outpost. 'Poor girl,' said Queen Sibilla. 'She's a danger to every single person in Fontania.' The King said I was not ready yet. Then he rushed out of his workshop. The Queen kissed me and said, 'Poor metal boy.' I was afraid. I ran away. It took days to find trousers. I am a failed experiment."

Mr. Coop let out a slow whistle. "You might well have been afraid. But I'd say Rocket John will be delighted at how far his grandson has come with his experiments. But—a girl is the great danger? No, young man, it sounds to me as if you were made to search for Bale. Officer Edgar said he'd been put on alert."

Dorrity's breathing had stopped again. Blood thrummed in her ears. Her throat trembled.

Mr. Coop took Metalboy's arm. "Best thing is to take you to the Watch House. You'll be safer there than in a boat shed. I'll send a message to the King. If he designed you to seek out bad magic, it makes sense that you came to Owl Town." Mr. Coop chuckled. "Just listen to me—chatting with a machine made by the King."

The pair of them disappeared. The door shut. Dorrity heard the bolt rattle.

Metalboy must be stupid. He could easily have pulled himself free from Mr. Coop. Or it could mean he still had to follow some orders. It could also mean that he was a real friend—he hadn't given her away, even with a backward glance.

Dorrity stayed huddled in the boat shed, surrounded by dust that floated in the last rays of sun. Today she had learned two terrible things. Captain Westrap, who worked for Count Bale, was hunting her. The King and Queen had said a girl was a danger to all of Fontania.

Her heart thumped with an extra beat as the fourth ending from the magical *Volume* seemed to swim in gold letters before her eyes. *Dorrity…was crowned Queen of Fontania.*

"No," Dorrity whispered.

⁓

WORK IN THE DARK

Dorrity didn't want to be Queen—it was impossible! What could she do? Who was there to help? Not Mr. Coop—nor Officer Edgar—not Miss Honey or Mrs. Freida. At the last town dance there'd been five hundred people, but she didn't think any of them would help her if they knew about this.

One thing was sure. Owl Town was dangerous now.

She crept from the boat shed and through reeds and undergrowth. Gidibirds shrieked. Starlings shrieked louder. Could she stow away on a riverboat? She heard townsfolk on High Street and outside the Owl and Pie. She crouched and listened. Gossip about the Royals again. It seemed they were definitely coming…possibly…maybe…

Farmer Ember and his dwarf farmhands were loading rolls of fencing wire from a boat onto their steam cart. Dorrity sidled up to hide beside the truck till the plaza was empty.

"I thought the last lot wuz bad enough," one of the farmhands was saying. "Forty big fellows with forty crates of equipment each, if I counted right."

"You can't never count right," said the other farmhand.

"Sometimes I can," argued the first. "But I couldn't see clearly because of the dusk."

"And it being in the Beastly Dark," said the second. "Which makes dusk dusker."

"Grumpy, they were, in their glossy black coats," said the first farmhand. "I'd be grumpy too, if I'd had to travel down through the Dark carting all them crates."

Dorrity thought she was well hidden, but Farmer Ember gave a chuckle.

"Hello, Dorrity down there," he said. "Want a fivepence?"

She managed a laugh that she hoped sounded normal. "No, I want a dollero." It was a joke she often had with Farmer Ember. She beckoned him so she could whisper. "Those forty big fellows. Do you mean somebody is already working at Eagle Hall?"

"For the last week," said Farmer Ember. "One of my sheep strayed that way. When we reached the hedge, we was threatened. The sheep never came back. Maybe it was et."

"Et?"

"Chops," said Farmer Ember. "Casseroles with olives and rosemary. Not to mention roasts, fall-apart perfection with herbed potatoes. Possibly someone even used the sweetbread and kidneys in fritters and fry-ups. But," he continued, "being threatened by guards, we kept well away. We'll mend that fence so it keeps an army out, or keeps one in. And we spoke to our nine remaining sheep very severely."

"Ha ha," Dorrity said to keep him sweet. "But I've heard

the Royals are still planning to work on Eagle Hall, not that they've started. There's been nothing definite in the papers."

"We just read what's in front of our eyes on the land and on the edges of the Dark," said one of the farmhands. "It's too gloomy further in to read much at all." He heaved the last roll of fencing wire onto the truck.

~

It was odd that only the farmer and his hands knew that someone was at Eagle Hall already. Had the people come the back way from Lake Riversea? Perhaps the King and Queen wanted to keep their arrival secret. But—Dorrity shivered at the thought of it. There might be another answer, also secret, to do with their being Count Bale's workmen, not the Royals' at all.

She rushed across High Street into the smelly lane between the butcher and the Owl and Pie. The tavern was rowdy this evening. The law clerk was singing with the steam-truck garage-man, though they had very different tunes and different words. It didn't seem as if anyone saw her dart into the alley for the back door of the Watch House.

The main door out on High Street had a large notice. The same notice, only smaller, was screwed on the back door:

Owl Town Watch House
dedicated to safety and security
of residents
no problem too large, no problem too small

Song and laughter continued from the Owl and Pie. The rollicking was good for Chippy O'Now's cash flow. It also meant Edgar would most likely be outside, watching for persons under the influence of roar-juice and being cheeky along with it. Maybe she could sneak in the back door of the Watch House and say a quick goodbye to Metalboy.

WATCH OUT IN THE
WATCH HOUSE

The back door opened into a tiny corridor. Dorrity checked the reception area. The notice board said who was on duty. For the last two months it had read **Officer Edgar Gizbett**. Now the only sign of him behind the counter was a rolled-up sleeping bag and a pair of neatly folded pajamas, blue with a pattern of anchors.

Now to find Metalboy. He'd be in a cell. The Watch House had only two, and the door that led to both of them was right here beside the locked cupboard with the spare swords and shotguns.

Dorrity would have expected a real person to lie weeping on the cell's narrow cot or to grip the bars, promising, *I won't do it again, never, never!* She would have expected a piece of clockwork to stand at attention or lie bent at the joints in a heap.

Metalboy was partly sitting, partly in a heap, picking threads off the ragged cuff ends of the knickerbockers. She crept closer to his bars. He jumped. She patted the air, for *Keep it down*. He frowned—a deep frown that put crinkles all over his forehead—then put a finger to his own lips.

Dorrity pressed into a corner near the foot of the bars. From here, the moment she heard Edgar, she'd dash into the corridor and squash behind the weapons cupboard. Metalboy crouched too. His bare feet looked rosy-blue, cold.

"I'm here to say goodbye." Her voice choked up.

He looked puzzled. "You didn't even say hello when you came in."

"Don't be difficult. I have to leave Owl Town. I…" She may as well tell him a bit. "Listen, Farmer Ember said the King's people had started work on Eagle Hall. But that doesn't sound right. They might be Count Bale's."

"Count Bale is the King's enemy." Metalboy looked scared and even sweaty. "And I must face him."

"No…" This would be hard. "Mr. Coop said he thought you were made to seek out Count Bale. But…the Queen said it was a girl who was dangerous." Dorrity bit her lip. "So now I'm sure they're all after me."

He lurched back against the stones of the cell. His hand went to his chest again. "But that's ridiculous. You're Dorrity. You're kind—"

"Not very." She felt embarrassed.

"And we had—" his eyebrows rose higher—"such fun. Fun, in danger." His hand pressed harder over his heart.

Her face flamed. She couldn't think of a word for worse-than-embarrassed. "You keep rubbing your chest. Is it a rash?"

"You have asked, so I have to tell you." His voice quivered. "There is a dragon-eagle feather behind my heart. It floated there and hid itself."

Great magic—so close to her. Her fingertips tingled where they'd been scorched.

"Why?" she breathed.

"Why what?" said Metalboy.

She had so many questions that her voice stumbled. "Did a d-dragon-eagle make it happen? Was it an accident? Does the King know? Will he want it—?"

Metalboy gasped and started to talk over her. "Count Bale must not learn I have a feather-scale inside me. He'd tear me apart and dump the bits he didn't want into the waste bin. All of me—all of me, gone!'

Dorrity was itching to know more. A dragon-eagle feather! The King and Queen had to be told all that was happening. But she also had to get away as soon as possible! "I have to go. Listen…"

His neck straightened the way necks do when folk are offended. "You listen to me! I have a brain. I heard all manner of things in the King's workshop and I understood some of them. I understand more as I go on and—"

"Shut up!" she hissed. "Sorry, that was rude of me. Shut up *please*."

"A please makes it better?"

"A bit," she said. "You see, I have to decide where to—"

"Decide means think. How long will you take?" His eyebrows were up.

"Oh, you're learning to be sarcastic!" She took a moment and tried to smile. "Metalboy, I have to hide. If Edgar works out I'm the danger, he might lock me up beside you, then you'd be sorry."

He blinked. "A joke. A brave joke. I have made a joke or two myself. But I'll never be brave enough to make a brave one."

She opened her mouth to say, *Force the bar—come with me...*

But she heard growling and scuffling out in Reception. A pair of boots dragged, another pair marched with purpose. She heard Edgar's voice, then another gruff voice she knew from somewhere.

She crept into the corridor and peered through the half-open door. Edgar had arrested someone in skinny black trousers.

"I say no to your authority!" The growling was Ruffgo.

"I say you've had too much to drink." Edgar was handcuffing Ruffgo to a rail on the reception desk, the rail being a cheaper option than a second officer. "Like it or not, sir, you are in custody for your own protection. It is dangerous to bellow *Down with monarchs of all ruddy kinds* to people who support the King and the Queen. Steam was starting to come out their ears."

Dorrity saw Edgar nip to the other side of the reception desk and pick up a pen.

"Now, your personal details. Name and address?"

Ruffgo growled.

"Prisoner gave a garbled reply," Edgar said.

Dorrity heard the crisp sound of a new leaf being turned in the Town Arrest Register and the whisper of pen on page. Edgar was writing slowly but he probably had to be neat. "Next of kin or contact person?"

More growling.

"You mean none? Poor you," said Edgar. "Now turn out your pockets."

Growling and clattering followed.

"Prisoner's belongings: one handkerchief, used, no embroidery. Have it back in case you need it," Edgar said.

Ruffgo's growl sounded slightly like *Thanks*.

"A Fontanian army knife—I'll look after that," said Edgar. "One five-dollero coin, packet of cherry chewing gum, piece of paper…what's this? A label from a can of army rations? Where did you get it?"

Another growl, this time with actual words. "That girl and that boy left 'em with Brian. Very tasty. I planned to visit the shop and order more."

"So," said Edgar, "purpose of your visit to town. To order supplies."

"Purpose of visit, catch the girl and the boy!" roared Ruffgo. "Loss of income!"

"There's no boy in the town," said Edgar. "Mr. Coop brought in an experiment resembling a boy—I saw what could have been oil-holes or dimples. And there is one girl."

Dorrity cussed to herself.

Ruffgo let out a very long growl. "She made me slip on an ogre-wood blossom in front of my brother-in-arms. It's disrespect."

Edgar slammed shut the arrest book. "Your temper's in tatters from roar-juice. You're raving. In fact you're talking mildly for an anarchist. I've heard worse from royalists. Now, into the cell till you can think straight and be polite."

There was the click of handcuffs released from the rail.

Boots scuffled (Ruffgo's) and marched (Officer Edgar's) towards the corridor. Dorrity crammed herself behind the weapons cupboard.

Ruffgo and Edgar reached the cells.

"There's the boy!" shouted Ruffgo.

"You could be right or you've definitely had too much roar-juice," said Edgar's voice. "That's the boy with the oil-holes. I admit to confusion myself. But Mr. Coop is sure he's the King's Experiment."

Dorrity drew in a breath. Now the anarchists would do their best—which meant their worst—to steal Metalboy and ransom him to the highest bidder to fund their cause.

But there was nothing she could do. She ducked through Reception and away into the back streets.

33

MAKESHIFT DINNER,
SECOND-RATE BREAKFAST

In seven half-minutes Dorrity had crept through Mrs. Freida's garden and into the house. She grabbed paper and a pencil and listened at the connecting door.

In the shop Mrs. Freida and Button were making a list of what to order in case the Royals did arrive. "They're sure to forget things. Mechanical eyebrow trimmers," said Mrs. Freida. "And we're low on those devices for helping you pull up your socks."

Dorrity made sure Button was the only one in sight through the crack of the door. She waggled her fingers at him and held one up in a *Hush*. He held up an ice cream cone. She waggled *No thanks* and beckoned. He reached a long arm to the door. Into his hand she put a note about where she'd be and what she needed. All she'd thought of was: *any left-over broken crackers*.

~

For seven years, Dorrity had snuck through townsfolk at dances and at gatherings in the plaza for gossip, laughter, and squabbles. She'd had seven years of creeping silently away to find safe places. She'd had seven years of finding nooks, crannies, and by-ways. Now she edged along twilit streets to the craft lady's shed. It was a place of strange but familiar sounds because the craft lady used glue guns, soldering irons, and a poker-work machine. They each meant a yelp whenever she glued or burned herself by accident. Her craft-y mistakes were in bins behind the shed. It made a safe spot for Dorrity to wait. And in this spot, if she cried, nobody would notice.

She cried so much that her nose dripped. No brothers. A queen, but lonely and sad. Each of the five endings was more useless or more rotten than the last. And she was the danger—to Metalboy, Owl Town, the King and the Queen.

At last Button appeared. In his arms was a box of crackers (broken). In his wordless way he asked where she wanted it carried.

"Just here for now. Thank you." She didn't want anyone to know her plans.

He pulled his head down—or maybe pushed his shoulders up, it was hard to tell with trolls—and sidled away. So her dinner was a few broken crackers—plain, salty, and cheese. She didn't dare enter the Dark tonight. When it was dawn, she'd carry the box to Metalboy's house.

It would have been nice to talk to Button. It would have been nice to talk to anyone. A feeling welled up in her nose like years of sobs but, thank you, she'd cried enough now.

~

With the first lifting of black to gray, she heard slow feet, huge feet, padding. She heard the *inph-inph* of something large sniffing. There, against the gray, was the shape of a head—the head of a bear still with a scarf round its neck.

She didn't move. But the head turned in her direction.

Whumph! The bear sounded just like Birkett in a bad mood.

Dorrity burst away from her hiding place, but in moments the bear had smothered her to its chest. It smelled like hot iron, musty ashes, damp sweaty socks. She struggled, tangled her fingers in the fur of its chest, and twisted hard.

Yow-umph! The bear let her go a little but kept a long black claw hooked in her tunic. How much of the bear was wild, how much was still the man she'd called brother, she didn't know and didn't care. Then it reached a paw, pad-side up, like a *Please*.

"Liar!" She swatted the paw and ran through the craft lady's gate to the morning mist that lay over the Dark and the ditch. As she scrambled up and out to the wasteland, she heard a *whumph* and thud of huge pads.

The bear paced over the Dark Road.

She ran faster through the briars.

There was a *whoof!* Dorrity glanced again and saw the bear tangled in thorns—probably only for a moment. She ran, darting and winding up through the trees. It was not the most sensible of actions before breakfast. And she'd had to leave the box of crackers.

~

Gasping, she stopped behind a tree and her knees gave out. She crumpled on a fallen branch. It broke under her with a

THE VOLUME OF POSSIBLE ENDINGS

loud crack and dumped her in a muddy puddle. She glanced around—no sign of the bear.

Early fingers of sun played through the leaves. Birds were chattering about worms or bad dreams. She scuffled to her feet and brushed herself free of bits of bark and a dead beetle. Carefully, with a glance in every direction, she squelched uphill. Sunlight grew stronger and flickered like scraps of gold on the forest floor, on toadstools, a pair of rabbits playing.

At last she saw the little house. The door stood half open, the way the anarchists must have left it. What if a wild pig, or a man changed into a pig, had nosed in and was eating the walnuts?

She climbed the porch and pushed the door wide. All she disturbed was the air. With one of the stolen hammers she smashed the walnuts. That made it a satisfying breakfast in two ways—one, to fill her stomach and two, to bash something.

What now? None of the endings was: *She lived the rest of her life in the Beastly Dark sitting on the lawyer's stolen cushions.* That made her laugh—just a puff. At the same time it felt like pins were stuck through her heart.

~

A DWARF IN
THE DARK

Dorrity sorted through Metalboy's pile of stolen clothing. Anything would be better than the gray tunic, striped brown now with muck, and leggings with so many holes they looked like a criss-cross of bandages.

It was amazing how swiftly Metalboy must have worked to collect all this without anyone seeing. Here was a pair of overalls wide enough to be Chippy O'Now's. Here were socks and slippers, all odd ones. There was a shirt, a pair of Dorrity's own leggings, an old tweed waistcoat of Mr. Coop's—and some unknown underpants. In a box she found one of the craft lady's gardening bonnets and a hat like a flower pot. There was a pair of Dr. Oxford's white rubber boots.

Metalboy had not got around to constructing a bathroom. But the kitchen plumbing was connected to a water tank. She rinsed her face and hands at the kitchen sink, and pulled on the leggings and two socks almost the same shade of green. With safety pins, she turned a blue tablecloth bordered with Miss Honey's cross-stitch into a wrap-around skirt. Mr. Coop's old waistcoat would do too, as long as she didn't have to see herself in a mirror.

Everyone hunting for Dorrity was on the lookout for a twelve-year-old girl. At a distance, with the flower-pot hat and rubber boots, she might seem like a dwarf woman with poor dress sense. She could find a way up the Dark, over the top, down to Lake Riversea and start life anew.

She tilted her head to pretend courage, marched to the stolen glass door and pulled it open. Outside, like a bundle of coat without any buttons, waited the bear in Miss Honey's scarf.

~

Dorrity stepped around it. Of course the bear would recognize her through any disguise. Birkett had seen her in costumes a thousand times. Was that right? She'd probably dressed up an average of twice a week over seven years which made…only seven hundred and twenty-eight.

The bear followed and *whumphed* on her neck.

"Stop it!" It had nearly toppled the flower-pot hat. "If you want that lost axe, go round the house and look at the workbench!"

The bear blinked and backed off. Dorrity kept on through the Dark. It was hard going in those rubber boots. She tripped and stumbled and stopped to check her direction. She wanted to avoid the anarchists, which meant heading east. On the other hand, the lowest part of the ridge was towards the west. She turned that way. The bear was still behind her, though at a distance. It seemed uneasy.

She strode faster, but the bear bounded up and tried to

grab her. She bashed its nose. "Stop me and I'll scream my lungs out."

It backed off again but kept following.

She came to traces of the old road. Here it was more overgrown than the bit nearer the town. It led up, which was useful—but then ahead she saw a high, prickly barrier. On the other side was the hum of voices, the sound of people hauling stuff around, the thump of hammers, the rasping of saws. Eagle Hall.

By now she couldn't look feeble in front of the bear. And she was so curious it felt worse than indigestion. A tall ogre-wood stretched its branches overhead. She kicked off the doctor's boots, tucked up the table-cloth skirt—and at last she was certain that the bear was Birkett.

With that resigned look he'd often had when she insisted on something, it held out its front legs to make a step for her to stand on. When she did, it gave a heave to help her grab the lowest branch. She swung herself up and stared down at it. Though its eyes were much smaller than Birkett's, in this light they were as brown, as stern, and as kind. The bear put a paw to its muzzle as if it would dab a dribble of kiss towards her.

"Get lost," she muttered, and started to climb.

~

Dorrity managed not to *ouch* when a twig stuck into her. She managed not to lose the flower-pot hat. At last she was high enough to see over the barrier of thorns.

Eagle Hall was like the picture on one of Mrs. Freida's very old stamps. There was the house, five floors high, with a square central turret and wide steps leading to a marble terrace. By now the Hall should have been a ruin. It should at least have been surrounded by scaffolding, with painters and builders tripping over each other. But the Hall looked new. It sparkled through shadow.

The glow of magic made Dorrity shiver—a dark glow, an oily glow like in her nightmares when she was small. It was the shimmer she'd seen when the flock of crows attacked Birkett, Mike, and Yorky on the Fribbleton Road.

She made herself stretch along a branch to see down into the grounds. There was no glow there, only wheelbarrows, concrete mixers, people digging. Some parts of the garden were planted with new shrubs and squares of fresh-laid lawn seamed like a checkerboard. Other parts were still a wilderness of weeds and sapling ogre-woods. Bigger trees had been felled. The saws were being used to cut them up. So whoever was working here hadn't—or couldn't—use magic to do the whole job.

Dorrity had another look into the grounds. Cold filtered through her. The workmen—they wore overalls and caps like people did. They handled tools and carried things about like people did. Many of them moved like grumpy people, or bossy, business-like or hassled ones, but many more of them moved in a strange jerky manner. Maybe they were mechanical, like Metalboy when she'd first met him...

No. Her skin prickled. This was bad magic. Wicked magic—unnatural, cruel magic. The creatures ran in the way that starlings do, hopped and darted like blackbirds or crows. They waddled or lumbered about, made sudden leaps like frogs. One had a normal man's arms but two duck feet. One had a sheep's head and hind legs, though the rest of him was human.

A bird-man stared up at her tree. She shrank back till she no longer saw him.

A man in a dark blue officer's cap strode out the main door of the Hall to the top of the steps: Captain Westrap, sword at his belt, and a pistol holster too. But the most scary thing about him was the satisfied smile. Then there was something even more scary. He looked straight at her ogre-wood.

"A spy!" he shouted. "Looks like a dwarf!"

~

Heart thudding, Dorrity landed on the forest floor and shoved her feet back in the doctor's boots.

Whumph, said the bear.

She grabbed the fur on each side of its neck. "You've cheated and lied! Leave me alone!"

The bear growled right in her face. She was terrified. But it pulled away and loped back into the Dark.

Should she run too? No, Westrap would expect a spy to head down the old road to the town—his guards would be listening for running. Right now it was safer to hide...

She heard shouts behind the hedge, scrambled into the thickest patch of bracken she could see and tried to quiet her breathing by thinking dwarf-thoughts to help her disguise. Dwarves probably thought the same as anyone else, except for wishing all their lives they were tall enough to see over the counter at the ice creams. How she wished she was back in ordinary Owl Town. She wiped her nose on the tablecloth skirt.

"Are you all right?" whispered a voice behind her.

Dorrity turned. It was Metalboy.

~

35

A POLICE OFFICER'S DUTY

"How did you get out?" she hissed.

"The officer let me," he hissed back. "This morning he said, 'Good grief, I'd hoped that I dreamed it. Mr. Coop expects me to believe a boy is a piece of clockwork?' He said, 'It is my job to preserve law and order. It is not my job to decide whether dimples are oil-holes or vice versa.'"

"Hush." Dorrity crouched down, hand on her hat so it didn't slip off. Wind breathed in the treetops. It might be wise to stay where they were for a few more minutes.

Metalboy wriggled closer. "The officer said if he'd been misled about an actual boy being clockwork he didn't wish to be responsible for that boy being shut in a cell. But I told him I'd started as clockwork."

"He still let you out?" whispered Dorrity.

"Am I beside you, or are you dreaming?" He gave her a nudge. "Another joke."

She listened for sounds from Eagle Hall. Still nothing. "Go on."

"The officer said that it seemed a message-bird had gone astray." Metalboy bit his lip. "I think that was my fault, when I ran away. But now he knows for sure that Count Bale is trying to return to Fontania. He said if a local police officer had been told that in his cells there was an experiment that was the King's secret weapon—and he also believed that the King's enemies were around—he would take the same action as he would if it was a real boy. He would unlock the cells. Then he put the key in the lock. Then he said, 'Rat-bum. It's stuck.'"

"Tell me later," muttered Dorrity. "Let's sneak off now. Slowly. Keep an eye out. That's just an expression."

Metalboy started to ease backwards, still whispering. "Mr. Coop must be right—the Count is the danger that the King made me to face." He scratched his wrists where he'd had oil-holes. "I remember now. Yes, Count Bale must be the great danger. Queen Sibilla said 'poor metal boy' and kissed me. I couldn't blush then…" He pressed both hands to his cheeks. "I'm blushing now. It feels funny."

"I said, tell me later." Dorrity crawled a bit further.

"But I want you to hear how I got out of the Watch House," said Metalboy. "I jutted my chin. I set a shoulder against the bars. I pressed so hard I nearly popped any last rivets. I forced the bars and squashed through sideways. And I ran! And here I am! I'll face the Count!"

"You can't!" said Dorrity. "If Captain Westrap knew you had a—" She touched her heart. "You know. They'd take you to bits to find the magic. The Count would use it. The King and Queen would truly be in terrible danger. We—"

That sense of darkness, of having to flee from something terrible, slammed over her. She glanced around—nothing. When she glanced back, still nothing. Metalboy had gone.

She rose to her feet, ready to run. "Where are you?" Her voice shook.

The Beastly Dark was very quiet. No rustle from a rabbit. No chirp from a sparrow. No breath of wind.

—

A FRIENDLY SMILE?

Go, Dorrity said to herself. She was stinging all over. *Run, no matter where!* She glanced back at the old road.

Something like a long pale skirt floated from behind a pine tree. A woman appeared, smiling, and too well dressed for the midst of the forest. Her skirt was soft pleats. Sharp-toed red shoes peeped beneath. She wore a red jacket with a high collar, a red hat with a jet-black feather. In small rushing steps she came towards Dorrity, still with that smile. It seemed fixed in place.

Don't make faces, Mike used to tell Dorrity when she was little. *If the wind changes you'll stay like that.* Then he'd make his face really hideous to make her scream and laugh with him. Dorrity nearly gave a little sob.

"Good morning." The woman's voice was soft as a dove's coo. It ought to have been soothing. Her eyes narrowed, though her mouth stayed in that smile. "What is your name?" she asked as if she already knew and found it tiresome.

"Children are not supposed to talk to strangers." From the corner of her eye, Dorrity tried to spot a handy fallen ogre blossom. She hoped Metalboy was well away—or at least well hidden.

The woman's smile hadn't wavered. Her head turned again as if she'd heard something. In a shaft of sunlight filtering through the trees, the feather on her red hat glinted blue-black. Then she came at Dorrity in another little run just like a gidibird. Fingernails as sharp as claws gripped Dorrity's shoulder. The woman laughed again and raised her other hand as Dorrity tried to wrench herself away.

Down through the canopy flew four soldiers with huge ravens' wings. Dorrity finally twisted from the woman's nails and dived for the undergrowth. But the woman grabbed her again by the back of the waistcoat. Dorrity kicked and struggled, but now the raven-soldiers seized her too. Within moments they'd tied her hands and ankles, and harnessed cords around her shoulders and waist as well.

The woman smiled. In fact, she'd never stopped. "They call you Dorrity," she said close to Dorrity's ear. "Did you know that *Dorrity* means *little doll?* You're just a toy. Whoever owns a toy decides on the game."

~

The raven-soldiers spread their wings and soared up to the canopy, dangling Dorrity beneath them. The ropes cut into her. She had no breath to scream for help. As she lurched past the first branches, she had a glimpse of Metalboy's gray eyes staring from the undergrowth.

Up, up—leaves whipped at her face—and suddenly there was the forest spread below. It glimmered with the creamy tops of ogre-woods like a vast frosted cake with the tips of pine trees for candles. Beyond the Beastly Dark she caught sight of Owl Town. The blue-gray of the Forgotten River rolled on from the town between steep cliffs.

Down swerved the raven-soldiers, down. Dorrity thought they would smash into the forest canopy. But now they were above the thorn hedge—then over the grounds of Eagle Hall. Hundreds of workmen and soldiers, animal and human, stared up at her.

The soldiers swooped Dorrity over the expanse of steps that fronted the mansion, up again past all five floors, over the parapet to where, rising in the middle, was the turret. Her thoughts shuffled like cards. If Metalboy found his way in, if Westrap captured him and discovered the magic he carried behind his heart, Count Bale would find a way to rule Fontania for all time. But what could Dorrity do—she had to deal with the scary woman, the raven-soldiers and Captain Westrap. Actually—maybe she could manage the Captain. After all, she'd done it once before.

~

LIKE IT OR
NOT

The soldiers dumped her down on the roof terrace. In the tangle of ropes she felt trussed like a chicken for cooking. A giant raven darted to peck at the ropes round her ankles. Another giant bird pecked the ropes at her wrists.

"Ow!" Dorrity rolled free.

She was still on hands and knees when glass doors in the turret slid open. It would be Captain Westrap...

Two raven-guards in glossy black uniforms stood there at attention. The room behind them was lined with books—the library? But two women in black uniforms appeared—they looked like ravens as well, though they had no wings—and they were pushing something out of the turret towards her.

For a moment Dorrity thought it was a giant stroller. She'd once seen a family of ogres trundling their baby along the riverbank—she'd never known that babies could scream so loudly, though of course it was a baby ogre. But this stroller was so grand it glittered. The wheels sparkled with blue stones. The sides gleamed with silver and blue in a feather pattern, the sort of feather that Captain Westrap had on his badge. She looked around for him, but he still wasn't there.

She looked back at the stroller. The blue coverlet had a silvery fringe. It was a stroller-throne. It didn't hold a baby. It held a man.

He was bald and wore what must be very expensive red pajamas with silver buttons shaped like feathers. Wouldn't they jab him when he turned in bed? He didn't look exactly old…

Dorrity didn't think she'd ever be able to explain how cold she felt at the sight of him. He looked as strong and thin as trip-wire, at the same time as tricky and unexpected as a spider web.

She struggled to her feet, rubbing her wrists.

The man's voice was distant like the ringing of a bell. "Do you know who I am?"

"I suppose you're Count Bale," Dorrity said. "You don't look like any of your pictures." It would be because he'd gone bald, though she didn't say so.

The Count's chuckle too sounded like the jangle of a far-off bell.

She was determined not to sound afraid. "If you are the Count, you shouldn't be in Fontania."

He only smiled, thin as trip-wire, tricky as spider web.

There was movement at the doors into the tower and the smiling woman stepped onto the terrace. Sharp shoes peeping, she walked to Count Bale and bowed.

The Count flipped a hand. "You've met, of course. But I'll introduce you properly. Dorrity—your neighbour, Lady Charlotta."

"We had a nice chat," Dorrity said.

The Count pressed his hands together in silent clapping. "You will definitely do the job for me, little Dorrity."

"I don't know what the job is," Dorrity said.

He flicked a hand at the raven-women. They wheeled him in his stroller-throne to the terrace parapet. "Come and see," he called.

Still unsteady after the flight in the ropes, Dorrity edged near him. He smelled sickly-sweet, like black nightshade. She knew the scent from gardening with her fake brothers. She looked over the parapet.

Below, Captain Westrap was directing the Count's people to work in the grounds. Whether they waddled like ducks, strutted like panthers or walked like ordinary men, they all seemed scared of him.

"So you see," said the Count in the stroller-throne, with his terrible thin voice. "I am here. I'm settling in. I'm undeniable."

"So far." Dorrity only just stopped her voice from shaking.

The Count chuckled. "You're either brave or somewhat stupid. Whichever it is, as I said you'll do the job. Aren't you going to ask why I've hunted you down?"

"You may as well say it out loud," Dorrity answered.

For a moment there was a flicker in the Count's pale eyes, as if he thought that she'd been brave. "Indeed, I may as well. You're my little relative."

His relative? Every nerve in her shouted, *Bad idea!*

"In families," his thin voice continued, "it's nice to share."

"I wouldn't know," said Dorrity.

"Let's not argue. Family arguments make life fun, but one at a time is enough." The Count's eyes glinted.

Lady Charlotta still hadn't stopped smiling. The raven-people opened their mouths, perhaps in smiles, but it looked more as if they clacked beaks that weren't properly there.

"Jasper and Sibilla's branch of the family have had it their way for a very long time," said the Count.

"Not really," said Dorrity. "They had to live like ordinary people for years before—"

The Count let out a high wheeze and slapped the silver-edged coverlet over his legs. "They weren't on the throne but they lived very nicely. The thing is, I should have been King. I had far more idea how to rule a country than my young brother who snatched the throne from me. As for King Jasper and Queen Sibilla. Two monarchs? Where's the logic in that? It's confusing."

"Not for most people," said Dorrity.

He took not a skerrick of notice. "Therefore it is essential that you are crowned Queen."

So what she'd feared was true. She felt dizzy and sick.

But Count Bale continued in his wire-thin voice. "I can't be King, because I've been banished. That banishment can only be lifted by another monarch. We must pay some attention to the law. And you have a claim to the throne, Dorrity. Some say a very great claim. Though of course you won't know about that." He let out a whispery laugh. "So I will inform you. I had a daughter who had a daughter, and she came back to Fontania and married a Ludlow, and they had a daughter, and so it went on…" He ticked off on his fingers. "You're a four times great-grand-daughter, maybe five. A connection to both sides of the current royal house. More than enough for my purpose. Oh, she looks stunned. Steady her, please."

A strong raven-woman held Dorrity's arm.

"You'll never have a scrap of magical ability," continued the Count. "That's a benefit to me, so it doesn't matter."

"You're not supposed to be here," Dorrity whispered.

The Count waved a thin hand. "Yes, that's what 'banished' means. I thought I'd explained. As soon as you're Queen, you'll sign a proclamation that says I'm welcome again. I've already written it."

He reached into a pocket on the side of the stroller-throne and held up a roll of parchment. "You'll read it out at the right time, then put on your signature."

Bad idea, bad idea! "If I'm Queen I could refuse," said Dorrity.

The Count gave a grin. "I'm two hundred and thirty-three years older than you. I know how to get my way. I win in the end."

"You failed at something." Her fingertips prickled and stung. "You only managed to make Yorky a quarter rooster."

Lady Charlotta let out a giggle like a tiny chirp.

The Count stretched a skinny arm and pointed. There was a flash, a hiss and a singed smell. With a scream of pain, Charlotta collapsed to her knees...she cried out again and began shrinking in size. Her arms turned to tiny wings...her legs to red bird-stilts. Her smiling mouth became the beak of a small gidibird. It lay as if dead on the terrace.

Dorrity steadied herself again on the raven-women.

"When I was young, I was far too much of a good boy. I've made up for it." Count Bale grinned at the bird. "And that's what happens now when I'm annoyed." He turned to Dorrity. "Failed with Yorky? No. It was the idiot who wielded the enchantment for me. I turned him into a pumpkin. We had plenty of pie." He smiled as people do when they remember good meals. "So, Dorrity. Welcome home. And don't argue. Like it or not, you will be Queen."

HOME LIFE,
HA HA HA

PUBLICITY
PICTURE-GRAPHS

There on the high terrace of Eagle Hall, the words of the fourth ending swam in front of her again: *Dorrity, with a sad lonely heart, was crowned Queen of Fontania. The End.*

With each shaky breath she felt worse and worse. She didn't dare let out a word.

Count Bale laughed, a whisper thin as wire in the wind. "Such a well-behaved girl. But we won't have a monarch dressed like that." He pointed at Mr. Coop's over-large waistcoat. "And rubber boots? For crying out loud."

He waved his hand again. With another sizzle and a smell like scorched tea towels, the gidibird flapped a feeble wing on the marble terrace and stretched back into Lady Charlotta with the tiny red shoes, the floating skirt, the red velvet jacket. Charlotta gasped and shivered. She still smiled, but beneath it Dorrity saw how the change had hurt, sharper than knives.

"Take the girl away." Count Bale turned the glittering wheels of his stroller-throne. "Dress her for the official pre-coronation picture-graph session."

Two raven-guards appeared and took Dorrity, one arm each. "Let me go!" she cried. But they trundled her into the turret as if she had wheels like the stroller. Lady Charlotta hurried behind.

The room inside had silver and blue decoration, feathers and crowns painted and stuck all over the walls, sofas covered in purple fabric with silver piping. Dorrity was whisked out and down some stairs, into a corridor—this must be the actual top floor of Eagle Hall now—to a very grand door.

The door bore the sign of a crown. The true crown of Fontania was a delicate set of circles with red stones. This crown looked more like a workman's helmet, with holes cut at random and sparkly bits added to fancy it up.

Lady Charlotta thrust the door open and strutted in. The guards shoved Dorrity after her and slammed the door.

It was a huge bedroom. The enormous bed had that helmet-crown sign at the head. The crown sign was also on top of a full-length mirror. There was a sofa with fat cushions, a wardrobe, a desk, all with more ugly crowns.

Charlotta made a sort of whistle from the side of her unending smile. If she'd been a real lady, it would have been unladylike. For a gidibird, it suited fine.

Two women bustled in from a side room. One had a hopping walk that Dorrity now knew meant she'd been born, or rather hatched, as some sort of sparrow. The other walked like a tired real woman who was bossy because of it. They shunted Dorrity to a door. For a moment she thought she'd be locked in a second wardrobe.

It turned out to be a bathroom. A bathroom for just one

bedroom? Is that what a queen had? "What a silly waste of plumbing!" Dorrity said.

But already the sparrow woman had turned on the shower. She tried to thrust Dorrity in, still with her clothes on.

The bossy one jostled the first aside and turned off the water. "Clothes first, you pecking pest!" She shooed the sparrow-woman away then bustled out and slammed the door.

The window was locked and too high to escape from anyway. Dorrity may as well have a proper clean. She hadn't had one for days. But she was only just wet all over when Lady Charlotta barged in and turned off the water. She bundled towels around Dorrity and hurried her back into the bedroom.

A servant opened the wardrobe. It smelled musty, as if it had been closed for years. She pulled and smoothed Dorrity into a petticoat with a ruffled hem. She wriggled her legs into white leggings with ruffled ankles—they were awful! A dress of slippery white fabric was so dusty that Dorrity sneezed. It had ruffles right down to the hem, with a sash around the waist to hold the dress in. It made Dorrity look like a bunch of scrunched-up tissue paper.

Her hair was still wet from the shower. The sparrow-woman brought out a fat sort of gun and aimed it at Dorrity—she nearly fainted—but it just huffed heat at her till her hair was dry. In fact it was a very good idea. The women stood back and stared.

"It's very boring," chirped the sparrow-woman.

Dorrity looked in the mirror—her hair was its usual straight brown down to her shoulders, apart from a few floating-up wisps. She didn't think it looked that bad. But Charlotta jammed a white headband on her. There was no way stray hairs would escape now. Then it was the turn of the bossy woman. She rushed over and pushed Dorrity's feet into white velvet slippers. Dorrity had never imagined anything so foolish—they'd turn into wreckage in no time.

She had to admit that on the outside she was starting to look a tiny bit grand. But her eyes in the mirror were startled and scared. *Crowned Queen?* She already felt lonely and sad. She'd been right to want to hide and stay safe all her life. She wished she had never left Owl Town.

~

But having a picture-graph session didn't hurt too much.

Dorrity was hustled back up to the huge room that was the library. There she sat on a delicate white chair which was completely hidden by all of those skirt ruffles. The machine, with a dark round eye, stood on a tripod. The picture-graph man hid behind it under a dark green cloth. It made him look like a creature with two human back legs and three metal forelegs—she couldn't help but give a chuckle.

"Look serious, m'lady," said the man under the cloth. The machine let out a flash that dazzled her. "Superb. Now, try a smile. Ew, no good at all. Try serious again."

She gritted her teeth.

"Tone it down," said the picture-graph man

Aa-choo! went Dorrity because of the dust in those ruffles.

The man muttered a few dark things under the cloth. The servants squeaked and muttered amongst themselves. She heard *Poor girl*, a sharp *Shut up if you know what's good for you.*

Finally the man backed out, flapped some pictures around and puffed on them. Finally, he spread them on a silvery side-table.

Lady Charlotta and the servants huddled to see. Dorrity couldn't even catch a glimpse over their shoulders. One of the servants ran out and returned with the Count in his stroller-throne. Behind him strutted a man with a quiff of gray hair and a red bow-tie. He was carrying a green folder and a pencil.

Count Bale peered at every picture. "Not that one—she looks half asleep. In that one, she comes across as slightly stupid." He glanced at Dorrity. "Learn not to squint. A monarch who squints looks no better than a dodgy banker."

He turned back and rubbed a hand over his bald head. "I don't know—in these two she looks more or less pretty and not altogether mindless. Send that to the *Two-Daily Blast*. That one to the *Fontanian Weekly*. Read out the press release again."

The bow-tie man opened the folder. "*Relief in sight for citizens of Fontania.*" He cleared his throat and continued. "*A new Queen will be crowned this week. Lady Evergreen is daughter of Lady Lillie-betta of the Watcher Mountains and grand-niece of Sir Rupert Ludlow. Thus she has a claim to the throne on both sides. Lady Evergreen will have only the best and most efficient advisers working for her. Her rule will guarantee tighter control of the economy. The workers of Fontania will have higher wages and everyone will have more money in their bank accounts. This will take time so the public is encouraged to be patient.*"

"Lady Evergreen?" asked Dorrity.

"She was born in West Evergreen," said Count Bale.

"Let's have a potted history." He rasped his throat, folded his hands and began with a thin grin.

"What do I remember? Her mother, Lady Lillie-betta, was a royal cousin, distant but royal enough to be afraid when the Provisional Monarch was ruling the country a few years ago. She hid near the southern coast, and married a farmer. They were happy, quiet people by all accounts. The farmer died. Very sad." He shrugged. "At that point Lillie-betta sent a message to the Grand Palace which my deputy managed to intercept. I told him to hurry and find her. Who knows why, but she took a dislike to him and wouldn't trust him." He shrugged again. "She ran and ran, wouldn't settle anywhere. Months of running. What kind of life was that for her three-year-old girl? And it so happened that Lady Lillie-betta died too, hiding away in some country cottage." The Count's grin was hard as wire. "The little girl, Lady Evergreen—of course no one had any idea who she was—went to an orphanage. She's twelve now. Not a pleasant child in the experience of my deputy—that is, Captain Westrap." He gave a sly glance. The servants chuckled.

None of this could be true—it was all a story. Dorrity wanted to shake her head, but she was frozen to the spot.

"Apparently the child's completely spoiled," the Count added.

The servants chuckled again.

"Thinks everyone likes her," a raven-guard said.

"Thinks she is clever," chirped the sparrow-woman.

"Thinks she looks quite the little queen," said the picture-graph man.

The Count held up a finger. "So, Dorrity, soon you will become Queen Evergreen. But it won't be for long. You'll be a footnote in the history books soon enough." He pointed at the bow-tie man.

The man scratched his quiff with the pencil. "Something like this, Your Grace? *Queen Evergreen succeeded to the throne in mid-spring and by early summer was off it for good.*"

The Count wheezed like a far-off bell. "Scribble it down. Dorrity—stop sneaking looks for an escape route. Now take her to rehearse for the coronation."

The stroller-throne wheeled away.

Nothing seemed real—the ruffly dress, the sneering servants, the Count's sarcasm, the fact that she really was a royal relative. She felt as if her head had been punched from inside. But after all, maybe she was spoiled. Perhaps she did think she was more clever than she really was. She didn't want to be Queen at all, but being a…*footnote*?

She was afraid—and now she could remember being afraid before, when she was small, when each time it was meant to be safe, dark figures started to creep close, and each time it meant running away.

—

RULES AND
A RULER

Six guards, Lady Charlotta, and the two servant women bundled Dorrity back down to the grand bedroom. Two of the guards left, but four guards waited outside in the corridor.

Inside was another woman who looked more like a cat than a human. How did Count Bale prevent his creatures from fighting each other? She was sure of the answer: *fear of what he'd do with his bad magic.*

"Is there something to eat?" Dorrity asked. "I only had walnuts for breakfast…"

They took no notice. The cat-woman whipped out a tape measure. How long were Dorrity's arms? How wide was Dorrity across the back? Dorrity's stomach rumbled.

"Don't mutter, you'll bother the seamstress." The bossy woman prodded Dorrity's spine to make her stand straight.

"The coronation dress has to be perfect," snapped Lady Charlotta. "Advisers and journalists will be here."

How long was it from the back of her neck to her waist?

Ouch. The Count had left a claw on the cat-woman—maybe a mistake, maybe deliberate.

"You know it can't—*ouch!*—be a true coronation," Dorrity said.

"Family connections can't be denied," said the bossy woman.

"New rules will be enacted as soon as you're Queen," the sparrow-woman added.

"But they can't be rules now, before they're enacted," cried Dorrity.

"Turn around. Arms out. Stand straight," the cat-woman hissed.

In a side room began the *shhkk-shhkk* of scissors on silk, the whirr of two sewing machines in an angry duet. The half-made dress was rushed in. Again Dorrity was fitted and scratched (*ow-ouch!*). Then she was wrapped in a bedspread and told to sit down. Charlotta thrust a document into her hands.

The old rules. And, beside them, the new rules.

In one column, in very neat writing, the old rules said: *The coronation always takes place at the Eastern Lake where live the dragon-eagles who embody the magic of nature. The chosen monarch will wade into the Lake. The water of the Lake will confirm to the dragon-eagles that the monarch is the true monarch.*

In the second column were the new rules in spidery writing: *The coronation will take place at Eagle Hall. Afterwards the girl will wade into the pond. By then it must be free of smelly weed and stocked with fresh goldfish.*

The old rules said: *The crown is wire of purest silver strung with beads of blood-red jasper to signify selflessness and courage.*

The spidery writing said: *The crown has to look very grand. Make it of some sort of hefty metal and paint it gold. It can have pretty glass if that's all you can find. Doesn't matter much what it looks like, only matters how it works and I'll see to that.*

The spidery writing continued. *As soon as the girl is crowned, more picture-graphs are to be taken...*

Dorrity let the paper flutter to the floor. This wasn't going to make her a queen. The country wouldn't be fooled by a false coronation. If only she hadn't tried to catch up with Metalboy. She hoped he'd gone to get help...

Lady Charlotta jammed the document back into Dorrity's hand. "Don't dare make the Count angry. Read till you know it perfectly."

"For goodness' sake!" snapped the bossy woman. "No one can learn when they're hungry. Bring her some lunch."

So bossiness was good for something.

~

Lunch came on a tray, such a late lunch that Dorrity reckoned it was early dinner. It was a slice of bread spread with something that looked rather like cat food. There had once been some delivered by mistake to the Necessary Shop, and Dorrity had been curious. She suspected this splodge was from just such a can. Luckily, there was also an apple.

The bossy woman folded her arms. "The child still looks a wreck. Fresh air might give her pink cheeks."

With a faint snarl, the cat-woman pointed to the sewing.

"For goodness' sake. She can have a few minutes!" The

bossy woman found a striped tunic in the wardrobe and flapped it out the window to shake the dust off. There were plenty of boots and shoes, but the only thing they let her have was a pair of slippers that might once have been fluffy.

~

The four guards marched Dorrity along the corridor and down a wide staircase to the huge front door. She stumbled in the slippers to the foot of the marble steps and set off in a clumsy walk around the grounds.

The sky was cloudy as if a painter had put streaks of white over the blue and had no idea what to do next. Whiffs of bad-magic bitterness seeped from the Hall.

Her nose stung with tears of self-pity. The coronation was the day after tomorrow. With all these guards around, she had no chance of getting away.

A group of the workers looked as if they might have been seagulls in their natural life. The cries of seagulls seemed to echo in her memory. She might have seen the ocean before she came to Owl Town. She tried to catch more memories of her very young years. There were still none of any doll. Nor of her mother or father, nor of home. Just of feeling so afraid—of having to leave home and run, of running from one place to another mostly at night.

Could she remember the orphanage? For a moment she almost had a picture in her head of another child. But it crept away again.

She stepped over a heap of rubble. Seagulls, yes, a squawking call. It began loud, then tailed off. *Wark wark wark.* Not a pleasant sound at all, but what else might be there behind the memory? She tried again. *Wark wark wark*. Far off in the direction of the Forgotten River, the starlings sang *Be caa-aareful*.

A group of workers in white overalls and thigh-high waders stared down at a pond. It smelled revolting. A small dredging machine had hauled up a set of rusty wheels dripping with slime, the broken back and legs of a chair with a burst stuffed seat, rusty cans. This was the pond she was meant to wade into? Oh—but the people in Owl Town would see the picture-graphs in tomorrow's newspapers. Thank goodness—they would come rushing...

No. Newspapers arrived in Owl Town a day or two late.

Dorrity lost a slipper and had to go back for it. She forced herself on past the side doors and windows of glowing Eagle Hall, past more clusters of bad-tempered workmen. With guards still following, she circled back to the marble front steps. More rubbish lay dripping and stinking beside the pond. She moved nearer the thorn hedge.

Beside an old brick wall was a stone seat. This might once have been the royal herb garden. Here was parsley going to seed and some spindly plants with creamy flowers. There were rustlings from the hedge, tiny peck-pecks, nibbling runs and darting sounds, the ordinary music of the everyday life of small things. Squirrels, sparrows, insects, and mice. Way back in her memory was the ripple of a stream, the hum of a bee, her mother singing, safety and calm.

A sparrow hopped up on the wall. Something larger scuffled under the thorn hedge. She heard a small *ow*. She leaned down as if she was examining the heel of her slipper and tried to see into the hedge.

"Dorrity," hissed a voice.

It was Metalboy.

Her heart didn't know whether to leap with hope or to plummet. "Be careful," she murmured in the way of the starlings. If the Count's creatures heard, she would say she was trying out bird calls. "Be very caa-aareful. Don't let anyone hee-ar you."

"What's happening?" he muttered. "Are you all right?"

"I know now why I am a daa-anger," Dorrity sang. "I'm going to be crowned Quee-een."

There was silence in the thorns.

"But then the Count will get rid of me," she crooned in a whisper.

There was silence again.

"Like—toss you in a waste bin?" asked Metalboy.

It would be worse than a waste bin. She didn't dare think of it. She pressed her hands over her eyes. Now that Metalboy was here, he was deep in danger. Both the King and the Count would want the feather hidden behind his heart. He and she might both end up in the waste bin or worse.

"Let's escape together," she sang in a voice that wobbled. "Please, come up with a plan."

Softly, Metalboy sang back from under the hedge. "What should it be-ee?"

In the distance was the *koff-koff* of anarchists' bikes. For a moment she hoped it meant rescue. But of course, the anarchists, like her brothers, were just out for money, not to save her.

Boot steps thudded beside her. Guards yanked her off

the seat. A soldier dived under the hedge. There was a yell—another yell—and the soldier scrabbled out, hand over his nose. Blood dripped down his chin. Metalboy had got away!

Dorrity started to laugh with relief. But a guard clamped her jaw shut. "Come out!" he yelled. "Or I'll use this!" He stuck a dagger to her neck.

But now Metalboy was scrambling out of the thorns and kicking the dagger from the guard's grip. He lunged for Dorrity and pulled her with him under the hedge. Thorns tore at her face. She screamed and thrust up her other arm to save her eyes. Behind her were shouts, barks, yelps, whistles, and caws. She tried to ignore the thorns as Metalboy dragged her forward—but then he lost grip of her wrist. A soldier's hand had her by an ankle—two hands, by two ankles.

"Run!" she yelled to Metalboy as the soldier tugged her back out of the hedge. While she tried to struggle to her feet, the guard set a dagger to her throat again.

But there Metalboy stood, surrounded. Soldiers had begun to tie his hands and feet.

"Get away!" she cried. "You can pull free!"

"But they would hurt you," he whispered. "And you're my friend."

Tears streamed down her cheeks. "They can't hurt me till I'm Queen!"

Metalboy's gray eyes stared at her. "Cuss! Have I missed my chance?"

"Go!" she screamed.

He tore at the ropes and dived for the hedge, but a shout

came from Eagle Hall. The air smelled singed. Metalboy froze, cramped in a half-crouch.

Dorrity swung around. The Count's attendants were carrying his stroller-throne down the marble steps and wheeling it over the grounds.

"What's this?" The Count twirled a finger for the guards to turn Metalboy to face him. He lay back and looked thoughtful.

"Take off his cap," he said.

A guard grabbed it. The breeze ruffled Metalboy's pale hair.

The Count sat up and tapped Metalboy's arm. There wasn't a *clank*. "Hmm." He gestured again.

The guards made Metalboy kneel beside the throne-chair. Count Bale pressed a hand to Metalboy's chest for a moment, then snatched it back as if something burnt. He peered even more closely at Metalboy.

"Dagger," the Count said at last.

A guard stepped up and presented a small dagger, handle first.

"Boy. Hold your arm out."

Metalboy, still in a crouch, blinked, then his arm twitched. He reached out as if to shake hands.

"Low on brains," muttered the Count, and struck with the dagger.

Metalboy screamed, hunched over his hand and collapsed to his knees. Drops of red splashed to the grass.

"Take him away. Lock him up," ordered the Count. "There's something odd about him. I'll find out when I have time."

"Run!" shouted Dorrity.

But the Count gestured again. The smell of scorching filled the air, and guards carried Metalboy off into the Hall.

"I have him tethered, little relative. Red rope or invisible, there's not much difference." The Count lay in his stroller-throne with a pleased sharp smile and a thin sharp laugh. "One more day to wait, Dorrity. One more day for the guests to arrive. By then all of Fontania will have read in the papers how much better their government will be with their new Queen. They don't have to know right away that you'll be temporary."

—

SULKING AND
SKULKING

"Out of bed," snapped Lady Charlotta next morning. "The day's full of things to do before tomorrow."

Dorrity dragged herself out of the sheets, her head fuzzy from lack of sleep. So much for the ending that said, *At last Dorrity had discovered who she was and all came clear.*

"Get to work on the rules!" growled the bossy woman at morning-muffin time. "You must know them by heart for the ceremony. And the dressmakers will be back any moment."

At least today they were feeding her. But the words on the pages kept floating around—she just couldn't catch them.

The cat-woman took ages to fit the coronation dress on Dorrity for the last time. "Keep still!"

"But it's taking so long…"

"Don't whine," the cat-woman hissed.

At last Charlotta hauled Dorrity down to the Grand Dining Room for lunch and to boss her about table manners.

Guards rolled the Count to the table on his glittering wheels. "For crying out loud!" he cried aloud. "Are you a mistake after all? Try eating with a smile and a nod for when you have guests." He tapped his spider-thin fingernails on a table knife and narrowed his eyes at her. "There'll be plenty of guests here tomorrow. Top journalists. Political advisers from Fontania and observers from other countries. People to impress. Nod. Smile. Now!"

Why was he anxious? Surely he could simply tether any guests and make them do what he wanted. She nodded, fake-smiled…Wait a moment. The Count had said something yesterday about his tethers. *Red rope or invisible, there's not much difference.* Did he mean the two were equally strong? But Mike—the goat—had arrived back in Owl Town with a broken red tether.

Dorrity kept nodding, smiled harder, put a round of carrot into her mouth and nodded again. Normally Mike kept bashing at anything till it gave way. He must have done that with the Count's tether. So "equally strong" didn't have to mean unbreakable. You'd have to be so very strong yourself, though…

A wisp of an idea came to Dorrity. There could be a way to get Metalboy out. He'd be able to find the King. King Jasper would hardly be Dorrity's friend, but he was far better than Count Bale for Fontania and everyone else. Her idea—yes, the fourth ending from *The Volume* gave her the clue to getting Metalboy away. It said, *lonely and sad.* She almost gave a give-away smile.

She turned her mouth down and sighed. "I bet none of the guests at the coronation will be my age."

"Of course not," said the Count.

She sighed again. "None of them will be a friend."

The Count rubbed his bald head and gave a thin wheeze. "Dorrity, you're a wangler just like my brother. That little toad always tried to wangle his own way. It was he who egged me to try shape-changing in the first place—but never mind. Justice is about to be done. Better late for me than never at all. Smile! Nod!"

Dorrity shoved more bits of carrot over her plate and let her mouth sulk. "But I'm lonely," she sighed again. "Can I play with that boy you caught in the garden yesterday for just a few minutes? Then I'll work really hard for the rest of the day."

"Save me from children." The Count clicked his fingers. "I don't suppose it'll hurt. Take her down to the dungeon for half an hour. But the boy has to stay in his cell. Keep a close eye on them both the entire time."

Dorrity nearly jumped down from the table but remembered it would be more convincing if she pouted and slouched.

Charlotta led the way, Dorrity in the middle, two guards behind. They marched through the main entrance hall and down one of the grand corridors. They reached a narrow hallway, then a door that led down a stairwell. Other doors led off it. One level smelled of coal. On the next, she smelled nothing much. On the third came the sweet poison smell of nightshade. Remember each door, she told herself.

The stairs grew darker, steeper, and reached a landing. Charlotta hurried to a door.

"What's further down?" Dorrity asked.

"Don't be a pest." Charlotta pushed open the door.

Dorrity lingered to look down the stairs. Cobwebs hung thick on the walls and from the roof. No one could have used this way for at least a century.

A guard's hard hand yanked her through the door, which led to another one on which a sign read: *Bulk storage for root vegetables*. Underneath, another sign said **CELLS**.

~

Before the guard closed the first door behind them, from up the stairwell came a soft thump like someone sneaking in a clumsy manner.

Charlotta pulled Dorrity with her. A single light on the wall lit a row of cages. There were gray-faced men and women, half-men, bird-women who stared at nothing, a frog-man tethered in red rope moaning softly to himself. Dorrity felt more terrified with every step. If she was unlucky, she might end her days in this dungeon.

Charlotta shoved her in front of a cell. In the poor light it looked empty. Dorrity held the bars and peered in. Something shifted in the gloom.

"Dorrity," Metalboy whispered. He crept forward, nursing the hand that had been stabbed. He had a red cord around his throat.

Charlotta flounced to a chair against the wall and muttered angry words to herself through the constant smile. The guards stood, hands behind their backs, and started whistling the same bored tune.

Dorrity crouched on the cold stone floor outside the cell. She whispered to Metalboy about the coronation tomorrow, the journalists and advisers who would come, though she wasn't sure he understood. "You must do your best to get out. I won't say out loud what's inside you, and nor should you…" She floated her hand like a feather over her chest. "But it might give you an extra chance, some extra strength. Just be inventive."

"What are you talking about?" Charlotta demanded.

"I'm explaining a game, he's not very bright," Dorrity said in a rush. "Sorry," she added to Metalboy. "Listen, if you feel the tethers loosen at all…" She whispered about the stairwell, the flight of steps that continued down. "It might be a way out." She risked a glance over her shoulder at Lady Charlotta playing now with the folds of her floaty skirt.

When she turned back to Metalboy his face had flushed. "I was right. You are kind. You want to help me." He looked so pleased and shy that she felt embarrassed.

"If I'm honest, you're my only chance now," said Dorrity.

He looked smug again. "No, I think it's because you like me."

"Shut up. Just escape. Tell everyone I don't want to be Queen. Look," she whispered, "the Count needs a red tether on you as well as invisible ones, and a dungeon and guards on top of that. Doesn't it seem a bit odd? See if you can force the bars like you said you did at the Watch House."

He bit his lip.

"Try now, just to see," she hissed. "Please."

Metalboy rubbed his chest, took in a breath and gripped the bars. Nothing happened.

"Oof." He tried again. Nothing.

She pulled the cuffs of her dress over her hands. "Keep

still." She reached through the bars and tried to loosen the red rope from around his neck. At first it didn't budge. Then the knot slipped a little. She settled the cuffs again over her fingers. The fabric blackened, her fingertips stung, but at last she slid the rope off over his head. It fell to the floor and writhed for a moment.

Metalboy's hand moved to his throat, then to his heart.

"Don't." She rested a hand on his chest too. "The Count mustn't learn you're the Experiment and never ever about the..."

Something made her stop before she said feather. There'd been a change in the air behind her. Lady Charlotta's chair scraped on the floor. Metalboy looked over her shoulder. His eyes widened. There was the tread of soft slippers, the scent of nightshade.

She turned—it was Count Bale, on his own two feet. Lady Charlotta stood with her head bowed to him. The guards stood at attention.

"Dorrity." The Count's eyes shone as if he were young and not over two centuries old. "Soon-to-be-Queen. You do have courage. Trying to free your friend."

He smiled so widely that for the first time Dorrity saw wrinkles on the Count's face, pleats and creases, furrows and folds. He fumbled in a pocket on his fancy pajama jacket, produced a small stick, gave it a shake, then pointed it at the bars. A sizzling glimmer played over them. "That will keep the boy double-tight."

He clicked his fingers. "Take the girl to her room and triple the guard."

CORONATION
DAWN

Dorrity opened her eyes in the very grand bedroom. This was the morning of Fake Coronation Day.

She climbed from the bed, shoved back the curtain and stared down. Beside the pond were a crushed metal bucket and half of a skeleton so big it might have belonged to a bullock. Workers still slogged away at the dredge in their white waders. This morning they wore masks over their noses. A stench like rotten soup rose as high as her window. It was obvious that even if the pond was clear of rubbish by coronation time, the water would still poison her.

Charlotta rushed in without knocking. "Have a bath! Here's your breakfast. Hurry up!"

"Which one should I hurry to do first?" Dorrity asked. "Breakfast or bath?"

Charlotta's head jerked like a hen's—oh, Dorrity remembered actual chickens. But where had she seen them? Not in Owl Town.

"In fact I'm not especially hungry," she said.

Charlotta rushed over, hand up to slap Dorrity. But she glanced out the window and stopped. She'd seen the pond.

"And there's no point in having a bath if I must wade in that," Dorrity added. "It's all right. I know it's not your fault."

Lady Charlotta's smile, though it was fixed, trembled a little. "The guests are gathering in the Grand Reception Room. They're all in bad moods. They flew to West March in air-cars, came on to Owl Town in hired cars and steam buses, and they've had to trudge up the old path this morning." She sounded worried and glanced at the pond again.

"I won't scream," Dorrity said. "I'll behave like a queen as far as I can, though I'll just be a fake one." A random queenly thought came to her. "You like that frilly silk dress I wore before, don't you?"

Charlotta's chin gave a suspicious tilt.

"Have it if you like," Dorrity said.

Lady Charlotta's head jerked again. "Thank you!"

It might be interesting, being a Queen and being gracious—but Dorrity thrust the thought away. She listened for any shouting or alarm that meant Metalboy had managed to escape the Count's tethers. But there was nothing. The only thing to do was try to be dignified.

Bird-women as well as Charlotta were at Dorrity now, with hairclips and combs, coiling and braiding. In came the cat-woman with the coronation dress. Now that the pins were out, it looked beautiful on the hanger. That was a surprise. But Dorrity was sure it would look very wrong when it was actually on her.

First she had to climb into a petticoat with a standing-out hem. Second came another with a bigger standing-out hem. The coronation shoes were silver leather with tiny gold heels. Charlotta and the cat-woman slipped the dress over Dorrity's head and counted the tiny pearl buttons down the back as they did them up...*ninety-nine, one hundred...*

At last Charlotta turned her to see in the mirror.

The dress draped over the petticoats like a mist drapes over early morning. Even the freckles on Dorrity's nose seemed golden rather than sandy. Charlotta pip-pipped. The cat-woman purred.

There was a tap on the door. The Count wheeled himself in. Today his pajamas were gold, the coverlet scarlet. He eyed Dorrity.

"Good gracious." His wheeze seemed pleased. "She looks just the part." (Dorrity felt herself blush.) "String this on her."

He handed a small red box to Lady Charlotta. In it lay a golden chain with a pendant shaped like a feather. Charlotta strung it around Dorrity's neck and gave her a pat.

Dorrity stared in the mirror at the girl who looked as if she could in fact be a queen. Then she closed her eyes to wish that Metalboy had escaped in the night, that he was somehow talking to King Jasper this very minute, before Dorrity had to become a false queen...

Her hands flew to the pendant. "It's getting hot! It hurts!"

Count Bale's eyes had narrowed. "You'll wear it till the coronation's over. It warns me of any treasonous thoughts you have against me."

She opened her mouth to put him right—treason was

being disloyal to the monarch or the country. The Count wasn't the king of anywhere.

Ow—the pendant burned again.

"No, I'm not King yet," said Count Bale with a spider-thin chuckle. "But *yet* is the word that is so important."

~

CORONATION
GUESTS

The Count's throne-chair led the way along the widest downstairs corridor. Dorrity followed, twelve guards in crisp blue and silver uniforms marching behind her. For a moment she stumbled. Two guards took her arms and carried her, just as Yorky and Mike did when they lifted her over tricky, rocky road when she was small.

The Count wheeled himself into an alcove and disappeared. In the same moment Captain Westrap emerged to stand beside Dorrity.

"Forgive me for not welcoming you to Eagle Hall when you arrived." With a sarcastic bow and cold grin, he ushered Dorrity into the Grand Reception Room.

Fans of huge feather-scale arrangements hung on the walls. Dozens of silvery vases filled with silvery ferns and silvery feathers stood about. Even more dozens of people stood about too, with sour murmurs, sour remarks and opinions. An elegant silvery throne had been set in front of a great silvery screen. Where was Count Bale? Another screen stood over to one side. Dorrity bet he was behind it. He couldn't let himself be seen, of course—he wasn't meant to be in Fontania at all.

Captain Westrap bowed again in that caustic way and led Dorrity towards the throne. "You know the rules," he muttered. "You're not permitted to sit at the moment. Not till you've been confirmed as Queen in the pond."

In a daze of fright she muttered, "I'll drip all over the floor."

He grinned again. "That's why we have servants and mops."

Dorrity put her chin up and tried to stay calm in case the feather pendant scorched her again. The important people from the cities and other countries filed past and gawped and bowed. They all had name-tags that meant nothing to her. She had never been surrounded by so many people she didn't know. Now the coronation dress made her feel like a child in a costume. She wanted to cry that it was all a mistake and fling herself at the sturdiest guest. She thought he looked slightly like Birkett. Tears filled her eyes. She tipped her chin higher so they wouldn't fall.

Would she remember what she had to say during the ceremony? She should just shout a lot of nonsense…

The pendant stung her neck. She forced her mind to go blank.

The Count's official stepped forward. With his gray quiff extra-well brushed, he wore a scarlet bow-tie and duck-tail jacket. There was some singing from a choir of the Count's people and a sort of slow chanting from the official. He wiggled a finger at her when it was her turn to speak. She must have managed to do the right things at the right time, because nobody said *For goodness' sake, silly girl, try it again.*

An attendant stood in front of her with a crown on a cushion—an ugly crown with stuck-on glass. The official placed it on her head and twisted it to make it sit on her plaits and coils. It felt heavy as a brick.

A sudden roar of applause startled her—clapping and cheering from the creatures Count Bale had serving him, the bird-women, dog-men, the guards. Dorrity caught sight of Lady Charlotta. It didn't look as if she was wholeheartedly cheering.

The guests didn't clap at all. They looked serious, examining Dorrity. They must know that the coronation was just part of Count Bale's plan to return to Fontania, though they wouldn't know he'd sneaked back already and was hiding behind that screen. Fontania would be plunged into civil war. Friends against friends, families against families, brothers against sisters. Good magic against bad magic.

~

"When is the wading into the lake?" said a clear voice from the watching crowd.

"They tipped fresh goldfish in half an hour ago," said somebody else. "Is the pond going to stand in for the lake?"

"Dear-me goodness," said a foreign voice. "Now see and look! Already many dead goldfish they be hauling out."

"It can't pretend to be a coronation without some sort of wading," said an important-looking lady with a fine cashmere shawl.

"I don't want to waste a message-bird on a half-coronation," muttered a journalist.

238

"No message-birds until Captain Westrap gives permission," cried the official.

"Nobody can expect a child to wade into that sludge," said an important-looking man.

Dorrity closed her eyes and steadied herself.

Footsteps hurried into the room. Dorrity's eyes flew open. She saw the screen that hid the Count trembling a little. He'd be peering through to see what was up. Attendants and guards were whispering to a workman in overalls. Captain Westrap strode over to them.

A younger journalist leaned on a windowsill and craned out. "There's been an accident! Someone fell in—has he drowned? They're wearing masks…good grief, he's poisoned. The water's toxic!"

A guard marched across and the young man was suddenly on the floor.

"Take him to the—er—sick bay," said Captain Westrap. "He must have…fainted, perhaps, with the excitement."

Guards carried the journalist out. Westrap strode to the screen and disappeared behind it for a moment. He returned and gave Dorrity another mocking smile.

"An announcement!" he called. The crowd hushed. "The ceremonial pond is not quite ready. We'll fill in the time with refreshments." He leaned down to murmur in Dorrity's ear. "I am so sorry, Ma'am."

She managed to give him her own sarcastic look.

Guards surrounded her on three sides while guests were offered pastries on silver plates and tall glasses of roar-bubbles. They glanced outside, glanced back at Dorrity and the crown. They looked suspicious, disapproving or plain curious in a way that made her wish for the courage and the energy to give them a kick. The crown felt more like stone as the minutes went by. She reached up to ease it. The rim pressed tighter.

"Ma'am?" asked a well-dressed older journalist. His black hair had gray patches above his ears like folded-back wings.

"Sir, stand back," said Captain Westrap.

The man tapped the name-tag on his lapel: *Crispin Kent, President of Fontanian News Network*. At first Dorrity thought his eyes were sly, then she realized they had a twinkle. "Exclusive interview," he said, "by award-winning journalist?"

Captain Westrap glanced at the Count's hiding place. "Caution is wise," he muttered to Dorrity and took a step back.

She reached to the crown again but didn't dare touch it.

"Ma'am?" asked Mr. Kent.

"It's…heavy. I'm not used to it," she said.

"No, Ma'am." Mr. Kent eyed her as if he was trying to figure her out, and sipped his roar-bubbles. "What are your thoughts on this unexpected occasion?"

"Everyone came here on very short notice…" said Dorrity. The crown gave a warning squeeze. "It's so kind of them," she added fast.

The crown released a little. She had to be careful. She had to be calm. She smiled at Mr. Kent but felt her mouth quiver. "I am very pleased that everyone who has come here today is so worried about what is happening with Fontanian government."

She kept her eyes wide and tilted her head. Was he sharp

enough to understand what her eyes said? *I want to get out!*

His own smile turned a little wiser at one side.

"Because you are a journalist, Mr. Kent…" she began.

He bowed again. "I have many years of experience."

She bowed too. "So you must have a good understanding of how the people of Fontania want to be ruled. I have studied history myself, you know."

"Ah," said Mr. Kent. "That would be tutored by Mrs. Freida? And by the wonderful Mr. Coop for mathematics, so I have heard."

Behind her Captain Westrap gave a warning cough. Again the crown felt heavier. Dorrity made herself stay calm, calm…

"Teachers sometimes misunderstand what a child means," she managed to say. "And that can lead to a child feeling betrayed. It can be difficult for a child who isn't told the whole truth in the first place."

The crown gave a threatening squeeze. Mr. Kent was frowning now. Maybe he didn't understand her either. Dorrity held her head straight. The crown was heavier, heavier.

Mr. Kent bowed again and murmured so that only she could hear. "If I were you, I'd pretend to faint. It might help you escape the pond."

Captain Westrap stepped up and set a hand on Dorrity's arm. He gave Mr. Kent a chilly stare. Mr. Kent moved away.

"Be very careful, Queen Evergreen," muttered Captain Westrap.

Dorrity felt as if she really would faint. But from somewhere there came an idea. A real queen, once she was crowned, would give a speech.

~

The silk coronation dress whispered like water around Dorrity as she walked forward.

"Stay where you are!" hissed Captain Westrap.

The crown gave a warning throb. She gave a regal nod to Captain Westrap, continued to the middle of the Reception Room, then nodded to the guests.

"Ladies and gentlemen," said Dorrity.

The murmuring stopped. Her hands twisted together, which wasn't queenly, but, after all, she was only a distant connection of the royal family. The crown throbbed again but she wasn't too worried. It would look very wrong to everyone if the Count harmed her now.

"Let me say a few words before the…the wading into the pond." She managed not to shudder. For a moment some of the guests looked genuinely sorry for her. That helped her go on. "You have all come a long way to be here today. It is a—" she took a moment to choose the word— "a *surprise* to be crowned. I am sure I do not deserve such a…surprise."

Mr. Kent's wise smile encouraged her to continue.

"In fact, many of the people of Fontania will be astounded." The crown throbbed hard. "Let me say how much I want Fontania to have a…a monarch who listens to what the people want and acts wisely." The crown gave a squeeze but not as hard. "I have been brought up in Owl Town with people who were kind to me. That's all I want for any child—but, till recently, I had never met another child properly. Did you know that?"

There was a murmur, and more of the people looked sympathetic.

Dorrity hurried on. "Maybe I knew other children before I came to Owl Town but I don't remember. Anyway, I just want to say a bit more." She made herself smile. "In the last few days I have met someone who has been very interesting to get to know…" The crown relaxed on her head. Count Bale probably thought she meant him. That gained her a moment.

"That someone…is actually the King's lost Experiment."

A clamour began, gasps and chatter. "What? The King's Experiment?"

The screen jiggled. The Count would be wondering how to handle this. The crown started to tighten. He'd obviously decided.

"Let me finish," Dorrity cried with a great effort. "People think it is neglectful of the King to have his own workshop and not pay more attention to his country!" The crown relaxed—she had another moment. "But I know he's trying to understand the boundaries between machinery and magic. He deserves to try…" The crown squeezed hard… "King Jasper is working for the good of…"

The crown squeezed harder. Dorrity's hands flew up, but she couldn't budge it. She let out a whimper.

Lady Charlotta swooped over and threw a silken shawl around Dorrity's shoulders. "The young Queen is over-tired. She needs to rest."

"She can rest when she's waded into the pond." Captain Westrap beckoned the guards.

"That vile soup can't represent the Eastern Lake!" cried a woman adviser. "This whole coronation is clearly nonsense."

Dorrity swayed on her feet. Guards approached but

didn't seem too sure what to do with a fainting girl Queen. Nor did Westrap. Mr. Kent was beside Charlotta now, eyes fiery with interest.

The crown was so painful that the room had dimmed. Dorrity staggered.

"A good time to faint, Ma'am," Mr. Kent murmured.

"He's right," Charlotta whispered. "Pretend to faint."

"This will be an excellent story," Mr. Kent muttered. "Well done, Dorrity."

"We have been tricked all!" cried a foreign official. "This is not rightful coronation. Right now I decide to be leaving!"

Dorrity heard the rasp of swords pulled from their scabbards, loud orders for the guests to stand back with their hands up. Fainting was an excellent idea.

—

BOOTS

Dorrity's eyes opened. She lay under a thin cover on the bed in the grand bedroom. She felt hungry. That probably meant she wasn't dead yet, so she sat up.

The crown was gone, and her hair had been taken out of those plaits and coils. Something swayed near the wardrobe—the coronation dress on a hanger, moving in a breeze. Faint gidibird cries through an open window said it was morning. Had she escaped the pond? She started to climb off the bed but her legs tangled in the coronation petticoats. She must have slept in them overnight.

Out in the grounds she heard arguing. She stumbled to the window. The journalists and advisers milled below. They looked bedraggled as if they'd had too many roar-bubbles and slept with their clothes badly buttoned.

Dorrity tried the bedroom door. Locked. She thumped with one fist. She thumped with two.

After a moment the lock rattled and the door opened. Charlotta sidled in, little red shoes peeping. "What is it?" she said through the fixed smile.

"Breakfast?" Dorrity said.

Charlotta's smile seemed a great strain. "The coronation guests are racing through the supplies."

Even a fake queen needed breakfast. "Send them home," said Dorrity. "Order supplies. Can't the Count magic some up?"

For a moment Charlotta's smile seemed real and sad. "You're a brave child. You let the guests know you don't want to be Queen..." She fluttered the pleated skirt. "But now the Count won't let them leave. They're angry." She glanced at the window. "As you can hear."

Dorrity sank back onto the bed.

The bird-woman moved closer. "Take heart a little," she murmured. "Yesterday the journalists wrangled and tried to confuse each other. This morning they're sticking together. They're taking turns to send out message-birds when they think nobody's watching."

Maybe Dorrity could take heart. "You mean the Count's tethers can't stop them?"

Charlotta's eyes glistened, perhaps with tears if bird-women wept. "He will stop them very soon." She used a comb on Dorrity's hair and breathed in her ear. "Eagle Hall is large, but he has explored a great deal of it again. He left many of his secrets here when he was banished— experiments of all sorts, machines and magic."

"Can you help me get away?" But Dorrity knew what the answer would be.

Charlotta just tugged her hair (*ouch!*). "The Count will give me what he promised. I will be a real lady with fine clothes of my own rather than a queen's cast-offs. When I'm a real lady, my shoes won't hurt."

"If the shoes put you in a permanent bad temper, take them off," said Dorrity. "What's better about being a lady? I'd love to have a nest near the riverbank."

Briefly Charlotta's eyes closed. A drop of moisture trickled to meet the fixed smile. Then she rapped Dorrity with the comb. "I must tell the Count that you're awake. You're lucky—he's decided the pond is more trouble than it's worth. It would kill you at once, in front of the journalists. It's more important that you make the First Proclamation."

"It isn't my fault if your shoes hurt," Dorrity whispered. "It isn't my fault you made the wrong choice." She'd made her own very bad choice. She should have run from Owl Town the moment she knew Westrap was after her.

Her voice nearly broke. "When is the First Proclamation? Let's get it over with."

Charlotta let out a chirp between amusement and exasperation. "You're a complicated child, a foolish child. When the First Proclamation has been made, the Second is next."

Dorrity blew her nose so she wouldn't actually cry. "That makes sense."

"You've no more sense than an egg," Charlotta cried. "Girl, after the Second Proclamation, the Count won't need you and he'll get rid of you!"

~

Charlotta hurried away and slammed the door.

It slammed open again at once. In flounced the cat-woman. She carried those white velvet slippers and a new dress for Dorrity, the yellow of…mustard.

Dorrity couldn't fight the big things. And she didn't mind mustard on a potato. She would even say yes to mustard on toast if that was all that was offered right now. But a mustard dress? For what might be the last dress she wore in her whole life? As for those slippers…

"No," said Dorrity.

The cat-woman snarled. But Dorrity banged open the wardrobe.

There was Dr. Oxford's pair of vet boots. There were blue high-heeled shoes, a pair of small black flat-soles with diamond butterflies. She climbed right into the wardrobe and felt around. Her hand came upon leather, boot shaped, and her fingers touched something like cross-stitch. She crawled out again.

In her hand was a pair of ancient leather lace-up boots that might once have been crimson. Perhaps they were the boots of a long-dead Lady Someone, even a true Queen of Fontania. The treads were thick with dried mud, so the long-dead lady must have been very like Dorrity. Besides, she'd had red boots for her birthday, so these felt right. She rubbed the crossed laces and stood up straight.

"I am going to wear these," Dorrity said. "Until the Second Proclamation, I am Queen and you can't stop me."

⌣

QUEEN EVERGREEN
ON SHOW

The next minutes were a flurry. The cat-woman screeched and scolded, but Dorrity opened the window wider to stick the boots through and bash them clean.

The guests were still milling below. They muttered to message-birds, listened to birds that had just arrived over the hedge. Scraps of sentences floated up: "...unrest in West March...consternation in the City of Much Glass... Full-blown riot on Battle Island as you'd expect...City of Spires preparing for bread shortages...civil war...Who is the girl upstart?...doesn't show great dress sense...spend the rest of her short life locked up..."

Shouts rang on the far side of the hedge. Angry townsfolk. For Dorrity, or against her? Whichever it was, the Count wouldn't find it easy to win over Fontania. Dorrity figured that people in the cities would be much the same as in Owl Town. Everybody liked things to go on as they were, though more money would always be nice. As long as ships and steam trains were on time—stuff like that—they didn't want a government that interfered. What was clear from the shouts was that nobody was fooled about the Count being good for the country.

The cat-woman dragged her away from the window, hustled her into the ghastly mustard dress and jammed an ugly tiara on her head. Dorrity was sure it would be as dangerous as yesterday's crown, but at least it wasn't heavy.

~

Captain Westrap waited outside the Reception Room door. He was carrying a parchment with a fake-royal sign, a green ribbon dangling. "Green for good news, the Count tells me," he said through his cold grin.

Fright squeezed at Dorrity's throat but she managed a fake queenly smile and walked in.

The corner of the room was still screened off. Count Bale would be there again, probably in his stroller-throne. If he needed it sometimes but not others, his powers couldn't be as strong as he wanted—at least not yet. Otherwise, she'd never have been able to loosen the red tether on Metalboy. Oh—had he escaped yet? No, or she would have heard. Maybe he still could, though time must be running out.

Mr. Kent, President of the Fontanian News Network, had his eyes on her. She flicked him a smile. Captain Westrap gave a narrow glare.

Dorrity took a deep breath and read from the parchment in a voice with no emotion: "...*happy to perform my first task as your new Queen. Many years ago after the death of King Vincent of Fontania, his son shamefully banished his uncle Count Bale,*

who had been Noble Prime Adviser to King Vincent. By this First
Proclamation of Queen Evergreen…"

She stopped. She had nothing to lose. The more annoying she was to the Count, the better the chance for Metalboy.

"In fact I prefer be known as Queen Dorrity," she said.

The wire of the tiara stung a little. "Ouch," said Dorrity. "Anyway, this paper goes on to say…" The tiara stung again. "*Ouch!* All right, I'll read exactly what's written. *By this First Proclamation of Queen Evergreen, Count Bale is welcomed back into the Kingdom. Pause for applause…"* She looked at the guests. "I wasn't meant to read that last bit. Do you want to applaud?"

The journalists examined their pens and pencils. A few cowardly advisers pressed their hands in a medium pat-pat. Some put their hands together in a patting-dust-off sort of way. Three brave ones folded their hands up into their armpits. The foreigners shrugged and muttered versions of hooray, like *oo-rah, oo-raw* or *hu-roo.*

"All right," said Dorrity. "That's all." She rolled up the parchment.

"Did she say Count Bale?" asked a young journalist with a small message-bird clipped to his jacket. "He must be dead a century by now."

"Do your research before a job," said a lady journalist with embroidered mittens. "It's one hundred and ninety-five years."

"He was terribly ill, apparently, and should have died at that time," said Mr. Kent. "Ate something he'd been making right here in the vaults of Eagle Hall, so I believe. Overdosed on his own beauteen. But he didn't die. He just couldn't move at all for several weeks. It made him easier to deal with. That's how they removed him from the country."

The screen jiggled a bit. Mr. Kent looked unsettled but not surprised. "So, Ma'am." He bowed to Dorrity. "When can we expect Count Bale to return?"

Everyone looked at her. Then they looked at the screen. She could tell they were putting two and two together and coming up with a bad result.

"Um…maybe you could prepare your messages," she said. "It is usually best to…um…be prepared."

Captain Westrap stepped onto the platform beside her. "The Count will make himself available at the first opportunity."

Mr. Kent nodded to the Captain but spoke to Dorrity. "And will he be your Noble Prime Adviser, Ma'am, as he was to his younger brother?"

She put a hand to her heart without thinking. "I want Fontania to have the best government. Like…like it is said, children should be properly cared for, babies should sleep safe in their beds. That's…that's all I can…" Her voice gave out. She couldn't even find the breath to say *excuse me*. She jumped down from the fake-royal platform in her true-royal crimson boots.

Mr. Kent called out. "Ma'am! Have you actually met the Count in person?"

The tiara stung the sides of her head, so she stayed silent.

"Your hesitation means yes, I think?" said Mr. Kent.

Everyone murmured and stared at her, and at the screen.

Mr. Kent strode to the front of the crowd. "His reputation

is cruel. After all, it is a fact that his shape-changed creatures killed his brother, King Vincent. Count Bale is the last man any country would want as adviser to a new young Queen. And despite what has been in the papers for the last two days, Fontanians are fond of the King and Queen who rule already."

There was a very faint scent of scorching and Mr. Kent groaned—it looked as if he was stuck, unable to move. At the same time, Dorrity felt the tiara burning fiercely at her temples. She couldn't save herself. Perhaps she couldn't save Fontania.

But maybe she could still save Metalboy. She jumped back on the platform.

"Mr. Kent, guests—you need to see how—how kind— Count Bale can be." The tiara trembled on her head but didn't burn. "Listen. In the Eagle Hall dungeons, there is a boy. In the next three minutes he will be released…" The tiara stung badly. She yanked the thing off. It scorched her fingers and fell to the floor, where it steamed a bit. The guests gawked at it. One or two people screamed.

Dorrity continued. "The—the boy—will walk through this room so you can see him. Then he'll walk free through the barrier hedge. Nothing will stop him. This will be proof that the Count has a heart."

She crossed her scorched fingers and didn't dare glance at the screen or Captain Westrap.

For a minute there was silence except for whispering among the guests, many mutters to message-birds from the sides of their mouths. Mr. Kent very slowly eased his limbs and tested his neck. He nodded thank you to Dorrity, but his frown was worried.

For another long minute there was shuffling, and muttering, and Captain Westrap's expression grew darker and darker. Another minute passed.

At last the footsteps of guards rang in the corridor.

They entered with Metalboy. She'd never seen a boy look so real. His knees were gray with dirt, his hair tousled, face smudged. His clothes were torn.

"You're free," Dorrity said. "Quickly. Go."

"Is the boy simple?" murmured a journalist. "Who is he, exactly?"

Metalboy gave Dorrity a very small smile. "Thank you," he whispered. Then he ran from the Reception Room, over the marble terrace, down the steps. Journalists and advisers followed and flung their message-birds into the air...but then Dorrity smelled burning.

Metalboy stopped as if he were a statue of a running boy.

45

THE EXIT OF
QUEEN EVERGREEN

Dorrity knew what had happened. The Count had decided to risk it, despite all the guests. He'd put tethers on Metalboy and on her again too. She couldn't move from the Reception Room. She couldn't cry out.

Captain Westrap strode out to the terrace and clapped his hands. The journalists and observers turned to him. "The Count is happy for the boy to go," he called. "But look—the little chap can't bear to leave his friend. I will speak to the Queen for a moment. Excuse us."

He marched back and hauled Dorrity past Count Bale's screen and into a side room. "Wait here out of mischief." He slammed and locked the door behind him.

She looked around. This room was faded and shabby. It had an empty shelf and a row of chairs fixed to the wall. On one of them lay the bow-tie man's green folder and pencil. She tried to pull herself up to the one high window. All she glimpsed was the top of the hedge. But she heard a few voices.

"Town shouldn't have been ignored for so many years…"

"Are those anarchist catch-phrases over the hedge?"

"Poor girl. This is awful…"

It definitely was. Dorrity picked up the pencil and wrote on the walls.

CUSS CAPTAIN WESTRAP

DOUBLE RUDDY CUSS THE COUNT

It was satisfying only for a moment.

She made a huge stretch and reached the window catch. It was old, loose, and rattled open. Count Bale's fault—he'd ignored the small things, so this was just what he deserved.

From the far side of the hedge came a roaring so deep that it must be a bear from the High Murisons. It was most likely Birkett, still waiting to be paid by the Count. The bear roared again. Deep goatly bleating joined it. Double-cuss to fake brothers as well.

There were shouts of "No gov-ern-mint! No gov-ern-mint!"

"Anarchy *doesn't* rule!"

"Out with the King and down for the Count!"

The door slammed open. "Out you come," ordered Westrap. "Act as if nothing's wrong. Go and speak to the boy, but be careful." His grin was more scary than ever.

Something not very nice was being planned.

~

Dorrity walked over the grass, smiling and nodding to the guests. When she reached Metalboy, she kept the smile on, as a real Queen would. "At least I tried," she said.

His gray eyes looked damp, but he was able to stand in an easier way now.

"Can you talk? The Count must want things to look normal for a bit longer." She still managed to smile.

He took a small breath, then a deeper one. "I…this might be useful. I escaped the guards long enough for a quick look. At the foot of that staircase is a huge door. Behind it, I heard a lapping like a giant animal."

"What sort of animal?" Dorrity asked.

"I said *like* an animal…" Metalboy stopped.

Someone's shadow loomed over Dorrity. She jumped, but it was only Mr. Kent.

He nodded at her. "Is your friend all right?"

"Thank you for asking," said Metalboy. "I don't know how to answer. Should it be true or just polite?"

"That's a very telling answer in itself," said Mr. Kent. "D'you know, if Count Bale was already in Fontania, I would guess that he was maintaining parts of Eagle Hall by magic—not necessarily by good magic."

Dorrity batted her eyelids so Mr. Kent would know she was using sarcasm. "But if the Count was here already, the First Proclamation would have been fake. What a shocking idea."

Mr. Kent grinned in his lop-sided way. "If a girl was being held hostage because of her brothers, the people of Fontania would understand."

"What if they were fake brothers who, for instance, worked for a Count?" Her voice cracked.

"So that's the way, is it?" He thought for a moment. "Mind you, many a bad man can learn the error of his ways."

"I bet just as many never learn or don't even care," said

Dorrity. "What if you could hear two of the fake brothers now—a bear and a goat?" Her hand bunched into a fist and she rubbed her eyes with it.

"I'm sorry," Mr. Kent whispered.

"I just want there to be a good ending." She touched Metalboy's arm. "For me and my friend."

Mr. Kent spoke kindly. "You're in the middle of politics, Dorrity. It's tricky and difficult to tell truth from lies and figure out where you should stand. And no matter how good a government might be, there's always somebody certain that something else would be far better." He shrugged. "But journalists aren't meant to take sides. If there was no unrest, there wouldn't be many stories. Stories are my bread and butter."

Dorrity couldn't help herself. "They're also your expensive shoes and plenty of roar-bubbles."

Mr. Kent chuckled. Metalboy let out a snort too.

"I did say *not meant* to take sides," Mr. Kent added.

A trumpet sounded.

At the same time, a sizzling smell laced through the air. The heat of magical tethers stung Dorrity's arms and shoulders worse than ever. She tried to struggle but it was impossible.

"What's this, what—" began Mr. Kent.

But she—Metalboy—Mr. Kent—guests and soldiers— every single person in the grounds swung as if they were trapped in a very slow dance, turning till they all faced the terrace.

There at the top of the steps was the stroller-throne.

Count Bale sat straight, wore a sleek new velvet jacket and smiled the spider-thin smile. He seemed skinnier than ever, as if something was being drawn out of him the way a balloon gets gradually smaller after a party. But Dorrity knew he was probably still going to win.

~

The Count's voice carried over his motionless audience. "This is a great day for Fontania! Thanks to the First Proclamation of our little Queen, I have returned. Here I am again in Eagle Hall where I worked for my brother, King Vincent. It is important to keep in mind that very few monarchs have the talent to rule a country entirely by themselves..." Smiling, he eyed the crowd and spread a bony hand. "And now our Queen Evergreen is in charge. She's a wise young Queen to have made her First Proclamation so early in her reign. She has also sent a wise invitation for me to come and be her tutor."

I ruddy certainly did not, thought Dorrity.

"I am proud to accept." The Count tipped his bald head as if to listen, then mimed that everyone had better clap.

The heat of the tethers faded on Dorrity and she sensed she could move. So, it seemed, could everyone. The political experts and foreign observers clapped silently at first, then a little harder as if it had occurred to them they ought—just in case—to make sure the Count liked them. All the journalists lowered their heads and scribbled in any spare margins of their notebooks.

"And now..." The Count clicked his fingers. The bow-tie official walked over and presented him with a roll of parchment with three fluttering green ribbons. "My first piece of advice to Queen Evergreen is to read her Second Proclamation right away."

~

The invisible tethers forced Dorrity to the side of the stroller-throne. The official held out the parchment. In the clutch of the tethers, her arms moved, her hands took the creamy scroll and her fingers unrolled it. She found herself starting to read.

"*Here is the Second Proclamation of Queen Ever…*" At least her voice was freed now. She might be going to die any moment, so in her loudest voice she cried, "Queen Dorrity!" and then returned to what was written. "*In the event of my early death… Count Bale shall be Regent. That means he will be King though not actually called King. After three months he shall be crowned King of Fontania as recognition of his abilities in the ways of—*" she had to stop for a moment—"*of effective magic.*"

That was the end—but her voice was still free. "The three months is just to make it look better," she shouted. "And you know that by effective magic, he means bad magic!"

The Count gave a cry of anger and tried to rise from the throne-chair. He stumbled. She felt the tethers slacken their grip and in that moment pitched the Proclamation at him.

The guests burst into movement too. Yelling and screaming, they ran for the hedge, tripped over guards— guards tripped over them. A bear burst in through the hedge—so did a goat—and a few anarchists.

A guard seized Dorrity, but Mr. Kent tugged her free and flung her towards the hedge…

"Run, Dorrity! Run!" Metalboy cried.

"Come on!" she shouted back. "Use the feather!"

She ducked under an arm, aside from a grab—thank goodness for all the years she'd spent darting away from her brothers when they played tag. She was into the hedge and scratches from a thousand thorns didn't stop her.

Then she was out the other side, silk dress in tatters.

⌣

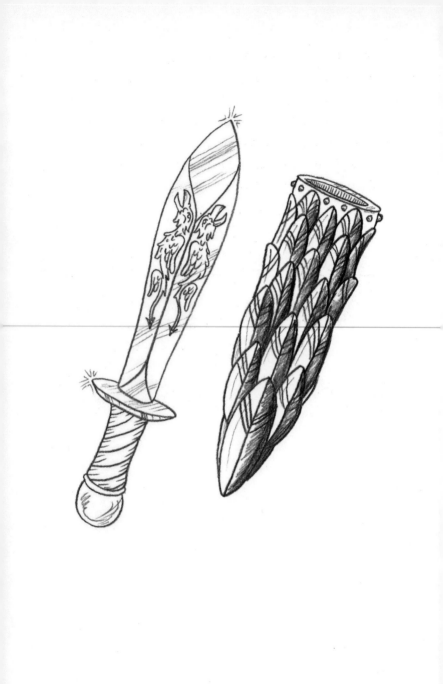

PART FIVE OF DORRITY'S TALE

MISTAKES
AND
EXPERIMENTS

46

HEADLONG AND HEADLINES

Dorrity ran down the old road to the town. A roar from a bear, *That's her!* from Ruffgo, shrieks and squawks, screams from a goat, the clash of swords and blasts of gunfire… She thanked goodness again for the crimson boots, excellent for speed and grip. Footsteps and ragged gasps sounded behind her. She risked a look—a gaggle of guests slipped and slid in their best shoes. She tripped on the skirt of that stupid dress and slammed into a slab of stonework. For a moment she lay bruised and winded.

Something rammed her shoulder. Before she could scream, she was boosted up and thrown out of the way of a raven-guard. The goat had saved her. Now it ran beside her down the path and used its horns to hammer branches out of her way.

The bear roared again. She was certain she heard Captain Westrap—*Get the girl!* Shots rang again—another roar. When she glanced back through the trees, confusion and fighting filled her vision. Troops of raven-soldiers strode with pistols and swords. The goat, huge as a horse, leapt back uphill and—*wham!*—slammed into Westrap.

Dorrity gathered her silk tatters and skidded on. All she could think of was what would happen to her friends if the Count became King. They'd be turned into animals or half-birds, treated cruelly just because they'd been her friends. Was Metalboy with her? She couldn't tell.

She sped faster down slope after slope and at last reached the edge of the Dark. She let herself stop and catch a breath. A foreign observer collapsed panting beside her.

"What happened to the boy?" she managed to ask. "Did you see?"

The man nodded. He had no breath to talk but made tying-up motions with his hands.

"No!" said Dorrity. But he nodded again.

She set off over the wasteland. On the far side of the old ramp stood a Fontanian army officer giving orders to a troop of soldiers. The Royal Army! They could save Metalboy.

The officer called to her. "Halt!"

But Dorrity was over the ramp and past him so fast it felt like flying in the crimson boots.

~

She kept on, over the Dark Road and into Upper High Street. Head down, she jinked and darted through groups of soldiers, clusters of journalists in clean fresh clothes. Steam cars and army trucks were parked in the plaza. A huge military riverboat was just scraping under the bridge. The wharf was crowded. Everywhere officers shouted orders, messengers ran.

At last she reached the shop. Her foot caught in the gutter and she sprawled beside the newspaper hoardings. Her knee stung badly.

A soldier stooped beside her. "Girlie, are you all right?" He gave a shout. "It's her! This is the girl!"

Dorrity stared at the hoardings. On each was a picture of her in the ruffly dress. She looked as if she'd just eaten something peculiar. On one the headline read:

Fontania Prepares for Civil War

Brave Neglected Child is our Rightful Monarch

The headline of the second paper said:

Fontania Prepares for Civil War

Upstart Brat Makes Claim to Throne

Dorrity scrambled up.

Strangers, townsfolk—all kinds of people—gathered, staring, exclaiming, pointing at Dorrity. The soldier reached for her, but a pair of strong skinny arms scooped her out of his way. It was Button.

He carted her into the shop and stowed her on the shelf for broken crackers. Her knee dripped blood. The shop echoed with voices. Behind the counter Dorrity saw Mrs. Freida. At the connecting door was Mr. Coop.

"I have to see a general!" Dorrity cried. "Who's in charge?" In the chorus of bellows and shouting her voice was a peep.

"Quiet!" roared a voice even deeper than the bear's. "Quiet at once!" It was Button.

The townsfolk shut up with the surprise. The newcomers gradually shut up too.

Mrs. Freida started to say something, but Mr. Coop stopped her.

The shop door darkened with the bulk of a King's troll captain wearing metal gauntlets and helmet hood with a sun-visor. He lifted his visor, pointed at Button and spoke in deep rumbling Trollish. Button rumbled softly back.

Dorrity gripped the edge of the shelf. "I must see a general. It's important. I've got to get a message to the King and Queen at once."

"Girl has done nothing wrong?" The captain frowned, probably—with trolls it was hard to tell. But she definitely didn't want to lie to him.

"Um," said Dorrity. "Only what most children might. Like, not doing my lessons sometimes. Snuck off when I should have done chores."

The troll captain's mouth twitched. "Very bad. Like troll boy or girl. Come."

He lifted her down. People pressed back to make room. He clanged his sun-visor shut and tucked her under his arm like a sack of potatoes.

Outside, the jangle of military equipment smothered all the normal sounds of Owl Town. Everyone stared at her, with her feet dangling. It was only thirty or so of the troll captain's steps over High Street and the plaza to the town hall, but it seemed to take a year to cover them.

At the entrance, guards saluted. The captain set Dorrity down, put a hand big as a pork hock on her shoulder and ushered her in. The place was buzzing with the business of military people. Where was the commanding officer?

The captain pushed her past the hall to the meeting room. There, in a crowd of officers, stood a young man with untidy dark hair, a neat little beard and a simple uniform. He frowned down at a map spread on the meeting table. A pistol and its holster rested by his hand. At his belt was a scabbard with a dagger—the royal dagger? Dorrity's skin prickled, though the dagger wasn't magic—or not exactly. This had to be King Jasper.

"Sir," rumbled the captain. "Here is the girl."

The King glanced up. "Girl?"

Dorrity quaked in those crimson boots, but she'd had enough.

"My name is Dorrity," she said. "I know you'll have to lock me up. But right now just listen and don't interrupt."

~

THE VOLUME OF POSSIBLE ENDINGS

GETTING A
WORD IN

Three generals and several majors and captains (men, women, ogres, dwarves and one more troll) straightened up and looked dangerous. Dorrity recognized some from newspaper stories. There was a short lady with many military medals—she was Lady Major Alannah. There was a fairly old man—the King's father, Dr. Ludlow.

She opened her mouth to begin. But outside there was scuffling and raised voices.

"King Jasper!" It was Mr. Coop.

"Jasper!" That was Mrs. Freida. "Let me in or I'll talk to your mother!"

The King's frown grew deeper, but Dorrity saw he was interested, perhaps even amused. He nodded to the guards.

Mr. Coop hobbled in. At once Dr. Ludlow lunged forward to shake his hand.

Mrs. Freida hurried to the table, newspapers clutched in a fist. "This is a pack of nonsense and you know it. Your family has brought it on itself!"

"Madam, mind your manners!" It was Special Major Murgott—Dorrity knew he was a famous veteran. "Sir!" he said to the King. "We're pressed for time."

"Exactly," said Dorrity. "Please listen to me."

A guard rushed in and slapped a message on the table in front of the King, who opened it at once. "Ah." He clicked his fingers at the guard. "Thank you. Fetch him in."

The guard marched out and the King looked at Dorrity. "After all this time. We've been trying to find you for years."

"You should have looked harder," she said. "Sir…"

"My best spies weren't good enough." He gave a grin. "And before that your mother was excellent at hiding herself."

"Sir!" said Dorrity.

He raised his hand. "You'll be sent safely off in a corvette…"

"I have something to tell you!" cried Dorrity.

But the King was distracted by noise just outside and looked up at the doorway. He frowned again. "So. Here he is."

Yorky was marched in by a squad of guards. He wore a clean shirt with a clean jacket slung over the wing. His jaw was clenched. Behind him were Miss Honey and Dr. Oxford, who looked scared.

Dorrity took a breath to start talking—but she'd like to hear what Yorky said too. He'd better be quick.

The King surveyed Yorky. "My young cousin believed she was your sister. Yorkman, you'll have to speak on behalf of your…colleagues? Henchmen? What do you call yourselves?"

Yorky looked as if he'd faint but stood to attention with his jaw shut tight.

Murgott saluted. "I can make the traitor talk, sir."

"I've no doubt of it, Murgott," said the King. "Mr. Coop?" he asked. "Mrs. Freida? Can you give me a clue?"

Mrs. Freida's gray curls shook in a *no*. "They all seemed good brothers to Dorrity. And she's a good girl, I'm sure about that."

Mr. Coop nodded. "They were good brothers. They enjoyed her company. They grinned like loons when she did well with lessons. I suspected they had their secrets but that's normal in Owl Town."

"Dorrity?" The King turned to her.

At last he was asking her something. But her mouth had gone dry. "They lied to me…" was all she could manage.

The King rapped the table. "Enough for now. Dorrity has to be sent to West March for protection…"

"No!" Yorky lunged at the table. Guards hauled him back, but he spoke in a firm clear voice. "She was a little girl. She was four years old. We kept her safe from Bale and safe from you."

"You didn't set out to save a child in the first place," said Murgott. "You set out to capture a child for an enemy of Fontania."

Sweat broke out on Yorky's forehead. The wing was quivering. "Yes, we've been traitors to King Jasper and Queen Sibilla. But in the end we defied Count Bale. And I'd do it again."

"Sir!" cried Murgott. "Time's very short!"

"Yes!" cried Dorrity at last. "You have to save Metalboy!"

"Who?" asked the King.

"Your lost Experiment," she said.

⌣

SEVENTEEN WORDS,
IN FACT

The King looked surprised but not nearly as excited as she'd expected.

"My Experiment? It ended up here? For goodness' sake—it must have worked."

He clicked his fingers, and the squad of guards led Yorky away. Miss Honey and Mrs. Freida were shooed out as well, but Dr. Ludlow wanted Mr. Coop to stay.

"Sir!" Dorrity said. "I haven't finished. I've hardly begun. The Count made me read the Second Proclamation. It says he's allowed to come back, but he's been back for weeks. There's all sorts of his stuff hidden under Eagle Hall. Some of it's the original beauteen."

"Good grief, what a turn-up," said Dr. Ludlow.

Dorrity rushed on. "I think Count Bale needs it to keep himself young, maybe even alive. And Lady Charlotta's very afraid—she's just a bird—well, she's a woman—but she says he has weapons stored too…"

Suddenly everyone seemed much more interested. Why

were grown-ups so dense? Hadn't they come to Owl Town to fight the Count's people? Of course there were weapons. What else would they expect from an enemy?

"They're magical or mechanical or even both. Magical—do you get it? And Metalboy's up there, and the main thing is there's a—" She stopped. Should she mention the feather aloud in front of everyone?

King Jasper picked up his pistol and holster. "Thank you, Dorrity." He turned to his officers. "Now, best plan of attack on Eagle Hall…"

"You're not going, son," said Dr. Ludlow. "You've got an army for that."

"Sir!" Dorrity cried. "The Count stabbed Metalboy. It was awful. He actually bled."

The King swung to face her, shock in his eyes. Dr. Ludlow looked at her properly too. So did Lady Alannah—Mr. Coop—everyone.

"Red blood," said Dorrity.

"Amazing, sir," said Special Major Murgott. "Well done. Excellent experiment. But sir, we have to start moving. We'll be battling uphill."

There was uproar outside. A corporal dashed in—Dorrity recognized young Lord Hodie, hero of the Um'Binnian incident. Everyone said he'd been extremely brave, determined, and kind—but he looked so ordinary!

"This room seriously needs a door," muttered the King. "What is it, Hodie?"

"Flocks of birds," said Hodie. "Big birds in big flocks. Circling over the Hall."

"That's why Westrap drew back," said Murgott. "Gathering the troops for the attack. I might have known."

"Of course we knew," said the King.

"For goodness' sake, save Metalboy!" Dorrity cried. "All right, I have to say it. There's a feather-scale!"

The King gave a baffled smile. "Feather…"

Everyone was listening now. Too cussing bad for the King. Dorrity spoke as clearly as possible—seventeen words.

"There's a dragon-eagle feather inside Metalboy. It floated behind his heart while he was in your workshop."

The King paled. His hand went to the royal dagger at his belt. "So that's what happened! And it's in Metalboy? In Eagle Hall?"

"It was because you sneezed," Dorrity said.

"It's that dusty workshop," the Lady General muttered. "He has been told, but does he listen?"

"Please tell me the Count doesn't know about the feather," King Jasper said.

"He…he might. That bit is my fault," said Dorrity. "I said something just now—just before I escaped."

"When it went missing, the dragon-eagles told me not to worry *yet*. I'd say now is definitely the time to be very uneasy." The King's knuckles tightened on the dagger. "I have to get that feather. There's no option."

"Send a team," said Dr. Ludlow. "At once. An expedition to salvage the Experiment."

"We don't dare wait," said the King. "We must attack now."

AVALANCHE

Officers, the King, everyone began rattling orders and suggestions, but in a remarkably organized way.

Lord Hodie gave her a quick wink. But Dorrity—because the Count had tried to make her Queen—would be locked away now, probably in the corvette the King had mentioned. She hoped it would be in a cabin with a view, though she doubted it. She looked out the window of the meeting room, across High Street up at the Beastly Dark and the first afternoon shadows.

A flash lit the tops of the trees. A deep rolling sound came from the Dark.

She cried out. So did lots of older, braver people. Had the Count exploded Eagle Hall?

She plunged under the arms of generals and corporals, out to the street. The air smelled sizzled.

The flash came again. Another *boom!* filled the valley and rolled like thunder. The sizzling smell, more bitter and pungent, spread overhead.

"There!" Murgott pointed over the river, where the cliffs

were scarred with scorch marks. Flames rippled through the bushes and daisies.

A third flash lit up the sky. Glowing black lightning sped over the town and struck the cliffs. The most enormous roll of thunder yet deafened Dorrity. Flashes of red ran up the cliffs from top to bottom. Rock started to fall; a fog of dust billowed in the wind across the river. Smoke stung her nose and eyes and made her cough. Huge boulders rumbled and splashed; on and on the thunder rolled; rocks tumbled and jumped—the river seethed.

"Bale's dammed the river," Murgott cried. "He's trying to trap us!"

~

Dorrity's heart lurched. Shouts and cries rose from families on the riverboats. The Command Vessel swung on its moorings and rocked the wharf. Already the river banked up against the fallen rocks, and water lapped the edge of the bridle path. Before long it might reach High Street. How long before the bridge was flooded too?

"The Watch House." Mr. Coop started hobbling towards it. "Edgar! Empty the Watch House!" He roared back to Dorrity. "Get over the bridge! The town will be flooded in—" he glanced at it—"soon! Dorrity, go for the bridge! Mrs. Freida, get her to safety!" He turned and hobbled up High Street. "Flood! Get over the bridge! Flood! Flood!"

Dorrity could run faster than him. She sped down Arrow Street, shouting as she went, "Flood! Flood!"—down the Dark Road—"Flood!"—back up Shield Street, then round onto High Street.

Officer Edgar, helmet askew, shepherded a crowd of townsfolk to the bridge. Even in the last five minutes, the water had risen. There onto the bridge went Chippy O'Now leading the craft lady who led the hairdresser. The hairdresser led the farm workers who were leading Button who was wearing his hood. Behind them was Farmer Ember barking orders like a two-legged sheepdog. There went Mrs. Freida…no, she was turning back, screaming for Dorrity.

The law clerk pushed Mrs. Freida onto the bridge again and the crowd hid them from Dorrity's view. Edgar waved to—oh, to King Jasper! There he was by the fountain with various officers. Edgar was speeding over to him.

The Forgotten River was becoming a long lake that lapped at the avalanche…The river! She hadn't understood what Metalboy said before, about something down there *lapping like a giant animal*. It must be the river, below the dungeon of Eagle Hall.

Dorrity sped over too and yanked the King's sleeve.

"Sir," Murgott was saying, "if one of their feather-scales is involved, the dragon-eagles might arrive and help."

The King's frown was very scary. "The dragon-eagles are hardly a pair of trained canaries. They've their own ideas about how much they should or shouldn't help. They're not made for battle."

"They breathe flame, sir," an officer said.

"Do you want them to set the Dark on fire? Or boil the river?" snapped the King.

Dorrity didn't see why any wild creature, even a magical dragon-eagle, would come flying towards a battle. If anyone asked her, which of course nobody would, she'd say the dragon-eagles would be best to leave people alone altogether. She yanked the King's sleeve harder. "Sir!"

A squad of soldiers came tumbling down High Street. "Raven-soldiers! The town is surrounded!"

A shot rang out. Dorrity dived behind a plaza waste bin. She dared to peer out. Mr. Coop lay face-down on the road. Dorrity darted up, but was pulled back by the tatters of the mustard dress. She found herself crushed between a slim soldier and a brawny captain.

A loud-speaker boomed from the wasteland. "The river is rising. Owl Town is surrounded." Dorrity recognized Captain Westrap. "Jasper, give yourself up to Bale. It might save a few lives!"

Mr. Coop moved a hand and Dorrity heard him groan. Another shot rang out, and he lay still. A pair of soldiers wriggled on their stomachs and drew him to shelter. Mr. Coop might be dying. Tears welled up in Dorrity's eyes.

"Bring me a megaphone!" the King called.

A soldier hurried one to him.

"Stay under cover!" cried officers and Dr. Ludlow.

"Bale!" shouted the King. "Come and talk!"

"My name is Westrap. I'm in charge," Westrap bellowed.

"The Count is a coward!" Jasper yelled.

"The Count wants to live!" shouted Westrap. "I call that sensible. How sensible are you? His weapons were in the Hall for decades and you never came and looked for them."

"Some magic and machines should never be used!" roared the King.

"Poor excuse!" shouted Westrap. "Give in! Or do we have to destroy the bridge as well?" He let out a laugh. "No, the river will destroy it soon enough."

The bridge! Dorrity scrambled around to see. Water covered the lower path now and was halfway to High Street. Only the middle of the bridge was still uncovered, with a straggle of townsfolk marooned there.

"Surrender!" roared Westrap. "Surrender now, or none of you will be alive to feel sorry!"

Dorrity scrambled closer to the King. So did Murgott and young Lord Hodie.

"We seem to be stuck, sir," said Murgott.

For the third time Dorrity yanked the King's sleeve. "I know a way into the Hall," she said.

"It might be a good idea to listen to the girl, sir," said Lord Hodie.

The King stared at her.

"That is, I *might* know a way," she said. "Though it might not be a very good one."

"You'd better show me," King Jasper said.

—

CRAZY IDEAS

Dorrity wriggled back into safety behind the waste bin. The King, Murgott, and Hodie crawled with her on their bellies.

The stones of the plaza were thick with dust from the explosions, so that was handy. She smoothed a patch. "I'm no good at drawing. But I think it's something like this."

With a finger she drew a curve that was the river, then a few loops for the trees of the Dark. By the river she put a C for Mr. Coop's, then up in the Dark she drew a circle that was Eagle Hall. Then she drew how she thought the stairs in the Hall must lead down to a cavern where the river lapped.

"Because," she finished, "I think that here—" she pointed at the riverbank up from Mr. Coop's and drew an X— "is an entrance to an old tunnel. I always thought it was one end of a crumbled bridge." She dotted a line on her dirt-map. "The river might lead into the cavern under the Hall."

"A cavern," said Lord Hodie. "That could be perfect."

"Send the girl away till Bale's defeated. Then I *might* trust her." Murgott scowled as if he wanted to add, *the time-wasting brat.*

"It will be dark in three hours." The King squinted at the map, then at the river. "Any entrance will already be underwater."

"But there is the barrel-boat," said Dorrity.

"The barrel-boat!" Hodie's eyes gleamed.

"The pack of nonsense," Murgott said.

"With respect, put a sock in it," said the King. "Not you, Dorrity. I was talking to Murgott. Please go on."

"It's actually another idea that mightn't work," she said. "In fact, it can't work. Mr. Coop's the only one who knows how to steer it and he's never done it, it's all in his head. And now he's—" she couldn't say dying—"Mr. Coop's unconscious," she whispered.

The King buried his face in his hands. Murgott scratched his ears. What battered ones he had—from being a Special Major, supposed Dorrity.

Hodie scrambled off under cover and soon returned. "Coop's alive but, yes, he's unconscious. What can we do?"

Officer Edgar's head popped through into the huddle. "Sir…"

"Back off," said Murgott.

"This is my town, Special Major," Edgar said. "The King appointed me. I'm sure he has the courtesy to consult me at least."

Good for him! Dorrity almost giggled, though it was a serious moment.

The King gave a tiny grin and nodded to Edgar. "Officer, what do you know about the barrel-boat?"

"Crazy idea," Edgar said, "though there's no scientific

reason for it not to work. However, I don't see how a barrel-boat could help now, and anyway, Coop's out of action. He can't give permission to use the boat. Of course the army could just commandeer it. But then Mr. Coop's the only one who can handle it…" He glanced at Dorrity. "There is her, of course."

"This is no time for joking," said Murgott.

"Resourceful young woman," said Edgar.

"I don't trust her," said Murgott.

"Pipe down, Murgott," said the King.

Dorrity had always dreamed of using the barrel-boat. But it had never been tested.

"Sir," said Hodie, "the crucial thing is that there is a dragon-eagle feather in the metal boy. The second crucial thing is that the boy is up in the Hall."

"The most crucial thing," said King Jasper, "is even if the Count knows about the feather, it will take time for him to get it. So the final crucial thing is that we have to get the boy before it's too late."

A question burst out of Dorrity. "Isn't the very most important thing not to dither till we're definitely too late?"

VARIOUS WAYS TO
GET ON BOARD

The King beckoned an ogre general. "Keep the enemy busy—you're the chap for the job. Now, Dorrity."

As fast as possible, Dorrity led the King, the troll captain, and a small group of soldiers with weapons and tools—and Edgar—under branches of willows on the riverbank to where she thought the boat shed ought to be.

The flood nosed at the toes of their boots. Only the roof of the shed showed above water. Dorrity heard things knock about inside—light bumps, heavy thuds. The barrel-boat must have floated up out of its cradle.

"We'll have to go in through the roof," Lord Hodie said.

That was obvious. Dorrity already thought he was nice, but she hoped he'd be more impressive as they went on.

"Ropes!" called Hodie.

A soldier handed him a coil.

Murgott grabbed it, shoved Hodie aside and dropped it over his own shoulder. "If you're going to trust a girl, rely on some muscle at least."

"You can't swim," Hodie said.

Murgott gave him a filthy glance, worked his arms like windmills and disappeared under the flood.

An ogre-wood petal spun past. Dorrity thought it might have scooped the Special Major up and carried him off. But one of his arms flailed from the water near the boat shed and his hand clutched the roof. He wriggled up on his stomach like a soaked caterpillar and peered through the skylight.

"Spotted, one monumental barrel, sir!" He fastened one end of the rope to a bird-head finial and tossed the other upriver.

Hodie waded in and managed to seize it as it washed by. He tripped, submerged, and came up gasping. A couple of soldiers pulled him out. Others lashed the rope to a tree. Hodie grabbed a crowbar from a soldier, plunged back towards the boat shed using the rope, and hauled himself up.

The King spoke to the troll captain. "Remember, keep the enemy distracted near the town. But don't attack the Hall till you hear from me. I'll manage it somehow." He turned to face the river.

"Sir!" shouted Murgott from the boat-shed roof. "Don't be an idiot!"

King Jasper dived in and used the rope to reach the roof. Murgott looked furious. The King laughed at him and shook water out of his hair. Then the King examined the skylight, grabbed the crowbar from Hodie and whacked the glass. He struck again at the shards around all the skylight's edges. In another moment, Hodie had scrambled out of sight through the hole.

Heart racing, Dorrity waited. They might manage to get into the barrel-boat—but even if they got the engine going, the boat-shed doors were underwater and bolted tight.

Hodie's head appeared up through the skylight. "I estimate there's room for five inside the boat!" he yelled. "That's me and Murgott and who else?"

"Me!" shouted the King.

"No!" roared Murgott.

"I'm coming too!" yelled Dorrity. "You need me to start the engine!"

"I can start an engine!" Hodie called. "Even Murgott can—"

"You don't know about the barrel-boat engine!" Dorrity shouted.

"We'll figure it out," Murgott bellowed across the flood. "We're not taking a twelve-year-old girl."

"There's more to that boat than an engine!" came Edgar's voice behind her. "Go on, Dorrity."

She lunged for the rope, spluttered out a mouthful of river, and pulled herself across to the roof. Murgott had her by the wrist.

He hauled her out. "Stupid brat!"

"You don't know how to work the buoyancy chambers!" she shouted. "You don't even know where to go!"

"The girl's *brisketting* right," said the King. "Put that sock in it again, please, Murgott."

~

Murgott's curses burnt Dorrity's ears. He pushed Hodie back down through the skylight and disappeared after him.

Dorrity gripped the roof, about to follow, but there was a roar. The bear came pounding to the lip of the flood. Edgar flung himself out of its way. The officers on the bank raised their pistols. For a horrible moment Dorrity wanted to shout, *Shoot it at once!* But they were aiming past the bear and into the trees.

The bear flung itself into the river like a load of laundry, swam (astonishingly well) and reached the roof. It hauled itself on and shook drops enough to make a rainstorm. Then it rose to its hind legs and faced the King.

For a moment King Jasper stared right in its eyes. The bear gave a damp *whumph* and bowed.

"I assume you're one of the false brothers. If that's an apology, I'll deal with it later," muttered the King.

Shots rang out from the Dark. The men still on the bank scattered for cover. Dorrity slipped, but the bear caught her. The King hurried her through the skylight into the boat shed and somebody's arms. It turned out to be Murgott balancing on top of the barrel-boat. He set her down so carefully that she knew he would far rather drop her.

There wasn't much of the boat above water and the river was rising. Dorrity slipped again but gripped the bar along the top of the boat. She'd suggested to Mr. Coop that he should attach it, so thank goodness for that.

Outside, shots rang again. The boat shed darkened. The bear was trying to struggle in. It was so big it filled the skylight completely.

Whuu-uumph! The bear thudded down onto the barrel-boat. The wobble almost threw Dorrity off, but at least there was more light again.

Murgott had his head down the hatch of the barrel-boat and his rear stuck up. Hodie teetered at the fore end of the boat with the crowbar and tried to wham the shed doors open.

Whumph! The bear lumbered along the slippery barrel-boat, past Dorrity and the King, and stretched out a paw for the crowbar.

"Don't trust it, Hodie!" yelled Murgott, and dropped down inside the boat.

Birkett, as a man, had been even stronger than Farmer Ember. Birkett as a bear was stronger than Birkett himself. *Bam!* The doors were forced ajar. *Bam!* The river wrenched them from their hinges, and away they tumbled. Hodie toppled, but the bear hooked a claw into his collar.

Dorrity ducked down the hatch after Murgott. In the half-light she fumbled for the controls and tried turning them on. The engine hiccupped. The King and Hodie clambered in, then light disappeared altogether. It was the bear again, trying to climb head first through the hatch. It had stuck like a cork in a bottle. It groaned and roared. Such terrible breath!

"You're disgusting!" shouted Dorrity. "Breathe in!"

The bear *whumphed* to the floor, dripping wet. The smell of damp bear in a closed space was a stench she'd have liked to measure with scientific instruments.

In the gloom and smell she felt along the control panel and pressed a switch that she hoped was for the lights. It was. But they flickered.

Hodie and Jasper were at her shoulder. "Quick lesson, please!" gasped Hodie.

The barrel-boat swung to the side and bumped against the boat-shed wall. Dorrity lost her footing in the puddles they were all making from being so soaked. She scrambled up again between bear-legs and the legs of Murgott.

The lights flickered again. They sputtered but then glowed brighter.

"That switch is for the burner," Dorrity told Hodie. "It makes air out of water—at least it's meant to." She had no idea if there'd be enough air for a bear. "This button is for going lower—it lets in water for ballast—that means what makes the boat heavier and steadier…"

"I know about ballast," said Hodie. "Hurry on. This is really interesting."

Praise from a such a hero made her grin. "And that button forces air in to force the water out and let the boat rise. At least that's the simple explanation. I hope this bashing around won't damage the tanks."

"I don't like any of this," muttered Murgott. "Especially the girl. Especially the bear."

"I'm guessing this bear has come along because he doesn't trust me," said the King.

The bear's expression was unreadable. But then Dorrity had never been taught how to read a bear's face. *Whu-hummph.*

"Shut up, all of you," Dorrity said. "I'm trying to concentrate."

She felt water tugging at the barrel-boat. Had the engine

warmed up? Mr. Coop had said it needed a whole ten minutes. She hadn't been counting. Panic fluttered in her throat but she tested the forward control. Hodie had a keen eye on what she was doing. Her arms weren't long enough to reach all the controls from where she was, but she told him what do to and they managed to share.

The barrel-boat eased out past the broken doors into the river. It creaked and groaned—but it was moving. If only Mr. Coop was here for this moment—his barrel-boat, actually trying the river. *He's a genius*, she thought, fingers crossed for good luck.

If the boat stayed as it was, half-submerged, they'd be able to see what was coming downriver towards them. But soon the sun would disappear completely. When they started moving ahead underwater, they'd have to trust the lights inside the barrel-boat to show dangers—rocks, snags like sunken tree trunks, floating ogre blossoms that might whack over the portholes and stick there, if they didn't smash right through and cause a shipwreck.

"I'm getting the hang of it," muttered Hodie. "The flood's taking us to the middle of the river, then we'll try moving upstream."

"I'll want a turn," muttered the King.

"I'll respectfully wait till after you, sir," muttered Murgott. "But let me remind you, this isn't a lazy sea voyage such as you and I shared so long ago."

The King let out a snort. The bear let out a growl—but a longing sort as if it too wanted to try the controls.

"Don't turn that knob too far," Dorrity told Hodie. "It

comes off in your hand—oh, it didn't. Metalboy told me he'd fixed things."

"Metalboy?" asked the King.

"He said he'd tidied up in here," said Dorrity.

The King made a sound that was pleased and even proud. After a moment he spoke as if only he and Dorrity were in the barrel-boat.

"I hoped to make a machine to go where ordinary men couldn't or wouldn't dare, to gather information about the Count. I planned to send it to the City of Canals, where Count Bale was banished. But somehow the boy came here. He must have sensed this was where he'd find the Count. And now Bale has him captured." He shook his head. "But why would the dragon-eagles allow the boy to have a feather-scale? Who are they testing? What's going on?"

"Sir," said Murgott, "what's going on is that you've put yourself in grave danger and light is fading."

Grayish gloom filtered through the portholes and down the hatch.

Dorrity looked up. "We have to close that!"

Murgott swung himself up the ladder and stuck his head out to unclip the hatch from the outside. He let out a yell.

Dorrity couldn't make out the words but she knew what they meant. Captain Westrap! The barrel-boat swirled in a half-circle—yes, on the bank, through river spatters on the fore-window, she saw soldiers in the Count's glossy uniforms. Three of the King's men lay as if dead. And there was Westrap with a pistol aimed at the top of the barrel-boat. He fired, but the boat bobbed. He fired again.

Murgott cursed. The hatch unclipped at last and he dropped back inside. "Good workmanship," he muttered. "Too damn good. It nearly got me shot and nearly sunk us." He scowled at the bear and Dorrity.

She decided it was best to ignore him.

"Captain Westrap might guess what we're doing. Hold on!" She shoved the steering lever to port. "It needs to look as if we're being swept away."

The barrel-boat tilted. The double hull creaked—water rose past the portholes—but it all seemed fine. She let the river scoop them back in the direction of the bridge. The boat rolled—then Hodie's hands were on the lever too. Between them they steadied the vessel. The river stopped blinking over the portholes. The engine chugged in a steadier manner, though Dorrity's heart raced on.

"Let's see if we can nose up along the bank opposite Westrap," Hodie said. "Dorrity, how far before the tunnel into the cavern?"

"If in fact there is a tunnel." Her voice had bumps in it. "And if in fact there is a cavern too. If there isn't, I'm really sorry and we're in trouble."

"I said not to trust her," muttered Murgott.

"Trouble's part of the job," muttered the King.

"So is feeling seasick," muttered Hodie.

The bear moved away from him quickly—for a big man, Birkett had always been squeamish.

"Oops…" Dorrity spotted a pile of rocks looming ahead.

Hodie turned the lever to port. She lightened the ballast. A scraping sound came under the belly of the barrel-boat, and the boat bumped upwards. The water level dropped part-way down the portholes.

Something heavy landed on top of the barrel-boat—and a second thump followed. Banging, scraping—what was it? Dorrity tried to squint from a porthole but saw nothing.

Again something scraped at the hatch. Now she saw a pair of great black wings take off from the roof, circle, dart away and speed back. She had a glimpse of a fierce beak holding a steel pike. The hatch juddered as the giant bird jabbed it from above.

"We have to submerge!" cried Dorrity.

But there were too many rocks.

The gray light through the portholes made the men look very strained, even the bear. She should give them a boost to their spirits. "I can't think of any better people to be in trouble with." She couldn't stop a slightly sarcastic glance at Murgott. "But we have to submerge before the Count's ravens put a hole in the hatch."

Another scraping along the roof made Dorrity jump. A raven-soldier tumbled past a porthole. The leaves of an ogre-wood swished past as well.

"He's been swept off," said the King.

Hodie grinned as if he'd never had such fun in his life.

The bear said a satisfied *whumph*. Then it made another sort of sound that came along with an extremely bad smell. *Whumph*, said the bear, like a soft excuse me.

Dorrity pressed the button for the ventilation system. It seemed an excellent time to check whether it worked.

52

VARIOUS WAYS

"Keep a watch for Bale's soldiers returning," said the King. "I'd rather not submerge completely until we must."

"I hope to glory that Westrap doesn't guess what we're up to," said Murgott.

Dorrity hoped the same to glory-plus. At least it seemed that Murgott trusted her at last. She didn't blame him for not trusting the bear yet—she didn't quite, either.

It was very scary to have to try out all the systems in the boat's first venture. Dorrity knew it would grow stinkier with every minute underwater, but it wouldn't be good to over-use the ventilation system and they might not have any chance to pop the hatch for a quick freshen-up.

The last of the daylight glittered with dust from the avalanche. Water licked at the portholes. In creaks from the hull, spits and squeaks from the machinery, Hodie kept the vessel moving upriver. Dorrity peered out and tried to spot the brickwork that—with luck—would be a tunnel mouth. The King and Murgott tried calculating out loud where the tunnel might be and how it might link with Eagle Hall.

Way up in the Dark was a glimmer. It was too soon to be stars. But it could be lights in the turret of the Hall fading in and out through branches. Dorrity squinted even harder at the riverbank. There, overgrown with creeper, just above the rising floodwaters, was the top of the old brickwork arch.

She crossed her fingers that it was a tunnel. She crossed her fingers they would arrive in time to save Metalboy. She crossed her fingers that the King would know what to do when they got there—that they would in fact get there—and that the underwater lights would work so they could see if they actually got there.

She also hoped that Mr. Coop had set the lights of the boat to shine where they'd do the most good, as she had suggested. It wouldn't help if they only shone ahead, not to the sides as well. And what if the tunnel was blocked? She hoped that the reverse mechanism of the boat would work if it was needed. Once the boat was in a tunnel there might not be any space to turn around.

But she kept her mouth shut. She didn't want the men to worry any more than they worried already, especially the King. He had to be at his best to rescue Metalboy.

Hodie eased the controls to let water into the ballast tanks. The vessel began to sink. The portholes had a lower lid of gray river water...now the water level was at the halfway mark...now the portholes were completely under water. The engine chugged to hold the vessel at its lowest speed. Dorrity turned the light switch. A beam shone ahead onto waterweed and a submerged mouth—it was a tunnel.

Dorrity's heart leapt with excitement, thumped with fear.

She wanted to hurry and find Metalboy—but they must go slowly to save themselves.

Whumph, said the bear. Without thinking, she reached out and nearly patted it. But she pulled back. The bear wasn't her brother.

~

The barrel-boat crept on. Beams of light washed over walls of stone covered in moss and weed.

The tunnel split into two. "Stay in the larger one," whispered the King.

"Why are you whispering?" whispered Murgott.

"Shut up," whispered Hodie.

They eased past three more small tunnel mouths.

By now Dorrity was used to the dim rays of light. A couple of eels twisted past a porthole, playing with the beams in a sort of water dance. The walls seemed to be further apart now. The vessel moved on. At last she saw no walls at all. They must be in a cavern.

"Let out some ballast?" Hodie asked.

Dorrity eased the controls to make air push water from the tanks. Slowly the vessel rose higher. The water level dropped halfway down the portholes. It was too gloomy and blurry to see much above water except the narrow beams of light. Dorrity hoped there wouldn't be a bump up top that meant the roof was too low for the hatch to open.

Now the vessel rose high enough for beams from the barrel-boat to show the dark silk surface of an underground lake. Up ahead was what might be a landing slip and an ancient wharf. Hodie gentled the barrel-boat to sidle up and come to rest. Dorrity turned off the engine.

"Now what?" asked Hodie. "Three of us are not exactly enough to attack the Count from the rear."

Three of them? Did they think Dorrity was staying here? She saw the bear trying to count to four and then five on its claws. It gave her a very Birkett scowl.

Murgott put a hand to the lock of the hatch. "We'd better keep our voices down."

In half a minute he was up and out. The barrel-boat rocked. For another half-minute Dorrity squinted through a porthole as Murgott crawled backwards, down the side of the boat, and jumped onto the wharf. He slipped but righted himself then knocked on the porthole and made tying-up movements. Was there a rope?

Oh. A rope was one thing Mr. Coop hadn't thought about. Nor had Dorrity. The rope they'd used before was still tied to the boat-shed roof.

"You stay here. It might be safer," the King told Dorrity. "No—it might be safer for you to come with us."

She made herself grin, though her heart was top-speed. "I already told you I have to come too, sir."

"Is she always like this?" the King asked the bear.

The bear spread its paws in a bear-like shrug.

~

"Should we leave a boat light on?" asked Murgott in a low voice.

"Yes, if we want to see the way ahead," replied the King. "We haven't got flashlights."

In the chill and sour air, he led the way as they snuck off

THE VOLUME OF POSSIBLE ENDINGS

the wharf. It was slippery—Dorrity took special care.

"If there is anyone about, they'll have heard the engine," murmured Murgott. "But they wouldn't know what it was. Maybe the sound was muffled by the river. Or maybe not."

"Haven't I said before, pipe down?" asked the King.

He had his pistol and that royal dagger. Dorrity was the only one without any weapon. Murgott had a pistol and sword. So did Hodie—though all the pistols had been soaked in the flood, so she hoped they were waterproof. The bear, of course, had its strength, its claws, and its jaws. By now Dorrity was pretty sure it was on their side, or at least that it was against the Count.

"Sir," she whispered, "just one more thing…" She explained what she thought about the Count's grasp of his magical powers, how it was patchy.

The King nodded slowly and gripped her wrist in a friendly way. Murgott gave another mistrustful grumble.

Water lapped on the landing. The river must still be backing up against the rock fall. The cavern might end up completely flooded. They might not be able to get back to the barrel-boat at all. She wished her brain would stop thinking of terrible *mights* and *might nots*…

The King moved towards a flight of steps that just showed in the furthest reach of the beam from the barrel-boat. It led into darkness. They started to climb. Far, far up, Dorrity wondered if there was the faintest glint. Perhaps it was the chink in the doors that Metalboy had tried to spy through when he heard the river lapping.

Darkness pressed down and stifled her. She wished she

had stayed in the barrel-boat. But she couldn't complain. After all, she was a queen, if only a fake one. Climbing like this might help her dress and boots dry out, and it would keep her warm.

The bear loped beside her. Again she reached out—this time she gripped a handful of the scarf and fur on its shoulder before she realized and let go. She glanced back. In the weak light from the barrel-boat, the gleam of the underground lake rose and fell like quiet breathing. The barrel-boat floated like a toy in a grim bathtub.

Before long they had to grope their way, Dorrity on all fours. Probably the men and bear were on all fours too—she couldn't see. The glint ahead seemed no bigger. Dorrity had to stop now and then to tuck up the tatters of her silk skirt. Her legs ached.

The gloom became slightly less gloomy, then slightly less gloomy again. The chink of light showed the edge of each stair. It showed spider webs too, thick as netting on the walls and over their heads.

They came to double doors of heavy wood, the chink showing where they met. Across the chink was something thick, a bar or huge bolt on the other side.

Hodie peered at it. "Murgott," he whispered. "Are you strong enough?"

Murgott wriggled a hand through and tried to heave. "We need that crowbar. But it's still in the barrel-boat."

The bear snorted and pushed to the front. It sniffed and peered, managed to put a claw through, but that was all. It plumped back on its haunches.

A King, a lord, a Special Major, a bear—and none of them could force the door?

Dorrity moved along, feeling and pressing for any loose planks. They were fixed tight. Then, low on one side, she touched metal. Was it a bolt? She tried to ease it. It didn't budge. But she leaned against the wood, and the bolt squeaked a little.

"I'll go back for the crowbar," said Hodie.

"Wait." Carefully, so it wouldn't squeak again, Dorrity forced the bolt back by herself. A small panel moved open and nearly swiped her down the stairs. "Ouch." She steadied herself.

A square gap had opened in the door, big enough for a short person or a large suitcase. The bolt, she could see now, was a double-sided sort of latch.

"Well done," whispered the King.

The men muttered thank you. The bear's thank you was a soft snort.

"This is big enough for me, at any rate." Dorrity didn't bother to wait and just climbed through.

On hands and knees, Hodie wriggled and joined her. Then Murgott with a few groans and then the King.

The bear stuck its head through, but Dorrity shoved it back. "You'll get stuck again."

Murgott and the King together lifted the bar across the doors. The bear shoved through the gap at once.

"What is the plan?" asked Hodie.

"Very simple," muttered the King. He eased his pistol from its holster. "Keep your fingers crossed and trust to luck."

—

STORAGE FOR
ROOT VEGETABLES

Light only a little brighter showed through the cobwebs of
the stairwell. Their heads were all covered in cobwebs too.
Dorrity was glad the men were with her. At the same time,
it annoyed her how they pushed her to keep behind them.
She knew more about the innards of Eagle Hall than any
of them.

By the time they reached the landing, her legs ached
even worse. There was no time to complain. From higher
up came the scrape of crates and heavy stuff being moved
around, the tramp of feet, insults and bicker from bird-men
to real-men and cussing to hurry up.

The King leaned towards Hodie and Murgott. "We can't
go further that way. Bale's still readying for an attack."

"I think the dungeons are through here." Dorrity pointed
to the door.

Hodie, pistol in hand, inched along the wall and eased
open the door. Yes—the second door had the right signs:
Bulk storage for root vegetables and **CELLS**.

"Dorrity, stay back. You too," the King said to the bear.

The men stole through. Dorrity glanced at the bear. It glanced at her. Together they snuck along anyway.

She heard a hoarse voice. "Good grief, sir. You spring up in some unexpected places." It sounded very much like Mr. Kent with chattering teeth.

Dorrity, with the bear next to her, looked over Hodie's shoulder. There, locked in the cells, were the journalists and advisers who hadn't managed to escape when Dorrity did. She heard scrappy doleful singing, out of tune—*Liberty means that we decide—Ya-hah*...It was the anarchists, Dodger, Brian, Ruffgo, and even Cooker, locked up in the cell with the man-frog creature.

The King, Hodie, and Murgott had their fingers to their mouths, ordering silence. Dorrity wasn't sure that journalists and anarchists would obey. There were a few grumbles but soon they fell silent. It would only be because they wanted to be freed, but the reason wasn't important, just the result.

Already she was hurrying from one cell to the next along the rows. There was no sign of Metalboy.

"Where is the boy?" she whispered. "Where is he?"

Dodger waved through the bars. "That friend of yours? The Count had him taken away half an hour ago. There goes our income."

Dorrity closed her eyes and took a breath.

The King uttered the royal swear word and went to check the stairs again.

She heard Murgott's voice. "What are you doing with that?"

"We can't leave them all here," said Hodie. He'd opened an army knife and was reaching for the lock of a cell. He touched it, recoiled and hissed with pain.

Whumph. The bear stared at the bars for a moment, chose the two furthest from the lock and tried to bend them. By mistake, it leaned against the lock. Its fur singed and it let out a squeak. The smell of burnt bear hair was terrible. But gradually the bear managed to bend the bars enough to let a skinny journalist squeeze through. It was a small triumph but not nearly enough. The bear hung its head.

The King crept back. "Still can't use that stairwell. Too much activity."

"Sir," said Murgott. "If we can't go on, we must go back. You're not safe here."

"Murgott," said the King, "if the Count has learned about the feather-scale, I'm not safe anywhere. Nor are you."

Whumph, said the bear, particularly deep.

"Exactly," said the King. "Nor is Dorrity. Nor anyone in Fontania for that matter."

"Can you undo the locks with your dagger?" Dorrity asked.

King Jasper looked amused again but sympathetic and also more worried. All three of those things annoyed her. "If I use the dagger now," the King said, "Bale will sense it is in the Hall. It's too big a risk yet."

She'd got them this far. But so much for grown-ups, and so much for magic.

~

CROSS-STITCH

Dorrity shivered. She was still damp from the flood. She'd had nothing to eat since early in the day, here, in the grand bedroom of Eagle Hall, that one slice of toast spread with honey.

Mr. Kent spoke through his cell bars. "You look like a frozen rat." He handed out his jacket. "Don't argue. Take it."

She thanked him and slipped it on.

"I'm afraid we didn't save any of the evening rations," said a woman adviser—the one with the fancy shawl. "Not that they were tasty or anything—it was rather like sawdust with salt. Why not huddle beside the bear? I would if I could. It's rather handsome."

"No, thank you," said Dorrity.

"Then squeeze into that cell and lie on the mattress." The woman passed the shawl out to her through the bars. "And take this—I wish it was a blanket."

"No. But thank you," said Dorrity again. None of the prisoners had blankets and she already had Mr. Kent's jacket.

"Go on," said the woman kindly. "Just a borrow while you wait for the stairs to be clear."

Dorrity didn't trust her voice. She just smiled, slipped through the bars bent apart by the bear, and lay down on a very thin mattress. The shawl and tatters of the mustard-coloured skirt covered her feet, and she huddled with the jacket cuffs pulled over her hands. She hoped the Fontanian army was keeping the Count too busy to concentrate on Metalboy. She couldn't stand to think how afraid he must be. She hoped someone was showing him a small kindness, as two grown-ups had just done to her.

She huddled herself tighter and closed her eyes. The King murmured with Mr. Kent and Murgott. After a moment she smelled the bear. There it was, sitting against the bars. She rolled over and tried to ignore it.

Soon she felt herself sinking into a sort of dream, or was it a memory? Long ago, she had huddled like this and heard murmuring—younger voices but grown-ups' too, moving close and tending her. She'd been in a bed, with other narrow beds in the same big room. There'd been other children. If this was more of a memory and less of a dream, she might be remembering the orphanage, the one the Count said she'd gone to when she was small. The blanket there had been soft and warm, and something else nibbled at the edge of the memory. Cross-stitch—yes, she'd had a doll with a skirt edged in cross-stitch. It had blue eyes that opened and shut, and she'd held it at night.

Yes, she remembered as if the doll was right there beside her with the warmth of a blanket and kindly people. But there had also been sorrow, before that. Now in her memory she saw her mother sewing cross-stitch on the doll's skirt.

Her mother, sitting up in bed in a room with gauzy spotted curtains. It was not her own home she was remembering, but out in the yard was the gossip of chickens, the complaining of cows ready to be milked, the ordinary music of everyday things. In the dim cell underneath Eagle Hall, Dorrity could even faintly hear what her mother had said. *Look, each stitch is like a kiss, mwha! mwha! I'm going to send you somewhere safe. Someday you'll have friends and a family again. Just wait and see.* Tears began to seep onto Dorrity's huddled-up hands. Her mother had been ill and knew she might die.

Now she remembered going to the orphanage with the doll, then after—how long?—Dorrity had carried the doll to the matron's office. There stood three big men she'd never seen before. The biggest had brown curls and deep frown lines. The fair-haired man looked jumpy, a bit jittery. The youngest man had red hair and blinked at her, then gave her a wink. The matron asked, *Are these your brothers?* Dorrity held her doll tight.

They have letters and papers, said the matron, *with signatures and seals from the authorities.*

She can bring her doll, said the biggest man. *Can I see the doll, Dorrity?*

She held it up, the cross-stitch under her fingers.

His eyebrows rose. *A beautiful doll*, his voice rumbled.

What happened next? Oh—the big man came with the matron and Dorrity to fetch her bits and pieces from the room with all the beds. The little boy—her best friend, from the bed next to hers—was there, changing out of wet socks. She looked up at the brown-haired man, her new big brother, then back at the boy. *I've got three brothers now*, she said, *so you can have this*. Dorrity gave the doll a kiss that made its eyes rattle and put it into her friend's hands.

The big man, Birkett, had looked at her as if something had shocked him, as if his world turned inside out in that very instant. She remembered walking away from the orphanage, with scatters of sunshine over the path. The three big men talked to each other in short low sentences. The fair-haired one—Mike—looked even more jumpy. Dorrity wanted to cry for losing her friend, so she held up a hand for Mike to take it. He gave that same startled look as if his world had changed. But he took her hand and, after a moment, her third new brother took the other. Mike and Yorky swung her up and bounced her down, and she was bounced away from the orphanage with Birkett striding in front. Then she could remember being in Owl Town and seeing Miss Honey Dearborn sewing cross-stitch.

Dorrity sat up on the thin mattress of the cell in Eagle Hall, feet in her damp royal boots, in tatters of silk. But she felt warm in the borrowed jacket and shawl. She ought to feel sad, but inside it was more like a smile. Her mother had loved her. At the orphanage she'd had a real friend her own age. Her brothers—fake brothers—had tried to protect her.

She hopped down, over to the bear, and gave it a nudge. Its yellow eyes turned to her. It let out a whuffing sigh.

"This doesn't mean that I forgive you," she whispered. Still, she reached out a finger and drew a tiny X in the fur of its chest. It gave another small whuffle.

But she'd remembered the doll, the fifth ending of

"Dorrity's Tale." There were no more to come. Count Bale would appear at any moment. He had probably already found the feather and tossed all the bits of Metalboy into the waste bin. Now he'd get rid of the anarchists, the journalists, advisers, King Jasper, the bear, and Dorrity.

～

OUT OF STORAGE

It must have been hours—early morning—when the terrible music of marching feet came down the stairs. The door crashed open and in strode the Count's soldiers.

"Line up the prisoners!" shouted an officer.

Guards unlocked all the cells with a clatter of keys. It was lucky the guards were mostly half-birds and half-animals. They didn't notice or care that there were extra prisoners, some of them not even in cells. They didn't realize that the King was the King and that three of the extra prisoners had pistols in holsters under their jackets (Hodie and Murgott had hidden their swords). The guards didn't even notice that there was a spare bear. Perhaps they were used to imprisoned animals—they even let the frog-man out, poor creature.

Dorrity shrank behind other prisoners and held the shawl up round her face. Mr. Kent whispered to her, "Keep my jacket on. With luck, you might be mistaken for a cadet journalist."

"Good thinking," the King muttered at Mr. Kent's shoulder.

"Sir, shut up if you have any sense," Mr. Kent whispered.

"Don't speak to His Majesty like that," growled Murgott.

The King pulled Dorrity right next to him. "Shut up, Murgott," he said without moving his lips.

The guards bundled everyone out of the dungeon and up the stairs. Lights from the walls were misty in the cold air.

"Where has the bear got to?" Hodie said softly.

"Back in the shadows," Dorrity whispered.

The King muttered to Mr. Kent, who scribbled like anything, then tore the page out of his notebook. The King scrawled something at the end—a royal signature?—then ducked into the shadows himself. Dorrity thought she saw him tuck something into the bear's scarf. The bear sniffed the air and loped off into more shadows. Taking a message to the army? Maybe the bear would manage to get out through the hedge. But it was too late for help of any kind for her.

~

The raven-guards herded everyone along the grand corridor into the Grand Reception Room. Would she see Metalboy? Outside was the tinge of dawn.

The prisoners murmured—scared, cross, and brave all at the same time. The guards banged their pikes on the floor. A single set of footsteps sounded. In marched Captain Westrap. "Line up!" he shouted. "Quick!"

"Don't order us around!" growled Ruffgo.

"Just don't obey," Dorrity heard Dodger tell him.

Brian nudged Dodger. "You stopped being boss yesterday. Isn't it my turn?"

"Silence!" roared Westrap.

A young journalist held up what must have been his last message-bird. "Will there be a Third Proclamation, and what…"

A raven-solder punched him in the stomach. He gave a terrible groan. So everyone lined up in a more or less orderly manner, with Dorrity in the middle. The anarchists lined up too, though Dorrity saw how they pretended to be only doing it by accident.

Captain Westrap paced around, eyeing the prisoners. It would be terrible if he recognized King Jasper. Or Lord Hodie or Murgott. She expected him to recognize her any second.

Though there was no hope for her, still her nerves zinged and tingled. Metalboy was nowhere in sight. If she drew Westrap's attention, the King might be able to dodge off and find him…No—she was too afraid.

But how ashamed Metalboy had been about being a coward.

With a gasp for courage, she jerked an arm up at the elbow and waved her fingers. "Excuse me, Captain!" she cried. "Over here!"

~

Captain Westrap swung around. He started to smile, a narrow, mean smile. "Dorrity. You're a tricky girl. I saw you last night down by the river. How did you get back? What game are you playing?"

"But Captain Westrap, I'm not Dorrity—" She was horrified at the words about to pop out. "I'm the imaginary friend."

The captain's smile darkened. "Girl, you'll be a loss to the monarchy. Enjoy your last bedraggled moments as Queen Evergreen."

She might have thought of a clever answer, but a pair

of trumpets blared. The main doors opened. Raven-guards wheeled in the Count on his throne-chair.

"No applause yet," cried the Count.

The journalists glanced at each other. The anarchists slouched. The advisers looked as if their hands would like to hide in their pockets. Outside was a shot, then the rattle of a return volley. The Count cocked his head, tapped his fingers on the armrests and laughed in his thin wheeze.

"My lord!" Captain Westrap saluted. "Here is one extra guest you'll be interested to see." He pointed at Dorrity.

Count Bale craned his neck. "For crying out loud, her again? She looks like something the cat's played with. What has she been up to? No, don't bother to tell me."

"But sir, how did she get back in?" said Captain Westrap. "She's not to be trusted."

Dorrity glanced at the lemony look on Murgott's face. It was a nice moment. She gave him an upside-down smile to say, *See?*

The Count grinned in his spidery way. "Westrap, nobody can be trusted. She did a better job of publicity than I dreamed of, and in double-quick time. But I don't need her any more, because she brought me this." He gave a signal.

Again the blare of trumpets filled the hall and hurt Dorrity's ears. Four guards wheeled in a platform. On it was Metalboy, tied to a pole with red rope.

"I daresay everyone expects breakfast," the Count continued. "But you all have to wait. I've had my couple of cornflakes and very nice they were this morning, flavored with triumph. About-to-be-triumph, at any rate." He shone his pale smile at the journalists. "I need you to take plenty of notes. Things have moved faster than I had expected…"

Another burst of gunfire rang out, but he waved as if it were no more than pesky sandflies. "And I require this story to be sent to every news agency in the Nation of Fontania as well as all surrounding countries."

He reached up from the stroller-throne with his slender black stick and tapped Metalboy. "What you see here is one of Jasper's failed experiments. Failed, yes, because I have tethered it."

"That looks like a real boy to me!" cried the woman who'd given Dorrity the shawl.

The Count ignored her. "I admit it took me a while to figure out what the girl meant when she escaped. But I believe that inside this—" he tapped Metalboy harder, and Metalboy flinched—"is a feather from a dragon-eagle."

"How did you ascertain that?" cried a journalist.

"Shut up. Wait till question time," said Captain Westrap.

"I take no orders from anyone unless I think it will benefit me!" cried Dodger.

Westrap clicked his fingers. Two raven-soldiers dragged Dodger's arms behind his back and snapped handcuffs on him. "It would have been a benefit to you to have held your tongue," said Westrap.

Dodger struggled. "Free speech!" he cried.

"Shut up," said Brian. "Just for a while. Dodger, that's an order."

Ruffgo elbowed him again. "Told you we should have gone to the King…" A soldier tied a gag around his mouth and handcuffed him too. By now all of the anarchists were in manacles. Their eyes glared through their balaclavas.

The Count chuckled. He eased himself out of the stroller-throne, held onto it while he tested his legs, then stood up straight.

"Pencils ready?" he said to the journalists.

Dorrity's heart nearly stopped. The Count was going to remove the feather from Metalboy in front of everyone. But Metalboy could bleed—he was real! She took a step forward, but Mr. Kent held her upper arm. On her other side was the King. Was he going to use his pistol? No, his hand was near the royal dagger on his belt.

The Count raised the slender black rod. It let out a glow.

"Bad magic," Mr. Kent murmured. "Well, we will see."

Her fingertips tingled where magic had scorched them. She heard the King's breath hiss between his teeth.

Count Bale stepped up onto the platform beside Metalboy. For all his smugness, Dorrity thought the Count seemed still a bit tottery, and nervous.

Gunfire rattled again.

"As soon as I have the feather, that rabble outside will be worse than sorry," said the Count.

He pointed the wand at Metalboy.

Nothing happened. He moved a little closer, prodded Metalboy with a bony finger, stood straighter and pointed the wand at him again.

Metalboy began to look more pale to Dorrity. The Count flexed his hands and pointed the wand a third time.

Metalboy seemed more and more silvery. There was no

question now. He was slowly turning back into clockwork.

"No," Dorrity whispered. "No!" she said. "No!" she cried aloud. "Please stop! He's my friend!"

Metalboy turned to her with an effort and looked right at her. In his final movement he started to smile. Life went out of his gray eyes, but the smile remained.

Dorrity pressed both hands over her mouth so she wouldn't cry out. Hot tears fell down her face.

King Jasper glanced at her and touched her arm. He probably meant it to be comforting. It was nice of him, but her tears kept dripping.

The journalists scribbled hard. Lord Hodie glanced at King Jasper—the King began to shift from foot to foot. Murgott put out a hand to restrain him. The King nodded that he was all right, but his fingers tensed near the royal dagger—why didn't he use it?

The journalists were watching the Count closely now, pencils poised.

The Count grinned at Dorrity. "Loyal little thing," he said. "Perhaps I won't get rid of you after all. Maybe family should count for something."

Dorrity used the most scornful voice she could manage, even though it was soaked with tears. "Family didn't count for you. You let your creatures kill your brother."

"Foolish little relative." The Count smiled that thin, cold smile. "That was your second and last chance."

—

SECOND CHANCE

Count Bale turned back to the clockwork boy. He pushed the jacket aside, and there was the gray metal chest with a silver square, gold screws at each corner. With his fingers, the Count took out one of the screws and let it fall. Two— three screws—the square slipped and hung on the fourth, squeaking back and forward like a far-away cry.

Inside the boy's chest Dorrity saw a shape of dull red. The Count started to reach in for it.

The King took a step, but Murgott stopped him again.

Mr. Kent stood in front of the King. "Sir!" he called to the Count. "Are you very sure of what you're doing?"

The Count didn't even bother to glance around. "I've waited a hundred and ninety-five years for this. Just take notes."

"Even a villain should be warned!" King Jasper cried.

Hodie and Murgott looked appalled that the King had spoken. They each moved as if to protect him. But the Count stood unmoving in front of the metal boy.

The air in the room seemed to tremble. It felt to Dorrity as if something loosened and fell away.

"The tethers," the King whispered. "Bale's had to drop some of the tethers around the boy—Dorrity's right, he can't manage everything at once. If we're lucky, our troops will be able to break through any moment. Wait—wait…"

Count Bale slowly reached out again. Something silver began to glow deeper inside the boy's chest. The Count hesitated. Very carefully, fingers ready to grip, he moved again. But the silver thing evaded him and floated out—the silver feather shaped like a dragon's scale, lighter than thistledown.

The Count snatched for it, but the movement of his hand made the feather float higher. It hovered over the metal boy's head beyond the Count's reach.

The tallest of the raven-soldiers stepped forward, but the Count waved him down. "It's mine! I'm the only one allowed to touch it!"

"Selfish," muttered Mr. Kent.

"It's beautiful," murmured Brian. For a moment the feather dipped as if it might float towards the anarchist's head. Then it lifted even higher.

A rush of noise sounded outside—gunshots, the pounding of footsteps. Into the room rushed the bear, the goat, and a troop of Fontanian soldiers.

"Stop!" Murgott roared. "Delicate moment!" He raised his voice even further. "Shut! Up!"

The bear roared louder than thunder. Everyone winced, hands over their ears (except for the anarchists in their handcuffs). The feather danced close to the ceiling.

The Count, face twisted with fury, made a swift gesture with the black wand. Every sword, every pistol from the

Fontanian army—and from the Count's men too—and the King's, Murgott's, and Hodie's—clattered to the ground. The King didn't seem to mind, eyes fixed on the Count.

The feather still floated above the crowd, lifting, dipping, almost playful.

"Everyone's breathing!" shouted the Count. "Stop breathing! You're making the feather rise!"

The journalists sniggered, and the anarchists guffawed. The political experts grinned wryly.

"The point is, Count Bale," called Mr. Kent softly, "that your 'magic' doesn't really seem to do much. Just a shape-change or two? A little stop-'em-moving spell now and then? You see, no matter how we report it, suspicious members of the general public might say it is no more than clever training. Bears. Birds. A tad of hypnotism."

"I have magic enough to kill the lot of you," hissed the Count.

"Personally, I've no doubt of it," said Mr. Kent. "But according to my research, a genuine dragon-eagle feather will lend itself for a short while only to someone who has already earned it or who will earn it."

"I should have been King," cried the Count in his thin sharp voice.

"That might be true," said Mr. Kent. "But some would say that because of all you've done, you don't deserve it now. That may be quite another question, but after all *now* is what matters. And one other thing—the feather itself might summon a dragon-eagle. I'm not sure if that is in person or just in spirit. But if I were you…well, I'm just here for the story."

He stood back looking rather pleased with himself.

"I know what to do!" The Count beckoned a guard to help him down from the platform.

The clockwork boy, tied to the pole by the red tethers, stood silent, the dull red of his jasper heart just visible. *Move*, wished Dorrity, *please, move*. But she knew he couldn't.

Count Bale eyed the feather. It veered, teased down and veered away. The Count held up the wand. His spider-thin body trembled again, again. Sweat beaded his bald head. He tensed with a great effort and gestured at prisoners, the King's soldiers, bear, goat, and his own people.

Dorrity felt cold, very cold. She could hardly breathe against these tethers.

Slowly the Count turned and bowed to the feather. "I promise most solemnly that with a dragon-eagle feather-scale in my hand I will undo the magic that has brought us to this day."

Nothing happened, except that the King seemed to unfreeze. In fact he glanced at Dorrity again and gave her a wink.

"Possibly you need to be more precise, Count," King Jasper called.

Other people started to move—the tiniest bit.

"He's confused," an adviser managed to rasp. "He needs an adviser of his own."

The Count looked furious and gestured with the wand. The crowd stilled again. Dorrity felt an even deeper chill around her heart.

But the King could still move. He took Dorrity's hand

and squeezed gently. Her fingertips tingled, but this time it didn't hurt.

"I can advise you," she heard herself call. "After all, I'm a royal cousin. I would promise the dragon-eagle that the transformations made by bad magic will be reversed. I'd ask if that is acceptable. Then I'd ask if the rightful king could be acknowledged."

"Cross your fingers," the King said softly, still holding her hand so that she felt him cross his own fingers for luck. She sensed him using his other hand to ease the dagger from its scabbard.

The Count stared at the feather. It was motionless, still out of reach. "I promise," he cried. "The transformations of bad magic will be reversed! There. Is that acceptable?"

The feather hovered a moment longer.

The King raised his dagger high—the Count didn't notice and still hadn't recognized him. Westrap did, though—Dorrity saw how he tried to struggle against the spell that held him motionless. But the Count's cleverness and wickedness was working against him. Even his own Captain couldn't move or speak.

Slowly, behind the feather, a huge silvery cloud appeared. It billowed, and inside its glimmer formed the shapes of both dragon-eagles. Dorrity's heart—though chilled—gave a leap.

~ *Acceptable* ~ chimed a silvery voice, whether in the air or just in Dorrity's heart, she couldn't tell.

The raven-soldier nearest the Count fell to his knees and cried with agony. His glossy shape dwindled—a black bird lay flapping its wings, struggled to its three-toed feet (and the fourth pointing backwards) and blundered for the door.

The goat gave a bleat of anguish and brandished its horns. It collapsed and bleated again. Another shape seemed to fight inside the shape of the goat—then Mike staggered to his feet in his hiking clothes, and the goat had vanished.

It happened all around the Reception Room—cries of pain, crumpling to the floor, the struggle back into full human form, or the wrenching and wrestling from human form to animal, reptile, bird.

Dorrity felt the last of the invisible tethers loosen from her, and looked around for the bear. It stood on its hind legs, shaking its head. She saw flashes of Birkett in it already, but in its last savage moments it struck Captain Westrap to his knees. It snarled and pounced, about to rip him to pieces—then the last traces of fur melted away, and there stood Birkett in his brown travel clothes and Miss Honey's purple scarf, his hands upraised. He lowered them, blinked, and held his head as if he had the most awful of headaches.

The red ropes fell from Metalboy too. But he could no longer move.

"Enough!" The Count raised his hand for the feather to float to him. "Now it is mine!"

~ *Quite right* ~ said the image of one dragon-eagle.

~ *Your turn* ~ chimed the voice of the other.

Hodie and Murgott dived for their pistols—at last!—but the King stopped them. "Watch," he said.

Count Bale staggered. His upstretched arm dropped to his head as if he was dizzy. He staggered again. "Stop! What are you doing? Confirm me as the rightful King. Everyone deserves a second chance!"

~ *Not always* ~ said the silvery voice of a dragon-eagle.

~ *But here it comes* ~ chimed the voice of the other.

~ *By the way, Dorrity's right* ~ rang the words of the first ~ *Good idea to confirm the rightful monarchs after all this* ~

"At last!" cried the Count. A silvery glow fell around him, but he tottered. "What…what's happening?" He tottered again. At last, as he tried to right himself, he saw Jasper, dagger still held high, and the blade now sending out sparks of silver.

~ *King Jasper* ~ the dragon-eagles bowed. ~ *Send our regards to your sister Queen Sibilla* ~

"No! No..." But the Count's legs were growing shorter. His arms shortened too. His hair grew, thin at first, then thicker with a dark brown curl, then he went bald again with just a soft fluff. "No—no…" He toppled sideways.

An image of a dragon-eagle spread its wings, and a scoop of air lifted the Count into the stroller-throne. His clothes sort-of shrank away—or he dwindled inside them. Dorrity couldn't see how that worked. Then all that Count Bale wore was a diaper and little shirt, and he was very small indeed. There he lay, a plump baby on his back in the grand stroller, little legs kicking, plump baby-face red and offended.

Waa, said the Count. *Waa, waa!*

~

FOUR DIFFERENT
RIBBONS

Really the Count should have known better. Dorrity wasn't exactly surprised, though it had been awful to watch. This was not the kind of second chance the poor bad man wanted.

On the foot of the stroller-throne, a roll of parchment took shape. It had four ribbons: green, orange, red, and black.

~ *There is his story* ~ said the image of the larger dragon-eagle ~ *It will be kept in the Royal Library with an attentive librarian* ~

~ *Green ribbon for good news* ~ said the other image ~ *Because bad magic has been defeated. Orange ribbon for be careful, keep a watch in case danger awakes. Red ribbon for bad news because bad magic refuses to stay asleep. Black ribbon for somebody important being dead…oh, but he isn't dead* ~

The black ribbon became a spiral of smoke and drifted to nothing.

~ *King Jasper* ~ said the larger dragon-eagle ~ *we trust you to find somebody kind to take care of Baby Bale and teach him his manners* ~

The silvery cloud began to break up. The shapes of the

dragon-eagles glimmered a moment more and Dorrity wasn't sure exactly when they disappeared.

The King's soldiers started rounding up the Count's men, among them an extraordinarily sick-and-sorry-looking Westrap. They shooed the creatures into the grounds to fly away, gallop, waddle, hop, or scamper off.

Lord Hodie had found a key and took the handcuffs off the anarchists. It looked as if he was suggesting that they scram if they had any sense. With no arguing they vanished into the crowd.

Dorrity looked at the fat squalling baby in the stroller-throne. "I won't be the one to take care of it."

King Jasper chuckled. "If it's a true second chance, he won't remember any of this. All the same, I promise to make sure somebody keeps a better eye on him than the royal family kept on your mother and you."

He picked up Dorrity's hand again and gave it a squeeze. "Little cousin, I am very sorry indeed for what you've gone through. Forgive us. I believe we need someone with your practical and clever nature in the family."

She knew she was blushing. Outside, the sky was blushing too. Sunrise.

"I'll take you home." The King slid the royal dagger back into the scabbard.

She hesitated. A few paces away stood Birkett and Mike. Arms on each other's shoulders, they looked battered and dead-beat.

"Do you forgive them?" King Jasper asked.

She did. But right now there was too much she was

starting to remember—the doll, her mother, even a memory of her father with a warm smile in a craggy farmer's face, and also how scared she had been, and how distressed when her father and then her mother died and she'd had no one.

"No hurry," King Jasper said. "Rest with your friends in Owl Town till you feel recovered. Then you can travel. You've got cousins all over Fontania. Like my sister Sibilla. They'll want to meet you. You'll be a hero, too, because of the barrel-boat and your part in defeating Bale—an excellent part. Your picture will be in the papers for all the right reasons. That's so, isn't it, Mr. Kent?"

Mr. Kent gave a nod.

"And after all," continued King Jasper, "now Mr. Coop and you will want to test the barrel-boat in Old Ocean. You can't do that if you stay in Owl Town."

He was jollying her.

"Come on," said the King. "We should hurry."

But Dorrity walked on unsteady feet to the platform where the clockwork boy stood, heart there for everyone to see. She picked up his hand—cold, with a dent where the Count had stabbed him.

"He was alive," she whispered.

"I'm sorry," said the King. "The black ribbon was right. Somebody important is dead."

A silvery chime sounded. A wide black velvet ribbon took shape in the air and folded into Dorrity's hands.

"Where's his second chance?" she whispered. "The dragon-eagle said bad magic would be reversed. He should still be alive. Metalboy was good magic."

"That's true," said the King.

"You made him in the first place," she said. "He was my friend. My real friend."

The King didn't say anything, which was sad and annoying. Mr. Kent said nothing either. She wanted to kick both of them.

"Where's the feather now?" Dorrity cried. "Where did it go?"

Again the King didn't answer. It had gone back to the dragon-eagle it had come from, she supposed.

She sighed and draped the ribbon around her neck. But she couldn't go yet. She managed to hold her head high and look at Metalboy.

"Goodbye. Thank you." In her heart she added, *for the pleasure of your company*. She reached up and kissed him.

Then she and her cousin the King walked out and down the steps to the lawn in front of Eagle Hall. Various townsfolk and officers bustled in to take care of that baby, thank goodness. The barrier hedge began to sink down and become fat drifts of mist.

A sort of slumping sounded behind her. She glanced back. Lumps of Eagle Hall had slid to the ground like a mud castle on the riverbank when water reached it. The officers with the stroller-throne rushed out and rattled Baby Bale down the steps.

Dorrity sped back across the lawn to the terrace.

"Dorrity!" shouted King Jasper.

Weeds had already sprouted on the marble steps and flagstones. One side of the enormous entrance door caved in as she entered the Hall. A slab of the entrance hall slid away; the ceiling hung in clumps about to disintegrate. She raced to the platform where Metalboy stood. Her hands shook but she reached into the clockwork chest—the heart was fastened tight by golden screws.

Chunks of wall and ceiling dissolved around her with frightening slurps. But the chiming sigh of a great dragon-eagle surrounded her and somehow the jasper heart eased into her hand. She even seemed to hear a *thank you* from a friend, a *see you soon* in an up-and-down, natural boy's voice.

The chandelier crashed beside her and was sucked down into the gluey mass that had been the floor of the Reception Room. She turned—she'd have to jump to reach the hall and front door. It was too great a distance…but there was the King, hands reaching from the other side.

"Come on!" he shouted.

Mike hurtled on his two legs past the King and grabbed Dorrity up. Together they leapt—Dorrity landed on a safe bit of the hallway and stumbled. King Jasper and Mike whisked her up between them. She still clutched the jewel of Metalboy's heart.

Then Dorrity and the King were racing over the slippery, dissolving hall floor. Mike and Birkett shepherded them through the softening entrance, down the steps to firm ground. On they ran, past the stinking bubbles of the pond, and stopped where the barrier hedge had been only minutes before. Its last traces were sparkles of mist among scattered twigs.

Behind them was the ruin of Eagle Hall, honest old

wood beams and hand-hewn stone. The central tower with only a few broken windows still pointed to the sky.

King Jasper waited till she had caught her breath.

"I'm ready now," Dorrity said. She was pleased that he put an arm around her shoulder—she still felt wobbly.

"Look," King Jasper said.

There below, through the path scorched in the forest canopy by the Count's bad magic weapon, glistened the Forgotten River. The slow and steady force of water had begun to tumble away the avalanche. The flood was diminishing.

"The river was always going to clear its own path," said the King. "That's magic of its own kind. Ordinary magic." He looked at her hand clutched around the heart-jewel. "What an ending. That's only so far," he added. "Because things go on, one way or other."

She took a long look at the river. She and Mr. Coop would have to find the barrel-boat. Actually, he could ask the army to do the job. After all, he hadn't given his permission for them to borrow it.

Fontanian soldiers ushered them onto the path down to the town. There was no sign of the anarchists, just a *koff-roar* far up in the hills. The crowd was a cheerful riot of journalists, Lord Hodie, Special Major Murgott, and various people, ordinary, troll, ogre, or dwarf, rejoicing to be restored to their true selves. Animals and birds of all sorts called and cried in their various voices. A gidibird swooped down, tugged Dorrity's hair with its curved red beak and flew on past—very likely it was Charlotta.

At last, the ramp was ahead. A flash of red hair—it was

Yorky. He waved two whole arms when he saw Dorrity, Birkett and Mike. And there was Mr. Coop on crutches with a bandage over his head, Dr. Oxford scolding him.

The crowd carried Dorrity and the King down High Street to the plaza. The main wharf had been washed away entirely. The bridge was damaged, but heavy planks had been laid over the gaps. Dorrity saw Mrs. Freida and Miss Honey just starting across from the other side. Chippy O'Now and all the townsfolk who had fled the previous day hopped over the planks amid the music of chatter and joy at returning home.

Birkett raced on to help Miss Honey over the last steps. She didn't seem to need it. She thanked him anyway with a light kiss, then they were hugging.

At the fountain, Dorrity stopped. "You really think I should forgive Birkett and Mike and Yorky?" she said to the King.

"They risked their lives to keep you safe," said Jasper. "Yes, they began by thinking they could do what Count Bale wanted and earn some dolleros. But you know that as soon as they met you, they couldn't go through with it. And as far as they knew, I was as bad as Bale."

"They really are my sort-of brothers," Dorrity said.

King Jasper nodded.

So the five endings of her Tale had come true in their own order, their own time and their own way, but her actual story would go on. She looked at the jasper heart, warm in her hands. Metalboy's tale might have various possible endings too. She'd ruddy well work on it.

The morning sun strengthened. The sky filled with wing-whistle and song from a thousand birds soaring on many more thousand feathers, diving and whirling like a banner, singing of their release in their many ways. *Gidday, gidday, gidday, we're glad to be here!*

THE END

APPENDIX I

Dorrity's Tale—the Possible Endings

One ~ *Dorrity stayed in Owl Town and did nothing. She never saw Birkett and Mike again. Yorky lived with one arm and one wing for the rest of his life but never, not once, did he blame her.*

Two ~ *Dorrity returned from the Beastly Dark and the dangerous ways she'd had to go. Birkett and Mike thanked Dorrity with all their hearts, and Yorky welcomed her back with two whole arms.*

Three ~ *At last Dorrity had discovered who she was and all came clear.*

Four ~ *Dorrity, with a sad lonely heart, was crowned Queen of Fontania.*

Five ~ *Dorrity thought about her doll and wished she had remembered it sooner.*

Appendix II

The Anarchists' Marching Song

Ya-hah! Ya-hah! We do it all ourselves
Leave kings and queens on shelves
Shove prime ministers out the door
What the heck is a president for
'Cept to order us what to do?
Anarchists do it for themselves
Quick march! No rules! Ya-hah to any rules.

Quick march! Quick march! Quick quick march!

Freedom means that we decide
Whether to walk or run or hide
Liberty means that no one's in charge
Of whether dinner is little or large
Brotherhood means that we agree
Unless we happen to argue and bash Ow! Ow!
Freedom! No rules! Ya-hah to any rules.

Quick march. Quick march. Quick march march!

(*lento*) Sometimes we'd like a sister or wife
A child who could call us Father
But girls are too bright to lead this sort of life
At the thought of it, they're in a lather
Oh, clean sheets and a bathroom
A newspaper brought to the door
We wouldn't rely upon gossip
We'd live right next door to a store...
(*sigh*: ice cream...)

Quick march. Quick march. March march
march!

But never tell us what to do!
We'll decide what we will do
We'll march and fight to achieve what is right
When we decide what might be right
Brotherhood means that we agree
Though we argue and bash, ow ow ow ow ow
Quick march! Don't boss! Ya-hah! to any rules.

Con spirito

ff Ya - hah! Ya - hah! We do it all our-selves Leave kings and queens on shelves Shove prime min - i - sters out the door What the heck is a pres - i - dent for 'Cept to or - der us what to do? An - ar - chists do it for them-selves. Quick march! No rules! Ya - hah to a - ny rules! Quick march! Quick march! Quick quick march! Free - dom means that we de - cide Whe - ther to walk or run or hide Li - ber - ty means that no - one's in charge of whe - ther din - ner is lit - tle or large Bro - ther-hood means that we a - gree Un - less we hap - pen to ar - gue and bash *Ow! Ow!* Free - dom! No rules! Ya - hah to a - ny rules! Quick march! Quick march! Quick march march!

Lento

Some-times we'd like a sis - ter or wife A